3 DAYS IN 63

THE UNSOLVED MURDER OF FRANCES BULLOCK

GREGG CLARK

Red Press Co.
redpressco.com

ISBN 978-0-0000000-0-0

LCCN 2019942421

Printed in the United States

Contents

For Jimmy Clark, my father,
the rock many of us broke ourselves on.

"I could walk up to the killer right this minute and lay my hand on their shoulder—I wouldn't live long mind you, but I could do it."

—ANONYMOUS FRANKLIN, NC LAWMAN, 1965

AUTHOR'S NOTE

In the writing of this book—prior to, during, and upon its completion—three Earth-rattling questions never stopped rocking my mind. First, I asked myself; how do I tell a story as it actually happened with any degree of accuracy when the story is older than I am?

Second, given the story's grisly and sensitive subject matter, is it safe or sane to tell the story at all?

Finally, I asked; what kind of book will it turn out to be? The first question was answered in a most unorthodox way.

The Frances Bullock story is hands down the most tangled, cryptic, enigmatic tale I've ever heard in my life. When all the cards are laid upon the table, there is no way anyone could capture the entire story in book form. All of the deceit, the despair, the secrets, and the concealments weave together in perfect abstraction with no one piece complimenting another except in their contrasts. I realized, before writing a single word, that I needed a platform. I needed a common denominator, a common thread running throughout.

I had no desire to write a biography of the victim. There was no pull to write a chronological history of her life, murder and the mystery that ensued. I wanted to tell the story that was told behind closed doors. I wanted to tell the story the police officers knew. I wanted to tell the story my father knew. I wanted to tell the story that I knew. I wanted to tell the story through a myriad of unique lenses that spanned half a century, and I didn't know how to do so—until—the radio show.

An online radio broadcast out of Little Rock, Arkansas awarded me the platform, the denominator, the thread to be strung from start to finish.

With the online radio show reasonably answering the—how do I write the book question, I say reasonably for I faced reluctance and suffered self-doubt throughout the entire writing process, I was left with the nagging—should I write the book at all question—and the question of what kind of book it would end up being. The first of these two questions haunted me from the book's inception.

Should I write the book at all? Is it safe? Is it sane? I asked myself over and over again, and three answers came back to me like an echo from within a canyon without fail. They came as I began the book. They came while writing the book, and they came upon completion of the book—NO, NO and HELL NO!

Ever since the body of Frances Bullock was hauled from her home in a slick-zipped body bag in the summer of 1963, her story has remained taboo and dangerous to anyone willing to speak of it, investigate it or write about it.

Keeping in mind well-known threats that had been previously doled out to others, stories of career loss due to the killer's pursuit, even unexplained, tragic and untimely deaths that occurred seemingly in connection to those seeking answers, I braved the waters, but much was concealed in that pronoun of I. I say that I braved the waters. I wasn't willing to have others ride the rapids with me. That would have been unfair.

Ensuring that I was the sole occupant of my own metaphorical vessel demanded unforeseen alterations to my manuscript, leading me to my third and final question—what kind of book will it turn out to be?

A fictional work of considerable length and complexity is the loose definition of a novel, so from the beginning, I felt certain I wasn't writing a novel, for my content was true. My setting was real. The events I was writing about actually occurred.

After a while though, as I ruminated on the fairness of naming names, the fairness of revealing who had pointed an accusing finger or suggested a salacious theory, I ruled out Creative Nonfiction, Historical Nonfiction, Biography or straight up history in general, as fifty years is not nearly long enough a time frame to name drop—too many people still living—too many of their children still living, so I decided to play Dr. Frankenstein.

I decided to piece, stitch, clamp and bolt genres together. Blending Biography, Nonfiction, Narrative Poetry, Creative Nonfiction, History, and Fictional dialogue together, the book became a cohesive single unit—though a howling beast it still may be—for it had been born of multiple perspectives spanning two entire generations. In the end, the book took on novel form.

The amalgamation of genres for the sake of Cohesion came at a steep price though. The novel, unlike a work of Creative Nonfiction, demanded that I change the names of suspects, investigators, past and present police officers who played a role, no matter how minuscule—It demanded that I alter the names and sometimes genders of friends, family and a wide array of others whose names peppered the pages of my book so as not to force them down the white water with me, especially those with breath still filling their lungs. In a nutshell, I was ethically forced to alter the identities of many of the living, while, with the exception of suspects, police and special familiel investigators, I was able to allow the identities of the dead and those with no ties of any sort to the case to remain intact.

I realized too, upon close scrutiny, that I, out of necessity, had had to create dialogue and gestures, weather and nuance to bind fifty years of facts, rumors, speculation and disjointed stories from multiple perspectives into a single readable narrative, so calling the book a novel was no great stretch in the end.

If the Frances Bullock story is new to you, the necessary alterations to protect the innocent and the living will mean absolutely nothing. If you know this story backward and forward, you'll enjoy the puzzle of decoding who's who amid the pseudo names and genders. Either way, the necessary alterations are meaningless to the story itself, and for every name that has been changed, there are three that have not—hopefully in their static form, creating rich nostalgia for those who look upon this story as a piece of their past, a piece of their history.

In conclusion, the book you are about to read is the unvarnished, unburnished true tale of Frances Bullock's murder and beyond, culled from hundreds of hours of personal research spanning a quarter of a century and thousands of hours collectively when the research of others is considered.

The creative license taken for the sake of the story, sequence and comprehension adds, in a sense, another layer of mystique, if I may be so bold. So take this book for what it is, a true story mashed together from many people's memories—some still living, some dead—meant to tell the most comprehensive version of the story possible— a story, that if I've told it right, just might cast out some demons from the shadows or call down some angels from on high.

PROLOGUE

66 We'll call five minutes before we go live; that's just so we can chat for a minute, go over the protocol again. You might want to have a list of stories you'd like to tell or things you'd like to talk about handy just in case you get a little stage fright, but I'm sure that won't be a problem, you being a teacher and all. Dale's been poring over your website and Facebook page, and he's already made a long list of possible topics that he might bring up or ask about as well, so you'll be fine. Just between you and me, Gregg, what brought on an interest in such things, enough to start tours and all?"

"I've had the interest since I was a little boy, but actually Where Shadows Walk was my wife Pauletta's idea," Gregg informed, Tony, the DJ from the popular online radio show, Behind the Veil, out of Little Rock, Arkansas, who, along with his partner, Dale, would be spotlighting Gregg and Pauletta's Where Shadows Walk stories on their show in two weeks. "We were camping the next county over from ours. We had rented a cabin. Pauletta had picked up a flier in town earlier in the day advertising a ghost storytelling event the next night. She literally tossed the paper to me as I was building a campfire out back. I picked it up out of the grass, looked at it for a minute and tossed it into the fire."

"You could do that in Franklin you know," she said, "with all the history we've got."

"Long story short—I did."

"Yeah Dale's been teachin' me all about that history—Gem Capitol of the World, site of the final surrender of the Civil War, French and Indian War battles, Trail of Tears. Franklin sounds like one Hell of a place. I guess that's where all the ghost stories come from right?"

"Maybe so. Been enough death, that's for sure."

"One death, in particular, Gregg that Dale's been consumed with, and I'll guarantee he'll ask about in two weeks is Frances Bullock. That story's all over your newsfeed, and he found where three different newspapers had interviewed you about it, something about some presentations you did last month."

"I'd be happy to talk about it. There's a ghost story in it too, but it's more of a murder mystery. I don't know how interesting that would be to you guys, seeing as you wouldn't know the characters or the settings."

"Well, Dale won't leave it alone, so we'll see I guess. Tell me more about Franklin. To tell you the truth, we've never done a show about small-town ghost stories. Last week on the show we had an actual exorcist from Rome. No pressure!" Tony jokingly relayed.

"Rome, Georgia?" Gregg facetiously came back at the DJ.

"Rome, Italy smart ass," Tony replied with a healthy laugh chasing his words.

"Right, no pressure there," Gregg repeated with a laugh of his own. "Franklin—what can I tell you about Franklin?" Gregg rhetorically asked the DJ hundreds of miles away. "Well, Franklin, North Carolina is what you want it to be, meaning if you want it to be a backwoods prison that you blame for holding you back in life, never letting you breathe, it can be that; however, if you want it to be a hidden treasure, a salvation, a respite, a port in a storm, a place to grow and change, it can be that too.

It's a town where the Mayor wakes up early to take pictures of heavy snow or hard rain or pastel dawn breaking and has the pictures posted on Facebook before most people are even awake. It's a town of old buildings and fractured sidewalks, a town of graveyards and church steeples that stretch just high enough. It's a town with deep roots and unlocked doors. It's a town of waterfalls and crooked trails leading everywhere and nowhere at the same time—again depending upon how you choose to walk them."

"Damn Gregg! I wish we'd been on the air for that. Remember that, and say it just like that on the show in two weeks!"

"I'll try," Gregg's words rolled comfortable and quick.

"I understand the history and the ghosts being of interest Gregg, but what got you all bound up with a fifty-year-old murder case? You weren't even alive when Frances Bullock died. Hell, I wasn't even alive."

"Well, I'd been hearing about the murder from my dad all my life, but what made me want to create a presentation, actually do a show of sorts, came from the craziest place, a Bob Dylan song."

"What? A Bob Dylan song? Dylan wrote about the murder?"

"No, no, nothin' like that. Bob put out an album out in 1986 called Knocked Out Loaded. He had a song called "Brownsville Girl" on that album. I'd heard it many times before, but sometime last year, I really listened to the lyrics, and they just fit— something in Bob's words fit the story, fit the time, fit me, and I started piecing it all together, making something cohesive out of it. The song served as muse or inspiration somehow."

"Well, hopefully we'll hear some of the story in a couple of weeks. Gregg I'll let you go. Remember, we'll call five minutes till show time, and have that list ready just in case alright."

"Will do Tony. You have a good evening," Gregg finished.

Gregg had been picking up sticks in his yard the entire time he'd been talking to the DJ in Little Rock. One at a time he'd been tossing them into the tall grass at his yard's edge. He'd also been watching the mail carrier.

From where Gregg lived, he could see his mail carrier's white Jeep stopping and starting in the distance through the breaks in the trees, silently inserting bills, coupons, letters, and packages along the way.

As she noiselessly glided from box to box, Gregg's mind, like a ladle raised from hot soup, filled up with faces, among them, his own grandmother and a passel of others who'd long since filled caskets in cemeteries fixed on sunny hillsides and down dark crooked roads. The mail carrier had been important to them, vital in fact, someone they'd waited for.

They'd take folding chairs and tall five-gallon buckets of green beans to snap and string as they waited. They'd sit in their cars two or three hours prior to expected arrival times. At Christmas, tucked inside their mailboxes, they'd leave baked goods, rolls of Nickels or hand-knitted garments for their carriers. In spring and summer, they'd come prepared with boxes of okra, peppers, tomatoes, and squash to hand through their carrier's window, even if their carrier had handed them a hefty bill in turn, and if they couldn't be there at their mailbox, they'd leave boxes of the fresh produce for the carrier non-the-less.

As the carrier's Jeep squeaked to a stop at Gregg's own mailbox, he tossed the last stick he'd lifted from the warm summer grass and made his way over to her. Smiling, Gregg jogged the last twenty feet, assuming Sonya, his mail carrier had decided to place the mail directly into his hand as opposed to the mailbox since she'd stalled in her action and was holding his mail up in the air like a torch; however, as Gregg reached her window, he realized in quick time that it hadn't been his propinquity to the box so much as an obstacle in the box that had altered Sonya's normal routine.

"You'd better get this back in the house before Pauletta goes missin' it," Sonya said while gesturing with her letter-filled fist to the obstruction that had prevented her from placing the mail inside the box. The smile that accompanied her warming was as old as woman-kind, warm, yet earnest.

Gregg placed his free left hand on the carrier's warm car hood and crooked his head so as to see inside the box. He then smiled as well. Sonya, a delightful middle-aged woman with a contagious smile, feigned she was swatting at Gregg's head with the stack of mail she still clutched tight in her hand before placing it into his right hand.

"It's a Southern thing I reckon," the carrier said through clenched teeth and eyes closed nearly to slits— a glowering visage of comic disapproval that followed her initial warm smile. "How's your momma been gettin' on?" Sonya asked, changing trails in a blink—her face no longer contorted with maternal judgment and half-hearted scorn.

CHAPTER ONE
A SONG AND A SILHOUETTE

Something about that movie though,
well I just can't get it out of my head.
I can't remember why I was in it
or what part I was supposed to play.
All I remember about it was
Gregory Peck and the way people moved,
and a lot of them seemed to be lookin' my way.

- From "Brownsville Girl" by Bob Dylan and Sam Shepard

AUGUST 16, 1987

Gregg thumbed mindlessly through a year-old Field and Stream magazine that boasted an article on Trophy Deer, as his father, seated to his left inside the overly-warm Macon Barber Shop, made the capacity crowd of geriatric scarecrows guffaw at his imitation of the way one of his fellow police officers drove his squad car. Placing both of his hands on an imaginary steering wheel before him, one firmly atop the other, Gregg's father, Jimmy Clark, the Assistant Chief of Police in their sleepy, little, mountain town of Franklin, North Carolina, animating his eyes to Don Knotts' status, acted as if he was driving erratic and fast around a serpentine mountain curve. The barbershop roared with laughter. Gregg grinned. He couldn't for the life of himself figure out why his father's imitation was belly-laugh-worthy, but he'd learned years ago that what old people thought to be funny was quite different than that of young people.

The maroon, duct-taped, barber shop chairs were hot and sharp, failing to see a ten minute window without a warm backside cooking them all day. Where the seasoned tears weren't taped or the tape had pulled to one side or the other, exposed at least a portion of the sharp tears.

The hot room smelled of aftershave, chewing tobacco, day-old sweat, and cigarette smoke. Though Frankie, the barber, no longer allowed smoking inside the shop, many of the old-timers, his father's present cheering section, wore their day-old smoke in their hair, on their big callused hands and all over their clothes like a spider's web.

The radio was on, barely audible behind the big tales, jokes, and eruptions of laughter but loud enough to tug Gregg's attention into a standing position at the mention of Elvis. Joe Cunningham, a female Disc Jockey on Franklin's WFSC station, was asking Brenda Wooten, her DJ partner in crime, where she'd been ten years before when the news had broken about Elvis.

Gregg couldn't quite make out Joe's reply in full, as another gong of laughter drowned out the radio, but he sat up straighter and lowered the magazine he was feigning to read to his knees.

"Suspicious Minds," a late 1960s Presley hit, poured forth through the ancient green radio speakers like a welcome whisper from an old friend. Gregg instinctively jerked his eyes in the direction of the grinning barber, whose left shoulder was unintentionally blocking his view of the Bryant Funeral Home calendar that hung slightly crooked behind her, a calendar that everyone he knew and had ever known had lived and died by. Bryant Funeral Home calendars had been to Macon County residents in the early 20th century what family Bibles had been to residents of the county a century prior. Their twelve long pages with twenty-eight to thirty-one-day squares recorded it all: babies who'd lived and babies who'd died, wedding days, anniversaries, birthdays, Easters, church revivals, funerals, and homecomings. The calendars even aided in feeding families, as they also held the moon phases used for planting, and rarely was a family's calendar without the seasoned flyswatter, most often sharing the same nail.

Gregg waited impatiently for Frankie to move. Frankie Bowers, the lovely thirty-something-year-old barber with a wild shock of white hair splitting the middle of her otherwise glowing strawberry blonde hair—a characteristic Gregg had had ample time to ponder on, seeing as she'd given him his first haircut, his last haircut and every haircut in between—wasn't the town's only barber, but by reputation, setting, routine, and comfort, she had become the queen. Unlike other barbers Gregg had seen while easing past their sad and ghost town shops, male barbers, barbers who sat alone in their own raised chairs reading newspapers with glasses on the tips of their noses, Frankie's shop was never barren, never void of life. Gregg began tapping his right index finger on the magazine's cover as he silently waited for the amiable barber to lean into a sideburn cut, lean back into a laugh or step back to scrutinize a line or a fade, anything to expose the calendar date she was unwittingly concealing.

When an old relic in clean bib overalls, starkly contrasting others in the room, began to robustly mimic the thick accent of a Boston Yankee who'd made the dire mistake of asking for directions at a gas station he'd been haunting earlier in the day, Frankie finally leaned forward. Comb erect in hand, as if to smack the old fool for his devilment, the barber's lunge revealed the calendar page Gregg's eyes had been hungry for.

August 16th, Gregg whispered to himself. Gregg's father, upon hearing his son's breathy exclamation, glanced his way

3

but didn't inquire. It had been ten years since Elvis Presley had died, and WFSC was remembering him through story and song.

Gregg knew the date well, as Elvis had been an obsession with him for at least three years; however, due to the mid-day baseball game he'd been begrudgingly pulled from bed on a Saturday morning to play and the rush to the barber shop thereafter, and given that his nerves were stripped raw due to school fast approaching, he hadn't realized the significance of the day.

Gregg's friends often teased him for liking old people music. He'd even been to Graceland in Memphis, Tennessee earlier in the summer. Gregg's teachers always smiled when he showed up to class in Elvis and Jerry Lee Lewis t-shirts.

Drinking in the guitars and backing vocals of "Suspicious Minds," after the calendar page's validation, Gregg began easing out of the present. His father's words and gestures, so raucous beside him, quickly became white noise, so too the laughter and outbursts. Gregg slowly but surely began slipping his setting like a Cicada slips its shell. Gregg flew on the winds of his own imagination. In his mind's eye he soared over darkening mountains, fields, trains, towns and rivers, and though his form, clad in an itchy gray polyester baseball uniform that read, Tourists, across the back and with tangle-tied dirty cleats, still filled a chair in the Macon Barber Shop, Gregg had gone back to Graceland.

Amid the spongy carpets and fabric-wrapped walls, Gregg could see the gleaming casket through the doors bedecked with colorfully stained glass Peacocks. He saw the profile of the King, the bridge of his nose, his forehead, his dark hair brushed back. He smelled coffee brewing somewhere in the house, and the aroma of cool flowers was overpowering. He heard phones ringing. He heard muffled, disjointed conversations from distant rooms. He heard youth running upstairs, and he was alone.

4

He was alone with the dead body of Elvis Aaron Presley. He felt the carpet give beneath his size sevens, as he moved in closer, wringing his baseball cap in his hands. He could see the white shirt collar now. He could see the deep-as-a-well, facial pores. His fingertips touched the squeak-shiny casket. He smelled Brut aftershave wafting up from the dead singer. He was so close. He could count his eyelashes, his ears were....

"I've got to go in a minute," Gregg's father blurted out while grabbing his son's left knee, never realizing the chest-tightening shock he'd just delivered to his boy, oblivious to the fact that he had just pulled him from Graceland, flung him forward in time, back to a barbershop, back to old men and cigarette smoke, squarely back to 1987.

Gregg and his family, which consisted of his father, Jimmy, his mother Audrey, who worked at a local grocery store and his six-year-old brother, Scott, had just recently returned from Graceland, the home of the late Elvis Presley in Memphis Tennessee. Gregg had begged for three years, as he was a mammoth Elvis fan, to go to Memphis, to see the home of his hero, to walk the halls and see the stage suits, records, and cars.

As Presley, with passion, told an unknown someone that they couldn't go on together with suspicious minds, and amid the spurts of laughter, outside, a heavy rain had begun to fall. The wide picture window that started at Frankie's right elbow and ended near the front door's frame, bedecked in bold red letters reading, Macon Barber Shop, revealed to the room filled to capacity, a virtual torrent, a mountain deluge, and the sky that had been overcast and strangely foreboding all day was darkening with haste, like the closing of an eye.

"Here she comes!" An old man called out above the horde. Frankie turned away from the clean-shaven man in her barber chair, comb in one hand and clippers in the other, to look upon the rain. After placing the clippers upon the sink's edge, she pumped, with her freshly free hand, the boost release of her barber chair, easing her most recent customer to the ground.

"Hit's a gully warsher ain't it?" The clean and clipped old man piped up as he climbed spryly from Frankie's chair, pulling the thin crisp paper collar from his neck Frankie had neglected to retrieve as she'd been watching the storm arrive.

"Lord, I pray my winders are up," Frankie said with raised eyebrows and lowered mouth corners.

"If you need somebody to run and roll em' up Frankie, ... Bob Tallent will!" The oldest looking man in the filled-line of chairs croaked, while pointing a crooked finger down the row of wrinkles, denim and crossed lean legs to another old man sporting an aged gray fedora with a turned up brim and a wide toothless grin. The room, like before, filled with laughter just as a warm glow of lightning lit the dark street outside. Gregg's father checked his watch.

"Damn!" The off-duty lawman barked. "I've got to go jump off your momma's car. *I figured we'd be done by now."* He whispered the last part.

Gregg had spent the morning with his father, as his mother was working, and that wasn't the norm. Usually, it was his father who was working or getting ready to go to work or hanging out at work. He loved his job, but it did make for too much time apart Gregg felt.

Gregg's mother had taken a break at noon. She had planned on running errands, but her car wouldn't start. She'd called Gregg's father who'd told her he'd be there to jump it off when she got off work.

"You stay here!" Gregg's father commanded. "I'll be back in a little bit."

"No Daddy, I'll go with you."

"No, you won't either. Your momma will kill us both. School's just about to start, and you gotta get that haircut."

Gregg's father gently took his son's left knee again in his right hand and squeezed then stood up.

"Frankie, I've got to run meet Audrey. I'll be back to get him in a little bit." Gregg's father spoke without looking in the barber's direction, a bodily sign of his perfect ease with her, the men, the town and the time.

"It'll be a little while," Frankie said with a toothy grin, gesturing with her comb to the full house before her.

"Be good." Gregg's father instructed before pushing open the door.

"Now don't you melt out thire Jimmy!" A snaggle-toothed old man with snow-white hair and deep-socketed eyes said with a gaping grin.

"Cecil," the lawman said in reply while lowering his head in preparation for the downpour, "Steel don't melt, it rusts." Another round of laughter from the room and he was gone, swallowed up in sheets of blowing rain.

As the old barbershop door swung to a close, a fresh flash of lightning lit the world outside for what seemed to Gregg an obscenely long time, creating, in its wake, a mirage of high noon in the eye of the storm and illuminating, in its lengthy glow, two men in the street outside. One man, heavy-set and hunched over, running with a cardboard box over his head was making quick time toward the open door of the tiny grocery store that sat across the street. The other man, spare of frame, straddling a bicycle, seemed, for all the world to be ignoring the rain altogether. With his head held high, and by the look of his leg rotations, just a shade faster than a clock's hands turn, he wasn't paying the rain any mind at all.

CHAPTER ONE

As darkness again took its turn after the glow died, it didn't surprise Gregg at all when an old man leaped to his feet, slung open the rain-spattered door and yelled, "As much as you charge for Ground Beef Shorty, a man might figure you could afford you an unbreller!" Ribald laughter once again lifted the ribs of the room, as the old character continued, "and Ted, damn it, ain't you got the sense to git in outa' the rain?"

Gregg could hardly appreciate the gravity of the booming thunder that followed the next wild light due to the exclamations of the loud old comic and the simultaneous explosion of laughter, large, dirty, slapping hands, stomping work boots, thigh slaps, whoops, whistles and coughs his bellowed comments had elicited from the crowd that filled the storm-darkened barbershop.

The old jokester eased back into his seat, gripping the exposed metal armrests with both of his pale liver-spotted hands, and without missing a beat, continued his satirical diatribe.

"Ole Ted, I'll tell you what's the truth don't even know it's a rainin' no more than a dead man. They ain't no tellin' what he's been a drankin."

The howling crowd soon settled. It seemed the roller coaster of tomfoolery was slowing down, and the cars were coming to a stop. Gregg just listened and watched. It would be a hand-full of years before he'd understand what had been so funny about the man with the box and the man on the bicycle. Shorty Mason and Ted Love meant nothing to Gregg yet.

All of a sudden a fist of wind coldcocked the door halfway open, bringing with it the rain and a macabre late-summer chill. Gregg watched as several of the old locals shivered and lifted their shoulders. Frankie hastily jumped to the door, pushed it shut, turned the open sign to closed and flipped the top lock so as to prevent the mid-August storm from again crashing their party that had thus far been as lively as any Gregg had ever known.

Upon completing her task with the door and the clamorous wind, the grinning barber addressed the new old man who'd seated himself in her chair.

"Well Troy, I'm glad you got to see me today."

"Yeah, yeah," The old man drawled.

"You been up to snuff?" Frankie queried her customer, as she placed a worn stripped apron over him and pinned it behind his neck.

"Oh, I can set up and take nourishment, but I ain't fit to work." He replied without the benefit of any recognizable expression in his tone or on his face.

Another loud gust of wind blew against the building, and somehow the room that had been sickeningly warm, grew cool, and several of the old men gestured to such by gently grabbing their elbows or blowing through pursed lips.

"Thank somebody just walked cross all our graves Frankie." The old man nearest the door slowly drawled, while watching the pouring rain through the window. The day grew darker, and inside the tiny archaic barber shop, despite the month and despite the body heat, the room put on a thin veil of ice.

Headlamps, broken in shards by the rain, like Picasso-painted light, slowly passed outside. Elvis, so faint, was singing, "It's Midnight, and I miss you," and for the first time since Gregg had arrived with his father over an hour before, the barbershop grew silent and still.

"Let me tell you one on your daddy." An old man in the middle of the row piped up, splitting the silence. He'd leaned forward and craned his neck toward Gregg with a rolled up newspaper in his claw of a hand, acting as if he were attempting to smack Gregg's knee, though the newspaper was a good three feet shy of its target.

"My daddy?" Gregg responded with a gentle smile, again lowering the magazine to his knees.

"Your daddy." The old man declared with verve.

"Now don't go tellin' tales, Clayton!" Frankie reprimanded with a pointed comb.

"Ahhhh!" The old man replied, waving his rolled Franklin Press in Frankie's direction as if swatting at a bothersome fly.

"I could tell a passel of em' on your daddy," the old man continued, remaining in his novel position, his left boney elbow digging into the top of his left thigh. Several of the other old men grinned but stared at their feet or their hands, as if joining the old man in his merry yarn would somehow be risky, as if stories passed around about Jimmy Clark, the same man just moments before they'd laughed with, at, and beside of was somehow taboo now.

"Hit was bout two year ago, ole CD Jenkins's boy, way up in high school, rear-ended this feller down round Zickgraf Lumber. Well, this feller'd been goin' around town doing that, bowin' up on people, trying to git em' to hit him. Well, CD's Boy, I don't recall his name right off."

"Patrick," Frankie said, never taking her eyes or scissors off of her fresh customer.

"Patrick!" The old tale-teller went on as if he'd just remembered the name himself and hadn't been told.

"Now ole Patrick had done hit his breaks three, four times. This feller'd gun it and stop, gun it and stop. Finally, ole Patrick clipped him. Oh, that feller come a tearin' out a thire.

"You'll pay for my car! You'll pay for my damn car!"

"Ole boy bellered, swangin' em arms, mad as an ole wet hen. Well here come Jimmy. I's a standin' ire talken' to Cowboy, your grandpa, Virgil Rice, in the parkin' lot bout havin' me a hoe handle made when here he come. Well, it weren't but a breath, ole Jimmy had at loud-mouth sombitch backin' down."

For the first time since the stranger's story had started, the other old local color, who'd grown uncomfortably sullen, seemed to grin and agree with what the tale-teller said. The storyteller, as further evidence of what Gregg sensed was occurring, turned away from him and began looking down the row of faces toward the rain-peppered door, then, leaning further than when he'd begun the tale the other way, back in Gregg's direction, but beyond him, to the three old men sitting to his right. The old man was obviously seeking collective affirmation and concurrence from the gaggle of scraggly old timers wiling away their evening at Frankie's barbershop.

"Well," The old spinner went on, "CD, Patrick's daddy, he'd been at home workin' in his garden when he'd got the call tellin' him Patrick had been in a wreck, and hit weren't two minutes, here he come. He fishtailed that ole truck, skeered to death, and here come ole CD, huffin' and a puffin', that chest out, dirt all ore him, rollin' that baccer round his mouth, and there was Jimmy, all arned and tucked, shined up like a new penny, cause your daddy's always lookin' like he's got a funeral to get to. Man can see hisself in your daddy's shoes. Well, Jimmy put that hand up in ole CD's face."

"CD!" He squalled. "Patrick's fine. Calm the Hell down!"

"Your daddy's like a pissed off Copperhead half the time. Well ole CD hadn't spit that baccer since he'd been standin' thire, and that ole swill was a wellin' up. Thire your daddy stood tryin' to calm ole CD down. CD's just a fumin, 'and he's got to spit. Ole CD leaned at big heard over to spit, and God a mighty he laid a pool of backer juice all over your daddy's slicked up shoes. Me and Virg bout went to our reward a laughin'. Your daddy looked up at us like he'd slit our throats if he could, and I believe he would have too had God and half a Franklin not a been lookin' on."

"Betcha CD's hire didn't move a minute through the whole damn thang either!" The toothless, old man who'd earlier elicited the steel melting response from Gregg's father proffered. The room once again filled with laughter, but as the barbershop rang with merriment the old tale teller's eyes darkened and bore a wounded look.

"Hell far, I weren't watchin' his damned ole hire." The old man mumbled as he leaned back in his seat, seemingly disgusted at having had his thunder pulled from beneath him.

Gregg knew CD Jenkins, a highway patrolman who his father often carried on long conversations with while he and his mother and little brother waited impatiently in the car watching the two lawmen appear to have no concept of time, so he got the joke. CD wore a high sprayed pompadour of hair, kind of like Elvis, but gray.

For some reason, the party was over. As loud and comical as the yarn spinner had been and as off the cuff as the toothless man's quip about CD's hair had been, neither man had succeeded in lifting the spirits of the room to its former glory.

"Frankie, you know what this rain puts me in the mind of?" The toothless man queried the busy barber.

"What's that?" Frankie asked while carefully dusting the hair from the still-expressionless old man's face with a soft handheld brush, a brush Gregg knew all too well, for it tickled the life out of him.

"Reminds me of that night in 63 Frankie." The toothless man delivered with an ever-so-slight tilt to his words. "Hit rained just like this." He said again.

As Frankie pumped her most recent customer's chair to the floor, she cut her eyes in the toothless man's direction. "Now let's not tell that one," Frankie said with an earnest look in her eyes, far more earnest a look then she'd worn all evening, more earnest a look than Gregg had ever seen her wear. "We've got young'uns in the house," she added.

Gregg lifted his eyes from a picture of a huge ten point Buck near the back of the faded magazine that had over the last hour become his mock interest, his barrier for hiding. Frankie and the poker-faced old gentleman then stepped to the old blue cash register by the door. For the first time since he'd saddled the barber chair, the old man expressed a hint of humanity when he laughed at something Frankie whispered to him as he paid for his haircut. The man's response to Frankie's whisper, God knows why stayed with Gregg.

"That's why I'm a-leavin'," he said. "That's exactly why I'm a-leavin'."

Frankie lifted the lock and opened the door for the man, once again allowing in the wind and the rain. The man ducked his head prior to entering the torrent and in a blink was gone, vanishing into the dismal August storm.

"Come on up here sugar," Frankie called out to Gregg while popping her towel into the chair with a locker room snap.

As Gregg gingerly laid the old magazine in his seat and made his way to the barber chair, he distinctly recalled when he'd had to sit on a board in the chair and the Bubble Gum tin he'd always gotten to thrust his hand into upon completion of his earlier haircuts.

"Day looked just like this Frankie." The old man once again cast out, obviously ignoring the barber's body language and previous reluctance at biting.

"Thankin' of ole CD Jenkins from that tale put me in mind of CD Baines, and lookin' at your pretty face all afternoon, Frankie, got me thankin' bout, Ms. Frankie Bullock." The toothless man said with a child-like, yet wicked grin.

When again the barber wouldn't take the old man's bait, the room stilled to absurdity. Gregg believed he could hear the hair hitting the hard tiled floor. No one spoke or nodded or seemed to even breathe.

"Yeah, I remember," Frankie finally murmured, after too long a respite in the conversation, most likely uncomfortable with the silence the topic had elicited.

"Jimmy's a whole lot like ole Chief Baines was back in his day." The toothless instigator drawled. "Both men not big as a minute, and both as soon kill ya' as look at ya' half the time."

"Both of em' ride motorcycles," the old man who'd been seated at Gregg's right elbow mumbled, without lifting his eyes from the Franklin Press page he had folded in half before him.

"At's right!" The toothless man replied. "And, both of em's haunted too. Ole Chief Baines just stares off into space now. He ain't ever let it go."

As Frankie wrapped the paper collar around Gregg's young neck and pinned the worn striped apron from behind, he couldn't help but wonder what in God's name was this old man talking about.

"Ain't nobody can live out thire, and you know that, and a man a git hisself kilt just talkin' bout that damn case." The old man said this last part in a whisper as if he were telling a ghost story.

"Well, there ain't but one spring chicken in the hen house right now. The rest of us need every step we've got left, so let's not talk about it now; how bout that." Frankie finally said with wide eyes, intentionally animated and just a little wild. "She's gone, and it's done. It's done!" Frankie placed a special emphasis on the second done.

"Oh, I know," the old dog mumbled. "but hit makes a man wonder? Who stabbed that woman to death out ire? Who could have hated her that bad? Hit makes a man wonder." The old man finished his sentence by rubbing the snuff-stained corners of his mouth with his left thumb and forefinger.

Gregg's mind was racing with questions—*Who was Frankie Bullock, and who can't live where anymore? Who is CD Baines, and why would he and his own father be haunted and haunted by what? And what danger are they talking about? Who could get themselves killed?*

The rain, through the barbershop window, began to slack a little, and the thunder, as if on God's queue to bracket the scene, rolled again heavy and long, edging the death-letter of a day in black.

Frankie leaned over and lightly turned up the volume on the radio before tilting Gregg's head slightly to the left with two guiding fingers. As Frankie's agile digits made Gregg's scalp tighten and tingle, the old toothless scoundrel stared hard and longingly into the dark of the day, seemingly unaware of his surroundings, lost in some sordid setting Gregg, at the time, believed he'd never know or understand—time would prove him wrong.

Like a wild horse being reined in and saddled, steadied and stilled, one last time before the cryptic topic of conversation would die a mysterious yet instantaneous death, the old toothless character spoke. This time he wasn't speaking to Frankie nor to his dusty old cronies. He wasn't even speaking to himself. Gauging from the far-flung look in his wintery eyes, he was speaking to the storm itself when he asked, "Looked just like this, just like this that night in 63 didn't ya'?"

CHAPTER ONE

The bizarre late evening at the Macon Barber Shop that had been punctuated with bursts of lightning and thunder, cackling crows in filthy garb, secrets, sin, and rain, came to a close with a song and a silhouette. The song, Elvis' "Are You Lonesome Tonight," came seeping through Frankie's ancient radio like rising, murky, flood waters. The silhouette, a dark form clutching an umbrella, suddenly appeared at Frankie's door and mysteriously peered inside without knocking. Frankie, noticeably frustrated, with reluctance, walked to the door, but just as she was lifting her deft fingers to the lock, the figure turned away, and within seconds had disappeared back into the belly of the summer storm from which he had come. Frankie lowered her hand from the unturned lock. She might normally have called out into the rain an acceptance of entry or a gracious denial, but something in the way the stranger had so quickly fled made her blood run cold.

"Who the Devil was that?" Frankie asked as she made her way back to the chair. Gregg noticed afterward that the barber cast several fleet glances over her shoulder at the door and through the window.

The eerie departure of the silhouette left only the song. The rain continued to fall. Thunder still growled in the distance. Without his knowing, what would become the Genesis scene in a long strange movie Gregg would play a part in was coming to an end, and it ended properly with a ghost, a ghost singing from a dark and empty castle in Memphis, Tennessee, a ghost asking a mourning stormy southland if it's lonesome, if it misses him and if it's sorry the two had drifted apart.

CHAPTER TWO
TOO LATE NOW

Now I've always been the kind of person that doesn't like to trespass,
but sometimes you just find yourself over the line

From "Brownsville Girl" by Bob Dylan and Sam Shepard

JULY 26, 2013

"I was over at Eddie Poindexter's this morning. Frank was workin' on my ignition. I got to talking to a couple ole boys about Britches, Eddie's daddy. Did you ever meet Britches Poindexter?" Robert Shook, the curator of Franklin, North Carolina's Historical Museum asked his friend and fellow museum board member Gregg Clark while fishing around in his water glass for a plum of a piece of ice to chew on.

"Not to my knowledge," Gregg responded while wiping, with a paper napkin, a few drops of spilled water from the menu that lay before him.

"Oh Britches he was a character." The curator went on. "Loved to fish. He and ole Ferguson, his fishin' buddy, retired lawman, Lord if you found one you found the other, fished till they by God couldn't fish no more. Ole Riley Henry told me a good one on em'. You know Riley?" The curator asked, simultaneously crunching down on a piece of ice.

"Oh yeah, Riley and Wanda both, two of the finest people I've ever met. You know Wanda's grandma way back was Frankie Silver, hanged as an ax murderer in 1833?"

"Oh yeah. Now that's a story, but we'll talk about that one another day or we'll run out of daylight sure as the world," Robert said before picking up right where he'd dropped his last bread crumb. "Now ole Britches and Furguson, Riley said, was way up in age, went fishin' up on Buck Creek. Some feller or other was driving by, had his window down. Thank God he did. He heard one of em' hollerin,' 'Help! Help!' Well, he pulled off the road and listened, and there they was. One of em', I can't remember which one Riley said it was Britches or Furguson, but one of em' had fell in the water and couldn't get out. The other one was down in there with him holdin' his head up so he wouldn't drown. Well, that ole boy he fished both of em' out. Riley said he left em' standin' on the bank there like two ole drown rats just a hoo-rawin.''

"Sounds like a scene from a Jack Lemon and Walter Matthau movie," Gregg said, just before lifting his own water glass to his lips.

"Lord, Franklin's got a mess of tales about old characters like that. I've been hearin' em' all my life," the curator said. "You ever heard tale of Uncle Boney Ridley and Doctor Snipe McCloud?" Robert asked with an expectant grin.

"Just what I read in Judge Felix Alley's book," Gregg responded while checking the time on his phone.

"Ole Uncle Boney Ridley," Robert continued, "lived a way up on Cowee Mountain, up on Watauga. He stood nigh on seven feet tall and weren't sober a day in his life. Ole Snipe, his bosom drinkin' buddy, had found himself a medical book somewhere or another and started callin' hisself a doctor, and damn if people didn't let him doctor em'! They lived, best as I can tell, from the mid-1800s to around the 1940s, best of friends ole Boney and Snipe, and the stories, Lord have mercy!"

"I've heard some of em'," Gregg responded, less enthusiastic than usual, due to his being distracted about the evening that lie before him.

"Old Dr. Lyle had Boney up there in his office one time." The curator continued. "Doc Lyle he says, 'Boney, you're nigh on ninety-year-old now, and you still drink like a fish. I wouldn't strike a match in your vicinity. You'd go up like kindlin'! You need to stop!' The curator took a drink of his water before going on. 'If that's the truth Doc., I will; I swear to it! I'll quit today!' The curator said this part with a slur in his voice aimed at mimicking the old drunk. 'No, no, I don't want to hear it Boney. I don't want to hear any promise to quit drinkin'. I've heard it too many times.' Ole Doc Lyle gruffed back at Boney; Robert said with a grin.

'Quit drankin' Hell!' Boney shot back. 'I mean I'll quit smokin', and I don't know exactly where my vicinity is, but I know damned good and well they ought not be nerry a match stuck up in it!'

With his punch line delivered, the curator laughed loud, warm and long, a Southern man's laugh.

"I'd loved to have met both of em'," Gregg said, his response wrapped in a Southern laugh of his own. "We tell their stories on the tours some nights."

"You do?" Robert responded while looking to his wife for affirmation of how funny his story had been; however, he found her to be deep in conversation with Gregg's wife, Pauletta, about something they weren't letting the boys in on.

"Here we go," Robert said as the waitress walked up. The waitress, a lovely young lady with big grey eyes, held the group's dinner plates up her arm like just-toppled dominos, each one slightly overlapping the last.

"My Lord, I'd have that spilled everywhere!" Kathy, Robert's wife, said while clearing the space before her of her cell phone and keys. "That's one thing I knew never to try was waitressin'." She added with a forward head nod for emphasis.

"Me either!" Pauletta replied as the comment had been directed at her. "I'm as clumsy as a drunk mule as it is. I'd have it all over the place."

The waitress, fresh and seemingly wide awake in her life, smiled as she sorted out the order she wore up her arm like a cast.

"I've got a hamburger salad, ... two hamburger salads," she quickly self-corrected.

"That's mine!" Robert responded with a big, child-like grin, "one of em' anyhow."

"Then this one must be yours, Mr. Clark," the waitress said, erupting in a noticeably- brighter countenance and tone, as she gently placed the salad into her former teacher's hands.

"Yes ma'am," Gregg replied with a smile of his own.

"Fish Tacos?" The young waitress asked, still beaming.

"Over here." Pauletta kindly spoke, holding up one, lone finger.

"And...," the young waitress paused as she turned the dish in her hand, "a Marlon Brando Burger," she said finally as Kathy reached for the last plate. "Can I get yall anything else, some coffee?" The waitress asked as she pulled four fresh straws from her apron emblazoned with a faded logo that read, Motor Company Grill.

After making solid eye contact with the others at the table, it was Gregg, her former English and history teacher, who ultimately sealed the deal.

"We're all good Tasha, thank you."

The eager young waitress then scurried across the black and white checkerboard floor and disappeared around a corner.

"Sweet kid," Robert said as he lifted his fork to the huge slab of hamburger steak weighing down his green salad, not unlike an elephant squatting in a clover patch.

"Hold on Cujo!" Becky said while gently placing her fingertips atop her husband's hand that was already sawing with purpose into his still-steaming meat. "The Blessing." Becky reminded her hungry husband. After the four friends offered up a short prayer, Becky and Pauletta jumped back headlong into the conversation, right where they'd left off. Robert and Gregg, not unlike their wives, as if a bell had tinged, fell right back into talking about ancient history, the reason for the dinner date in the first place; however, strangely the historical topic Gregg felt certain would consume their meal time had been left off the table completely. Robert, who'd more or less thrown the initial conversational punch, raised his fork while chewing, a visual that indicated he was just about to speak.

"Did I ever tell you about the first mailman in Franklin?" Robert asked Gregg, with serene eyes, eyes that had settled and no longer darted in the direction of every color, flash or bounce while dismembering his steak. "He'd strap a lantern between his knees on snowy nights." The curator went on while chewing his dinner. "He'd tote the mail clear to Dillsboro and back, did it for years." Robert trailed off from the mailman story just long enough to ask Becky if she'd fed the dog that morning. She told him she had before she'd left for work. She then reiterated,

"She's fine till tonight." That's when Gregg heard it, the unmistakable hum, a needle drop that the whole world recognized, a soft intro that led to dark places in his mind. Within a breath, the click-clacking of knives and forks, the occasional cough or laugh from a corner booth, the metallic pinging of the front door when a patron arrived or departed, all swirled together.

Tasha, the young waitress who'd served Gregg's party just moments before, passed and asked if everyone was all still OK. Gregg acquiesced with a gentle head nod. As the young waitress once again disappeared around the corner, Gregg recalled her project. Tasha had been in Gregg's English and History classes several years back. She'd created a fine tri-fold project on the state of North Carolina. He recalled she'd done a little dance when she saw she'd received an A. Gregg recalled the scene with a smile that just barely bent his lips; however, his former student's youthful visage and her project and her childish little dance too blended and swirled with the chemistry of the room, when, "Are You Lonesome Tonight" by Elvis Presley rolled through the speakers, filling the room much like an ocean wave fills a child's sand castle moat. With every recited line and every Jordanaire hum, it became harder and harder for Gregg to remain engaged in conversation. The song was calling him back, back to a summer storm, back twenty-six years, back to a hot seat and a cold rain, back to a silhouette, back to a time before he knew of Frances Bullock.

"Isn't it Honey?" Pauletta said, placing a hand on her husband's left leg.

"Isn't what?" Gregg responded with a smile that peeled his skin clean off, his ignorance totally exposed.

Pauletta ran her hand, feigning annoyance, up and down her husband's leg.

"Isn't it dangerous what we're doing?" She rephrased the question, so as to give Gregg some content to grab a hold of.

"Hell, surely they're all dead by now," Robert scoffed, pushing his cleaned plate forward and placing his crossed arms on the table before him. "Oh, that reminds me!" the curator actually jumped in his seat as he spoke. "I brought that song." As Robert leaned toward his wife on the bench, obviously retrieving something from the back pocket of his jeans, Kathy spoke.

"I don't know," Kathy said, pulling something from her purse. "I think it's thin ice." She then became satirically saucer-eyed, lightly opened her mouth and allowed her lower teeth to jut out beyond her upper lip. A look that read, glad it's not me.

"It's not the safest thing I've ever done I guess, but I can't seem to let it go," Gregg said.

"Here you go," Robert said, unfolding what Gregg could already decipher to be a loose-leaf notebook page filled with hand-written lyrics in blue ink. "Ole Dave worked out a decent rhythm for it on the guitar, but I thought your brother Scott could do one better. "Three Days in Sixty Three" I call it. Done right, it would make a fine ballad, soft guitar, some dulcimer maybe.

As Gregg silently read the song lyrics the curator had written and had promised to bring with him, Pauletta picked up where Kathy had left off.

"I've told him a thousand times, I don't think it's a good idea, but I'm as bad as he is; I want to know who did it so bad!" Pauletta said while checking her phone for new Facebook posts.

"*Oh me too!*" Kathy whispered. "Me and Robert have turned it over and over, not like you guys of course, but we've laid in bed trying to figure it out, have we not?"

"We have," Robert mumbled, as he again fished around in his water glass for a piece of ice and watched Gregg's eyes for reaction to his creation.

"Get your hand out of there!" Kathy commanded! "We're in public!"

"We think we know who did it," Gregg said, never lifting his eyes from the hand-written lyrics. Their booth grew quiet. The restaurant seemed to grow quiet. There was even a pause in the constant music that had been streaming through the little diner, and just as Kathy was opening her mouth to ask, *who*, Gregg's cell phone rang, making all four friends jump like frightened children listening to a flashlight-camp fire tale.

As Gregg lifted his phone to his ear and lowered the lyrics, the other three laughed at how silly they'd just acted.

"We're just like a bunch of young'uns," Kathy giggled, "scared of our own shadows."

The corners of Pauletta's mouth dipped though when Gregg answered the phone, "Where Shadows Walk," a greeting she'd heard a thousand times before.

Four hellos later, Gregg ended the call and gingerly placed the phone beside the curator's lyrics.

"Well, who was it?" Pauletta curtly asked.

"Heavy breathing," Gregg responded, before taking a long drink from his water glass.

"Hell, I've waited my whole life for one of them calls," Robert quipped to lighten the mood.

"Stop it!" Kathy said, smacking her husband on the forearm.

"I don't think you should do this tonight Hon! For Heaven's sake how many have died?" Pauletta rhetorically asked, not taking her eyes from her husband this time.

"Too many," Gregg responded, "but look." He pointed up the street to the one hundred and eleven-year-old historical museum they'd readied earlier in the evening for the presentation. "They're already lining up," Gregg said with a devilish grin.

The next few minutes were a jostling mess of paying bills, scrounging for and into purses for sundry items, leaving tips, applying lipstick, wiping up water spills and Robert's rehashing and re-rehashing of his heavy breathing joke, each time garnering a smack or steely eyes from his wife; however, amid the hustle and bustle of ensuring he wasn't late for his own presentation, Gregg's mind again slipped off, and he became hyper-focused on his surroundings. The Elvis Presley song and anomalous phone call had thrown him. Though he'd made light of it to his wife and friends, Gregg, with great clarity, remembered all too well when his own father used to get the same phone calls deep in the night, calls with heavy breathing, carnival laughter from a pull-string doll, and sometimes, from the same doll, single, slim whispered words and phrases like BEWARE, STOP and BE CAREFUL!

Still clutching the unfolded song, Gregg and the others stepped from the Arctic cool of the Motor Company Grill, a modern restaurant made to look like a 1950s era diner complete with black and white checkerboard flooring and bright, red, shiny leather stools, into the sweltering, late-July, Southern Appalachian heat.

Regardless of the balmy late evening, Gregg felt a chill through his sweat. *Who had the unknown caller been?* He wondered. Gregg meticulously scrutinized the small picturesque Main Street before him. He stared suspiciously and somewhat expectantly up and into the blind-clad windows of the Bryant Funeral Home that sat across the street, a tall, lazy, white building that boasted wide high pillars, half expecting two mysterious fingers to split the blinds. Gregg looked long into people's eyes as they passed in their cars. He looked up and down the street, mentally searching the parked cars and doorways for the silhouette from his childhood, but nothing seemed askew.

The funeral home blinds hung still and unparted with no fiendish faces behind them. The drivers of the passing cars seemed to pay him no mind. There were no leering glances or knowing stares from even one of them. There was not a single hint of caution or concern apparent on any of their faces. Gregg could see no mysterious characters up or down the street, no lurking figures, no strangers lifting their eyes over lightly lowered newspapers or peering up from beneath gingerly tilted fedora brims.

"Should we even do this tonight?" Pauletta whispered to her husband while reaching out for his hand.

Gregg cast one final glance behind him through the restaurant's windows at the dining patrons, then, squeezing his worried wife's hand, said in a mischievous child-like tone, "We have to baby. Look down there. They've already paid. It's too late now."

Robert and Kathy, who'd gone on ahead to open the museum, were just disappearing inside when Gregg began to read Robert's song lyrics aloud to his wife. As the two strolled the short distance between the restaurant and the museum where people were either gathered in knots of conversation just outside the door or already entering, Pauletta listened.

THREE DAYS IN SIXTY-THREE
In this little mountain town-
the tragic news went all around.
Here in the middle of the Bible belt-
Our worst fears were felt.

It was on that dreadful night-
Dear Frances lost her life.
An evil killer runs free,
Oh Lord who can it be?

Chorus:
Three days in sixty-three changed life for you and me,
But the scales of justice will be weighed on that
Great Judgement Day.

Folks bolted all their doors,
That never were locked before,
And loaded up their guns-
A damn killer is on the run.

The law came from all around,
But no killer was ever found.
Fifty years has passed us by,
But her memory will never die.

Repeat Chorus:

"It's good," Pauletta said. I especially like the name, "Three Days in Sixty-Three." That would make a good book title wouldn't it?"

CHAPTER THREE
WOODLAWN

She said, welcome to the land of the living dead.

From "Brownsville Girl " by Bob Dylan and Sam Shepard

AUGUST 30, 2013

The night was warm. The stars were bright, and the moon was crescent. With his right index finger, Gregg followed the deep-cut grooves that read, July 26th, 1963 on Frances Bullock's tombstone, a brand new fifty-year-old death date.

Earlier in the day, Gregg had received a call from the dead woman's cousin, Janice Crane, a woman of her mid-sixties and one hell of a piano player. With a gentility afforded very few, the old woman informed Gregg that she was standing beneath a lofty Oak tree at the Woodlawn Cemetery, a wide field of grave-stones that spread across several acres of rolling grassy hills two miles north of Franklin, North Carolina. The reason for the woman's phone call concerned some long overdue business. Mrs. Crane's cousin, Frances Bullock, who, at the time of her death had been twenty-five years her senior, had been brutally stabbed to death fifty years to the day. The purpose of her call was to inform Gregg that her cousin's death date had finally, that very day, been cut into her tombstone, a long, long overdue chore. The fifty-year absence of numbers showing when Frances Bullock had died in no way reflected indifference or laziness on the part of her family, rather the opposite. They'd collectively felt, as no one knew which day of the three days she'd been missing she'd actually died on, an irreverence in guessing, so for fifty long years her stone had bore her name, the year of her birth and nothing more. To the casual observer passing by her stone, Frances Bullock appeared to be very much alive.

The missing death date hadn't been the only oddity concerning the slain woman's stone. The spelling of her last name had also been a source of stories, fodder for whispers, secrets, and speculation, for, in life, Frances Bullock had ended her last name of Bullock with a k; however, her mother-in-law insisted, upon her daughter-in-law's untimely death, that her last name be altered upon her stone. The older woman demanded the k at the end of Bullock be changed to an h. The reasoning behind her requested odd alteration was alien and enigmatic. She claimed the version ending with an h to be the more ancient and proper spelling of the name; however, years later, when she herself passed away, her own tombstone did not reflect the same change. The k was back.

For five decades, as the calendar pages turned, according to her stone, Frances Bullock appeared to be growing old somewhere, tending a mountain garden maybe, attending Senior Sunday school classes or bouncing laughing great grandbabies on her knees, when in reality, her bones had been resting beneath her marker since before John F. Kennedy's assassination.

It was the closure that relieved Frances' cousin, and after calling Gregg, the thirty-seven-year-old History and English teacher she'd recently become acquainted with due to the school teacher's inclusion of her cousin's story on he and his wife's Where Shadows Walk, Historic Ghost Tours of Franklin and their detailed historic presentations concerning her death and the mystery that shrouded it, the older lady felt she could let some of it go. "It's been a long time coming," Janice told Gregg on the phone that morning, while draped in the shade of the tall Oak.

"*Fifty years tonight Frankie*," Gregg whispered to himself as he removed his finger from the deep-hewn grooves of the freshly-carved marker. With twenty-six years of affiliation with the dead woman now in his metaphorical rearview mirror, Gregg felt comfortable in referring to her as her friends and family had in life, "Frankie." He felt he knew her well enough.

Sitting in the tall grass at Frankie's grave, his fingers laced together and arms wrapped around his knees, Gregg began playing out the upcoming tour in his mind. *Where Shadows Walk, Historic Ghost Tours* were his babies. Since he was a young boy, Gregg had devoured ghost stories, myths, legends and tales of the macabre, so when the opportunity arose for he and his wife, Pauletta, to start historic ghost tours of their own in their quaint and wildly-historic small mountain town of Franklin, North Carolina, they jumped at the chance. The tour coming up, the Woodlawn Cemetery Tour, was packed, a full house.

Gregg cast one last long look at the moon then unlaced his fingers. He then lifted from the grass the leather-bound journal that lay beside him. He opened it and began reading. The moon, that for all the world reminded him of a luminous fingernail clipping, handed down just enough light for him to read his notes.

"*Mother's Muddy Feet—I'll start with that one.*" Gregg whispered to himself. "*I'll do Eddie McKinley, Little Girl's First Home, George W. Meek, Dillsboro Vampires, Ada Munday, Nimrod Jarrett, Bayless Henderson, George Bidwell, Kope and Tim, Aunt Ma-*

halia, Boojum, Nathan Rankin, Dr. Lyle, and you Frankie—I'll end with you tonight Frankie." Gregg said as he closed his book.

Gregg sat alone at the grave of Frances Bullock in the night, an unthinkable act for most people, listening to the sporadic hum of passing cars in the distance and the occasional night bird's call. Frustration bubbled up within him, displacing the placid state of mind the night had thus far helped him set. A dog started barking beyond the dark trees at the cemetery's far eastern edge and not just any dog, the dog, the dog that Gregg knew with blind certainty could hear his footfalls in the grass each time he arrived at the cemetery, the dog that could bark himself hoarse, the dog that, if it so chose, could utterly strangle the life out of the dark and foreboding mood Gregg so desired to set with his tours by never letting up.

Clutching his journal, Gregg rose to his feet. After sending up a prayer to any member of the heavenly host that might be listening and might consider stifling the incessant barking of a pesky dog, Gregg allowed his left hand to rest easily on the grave he'd been seated in front of for the past several minutes.

"Be back later Frankie," Gregg said as he walked away. Headlights far below in the parking lot lit the cemetery's lower edge. The guests were arriving.

Thank God that dog stopped barking, Gregg thought to himself as he checked his phone for the time. He'd checked it at least five times in the last five minutes. He was nervous, and he couldn't quite put his finger on the reason why. Tours, in the beginning, always made him a little nervous. He never knew what to expect, who to expect. Gregg's tours generally turned out to be amazing, filled with swarms of starry-eyed people sponging up every last historical and bloody detail. But there were other nights, nights with men who wore angry cement stares as their wives and girlfriends smiled and hung on his every word, mouths agape, mesmerized by the stories of the small town's strange and often grisly past.

As Gregg waited in the glow of the last light for several acres that hung high overhead at the edge of the parking lot, he wondered what kind of tour he'd have. He thought of his wife and kids at home and how he'd laughed with them prior to his leaving for the tour.

"Headed to the boneyard boys and girls," Gregg had jokingly called out as he was preparing to leave, patting down his pockets and closing the long top flap of the gray canvas bag he always carried, a bag filled with LLC forms, flashlights, pens, and small tea lights. Gregg then lightly begun humming his usual go-to song, "Here Comes That Rainbow Again" by Kris Kristofferson.

"I'd wish you good luck, but you don't need it," Pauletta said while grabbing her husband by both sides of his shirt near his shoulders and pulling him into a big animated kiss.

Gregg and Pauletta had been married for twelve years. They had three wonderful children and a life so blessed, they both considered it spooky. Both were teachers, Gregg, an eighth grade English and History teacher and Pauletta, a vivaciously-spunky third grade teacher, and both were completely and unapologetically addicted to adventure, ghost stories, legends, history and the art of living. They were perfect partners, two crossed naked wires crackling and sparking.

Gregg, near blinded by headlights and lost in sugary thoughts of his wife at home was mentally putting himself into tour mode.

The next twenty minutes were a perfect storm of headlights, flashlights, scratched out signatures, greetings and silent prayers peppered with curse words on Gregg's part, as the damn dog had yet to stop barking at the far edge of the cemetery.

Men waited by open car doors, asking one last time if their wives wanted their jackets or umbrellas, even though the stars shone brilliantly above. Couples sank into dark patches of shadow silently offered by the overhanging trees, and laughter rang out as some young ladies ran around the building to relieve themselves, their boyfriends receiving slaps across their chests from the peeing girl's friends who hadn't had to go when they informed Gregg that their girlfriend's Appalachia was showin'. Tiny, red, head-high embers bobbed by dark cars as guests took their last long drags from cigarettes.

The giggling girls, seemingly college age, who had just moments before announced to several strangers their intention of peeing behind a building prior to their tour, finally joined the group waiting patiently in the tall grass at the graveyard's edge, and then, as if on command, everyone grew still and quiet.

The stars, after Gregg had led the group away from the last lights of the parking lot, looked for all the world like a field of Diamonds in the sky, and the slim wedge of a moon, teasingly slipping through the fingers of clouds, cast just enough light to outline each stone and crypt with a silky edge of moon dust. Before leading his tour group into the shelter of a small gazebo that sat blushingly close to the paved walkway for the first story of the night, Gregg raised his lantern to a shoulder-high stone and began to slowly read aloud:

"WE ARE THOSE WHO THE BURDEN BORE, AND NOW HAVE EARNED OUR REST. WE ARE THOSE WHO HAVE GONE BEFORE AND SLEEP ON OUR MOTHER'S BREAST. WE HARKED TO OUR MOTHER'S CALL. SHE WILL OUR VIGIL'S KEEP. SOFT LET EACH FOOTSTEP FALL. LET NONE DISTURB OUR SLEEP."

After thoughtfully reading, via his lantern's warm spill of light, the requiem poem carved eerily into the stone at the cemetery's edge, Gregg led the group to the small covered area. After they were comfortably positioned, Gregg began a story he'd only recently added to the Woodlawn Tour, an old story that he'd learned as a boy but had lost in print until recently. First, he built the setting, an 1870s Southern Appalachian farm, a crooked fence line and a very sick young mother who was tight with a child in her belly. Next, he told of the young mother's painful delivery, the death of her baby upon arrival and of the mother's subsequent death. Finally, verbally drafting for his audience a sad funeral, pre-dawn darkness, a figure clad in white and bending, dead, corn stalks, Gregg finished his tale of a dead mother supernaturally tending to her newborn child who'd been buried alive.

As Gregg painted the dead young woman's journey, a lank cadaver careening through corpses of corn in the night, he watched the eyes of his guests, rimmed in gold due to the lantern he'd placed at his feet. He watched them widen and shift. He watched as each man and woman, boy and girl leaned closer to one another. He watched them stare nervously over their shoulders. He watched them start at every sound the night served up, be it ever so faint.

After leaving the shelter, Gregg, looking for all the world like a mother duck guiding her babies through the night, stopped at one of the most unique tombstones in America, a life-sized statue of a boy in Huckleberry Finn garb lying on his stomach. What made the tombstone so unique though went far beyond his attire or the boy's state of recline. What made it stand out were the books. Beneath the boy's fingers, upon which his chin was cradled, were the books he was reading, Harry Potter and Lord of the Rings. There, Gregg told the unrelated but sad story of little Eddie McKinley, a ten-year-old boy who'd been found frozen to death in the year 1910 and the mystery and ghost story that accompanied the tragedy.

Gregg then led the crowd to a second tombstone near the little reading boy, this time a girl, again life-sized, just like the boy had been, the stones similar by sheer coincidence, wearing bid overalls and pigtails and carrying, on her back, a pack meant for flowers. Sometimes there were fresh flowers spilling from her pack, but more often than not the pack was home to funnel spiders and the twisted dead remnants of what at one point had been fresh flowers. At the little girl's stone Gregg told a terrifying tale of a young child's experience in a haunted house in the late 1800s.

As the night wore on, Gregg spun yarn upon yarn of gallows and ax murderers, disembodied voices and angelic visitors, demons, and witches. Gregg hoped that the guests were building the scenes in their minds, tasting the blood on their tongues, smelling each rich spade full of upturned graveyard earth and hearing the softest whisper or the loudest scream.

Toward the end of the tour, Gregg led his group to the grave of N.S. Jarrett, the wealthy Franklin, North Carolina socialite who'd been shot through the head by Bayless Henderson in the year 1871. He then told his eager listeners the subsequent tale of how Henderson was later hanged and his dead body dismembered.

Not six feet from Mr. Jarrett's grave, at the tombstone of his daughter, Ada Munday, whose life had been bold, wild and filled with daring, Gregg told of Ms. Munday's sad affiliation with Mitchel Mozeley, a twenty-two-year-old African American man who was aggressively dragged down Franklin's dirt main street in the year 1898. He told of the beating, the lynching, and the boiling off of his flesh in a pre-prepared wash tub alongside the Little Tennessee River.

Gregg could hear gasps in the crowd at the grave of George W. Meek, the eccentric millionaire who pioneered the science of recording the dead though EVPs. Gregg told of how Meek believed Franklin, North Carolina to be a thin place, a place where the veil between the world of the living and the world of the dead was paper thin, a place where ghosts walked. He told of Meek's first EVP captured in April of 1982, the first EVP ever recorded on planet Earth.

Stories of vampires, witches, Bigfoot, and pioneers came next, followed by a tale of the once demon-possessed home of the millionaire miner George Bidwell and his wife, Ella, who'd gone mad upon the death of her child.

Just before Gregg was to tell of the final surrender of the Civil War, he stopped one last time to have his guests stand at the graves of Captain Nathan P. Rankin and Dr. Samuel Harley Lyle. At Rankin's grave, Gregg talked of how the Confederate Captain had started multiple schools in Franklin. At Lyle's grave, he told of how the doctor had been the first President of the College of Surgeons in America and of how, when serving as a state legislator, he had been instrumental in creating the first law in America requiring school attendance of children. Gregg finished by telling his guests of Dr. Lyle's warm relationship with old Buck, the vagrant three-legged town dog of Franklin, and of how the dog had laid upon the good doctor's grave for days after his death.

Standing at the graves of Timoxena Siler Elias and her famous lawyer husband, Kope Elias, Gregg regaled his enthralled guests with the story of the final Confederate surrender of the American Civil War. Timoxena, who'd been ten-years-old at the time of the surrender and affectionately referred to as Little

Tim, had ripped the American Flag from the second story balcony of Dixie Hall, the fine home she and her family resided in on Franklin's Main Street, where it had been hung by Union troops as a public display of surrender.

Finally, it was Frankie's turn. Scaling the steepest hill in the Woodlawn Cemetery, Gregg led the attentive crowd to the stone he'd sat at earlier in the night, a stone he'd sat at many times before—he led them to the final resting place of Ms. Frances Bullock.

At the grave's edge, Gregg began his story, a story bursting at the seams with deceit and lust, betrayal and guilt, mystery and scandal, intrigue and ghosts, a tale both grisly and morose.

On some nights a full moon cast a net of warm light over the crowd as Gregg spoke. New moon nights made Gregg a mere voice in the darkness, but that night, with the crescent moon teasing with its glow, the illumination was near perfection, for the moon allowed mere glimpses of Gregg's guests. It lit their eyes, the bridges of their noses, light-colored garments. It offered ample light for guests to see several feet around them in all directions without blacking everything out like a new moon or making the night as bold as noonday like a full moon.

Huddled together in groups and pairs and complimented by the moon's perfect glow, Gregg's guests listened with rapt, undivided attention as he took them back fifty years. Like the ghosts of Christmas past, present and future had led Ebenezer Scrooge as a silent witness to his life, so too did Gregg lead his guests through dark haunted houses, to gruesome murder scenes and into cold, bright, autopsy rooms. He took them by the proverbial hand and eased them through pivotal scenes in the life and death of Frances Bullock. He unwrapped the legend of the slain woman with tender ease.

CHAPTER THREE

As he finished his tale and led the group along the sinuous paved path they'd previously trod, Gregg couldn't put his finger on the sinking feeling swirling around in his gut, but the feeling was real, authentic. Something was gnawing at him, chewing on his nerves. Had it been the barking of the dog? He didn't think so, for the dog had ceased barking early. Was he still concerned about the strange phone call from the previous month? This too he discarded, as the presentation on that night had gone perfectly; he'd even been privy to brand new information the following day.

"The radio show!" Gregg actually blurted out loud as he led his giggling, talking, whispering, and once-again boisterous crowd out of the cemetery. He had completely forgotten about the online radio show coming up.

Just as Gregg was turning to formally end his Woodlawn Cemetery Tour right where he'd begun two and a half hours earlier, the headlights of a parked car flashed on bright and blinding. The college girls squealed and grabbed hold of each other. Several people jumped and cursed.

"Oh my gosh! Oh my gosh! Oh my gosh!" One of the louder girls chanted.

"Who left the group? Are we all still here?" Another girl spun around, asking perfect strangers.

"We're all here." A tall woman near the back answered.

"Then who's that?" The loud girl asked.

The car, a dark-colored sedan, backed up quickly then sped away, leaving the group gawking, pointing, and excitedly speculating.

Shortly after Gregg formally ended the tour, the night became a synthesis of burning and turning headlights, slamming car doors and the rise and fall of voices both gentle and course. Cigarette smoke and laughter hung in the air. Kind words, gestures, and handshakes were doled out, and soon, with the last two tail lights bobbing out of sight, Gregg found himself alone again.

As was his custom upon completion of his Woodlawn Cemetery Tours, Gregg walked slowly to the edge of the big dark necropolis. From where he stood, where the parking lot met the grass, the warm lights of his small hometown in the east were beautiful, yet oddly foreboding, and though the night was sultry, Gregg stuffed his hands into the pockets of his jeans and ever-so-lightly raised his shoulders the way one does when a cool breeze catches them by surprise.

Gazing out across the vast expanse of lives once lived, Gregg couldn't help but imagine them. He did it every time, imagined the ladies in veiled hats and smooth finery, men in crisp dark suits and ties, children clad in vibrant colors and a wide array of hairstyles that gave away their place on the timeline of life. He imagined them all rising transparent, filmy and silent amid the tall and crumbling stones that bore their names and their numbers. He looked to the hillside. The slice of visible moon had slipped from behind the clouds and lit the top of Frankie's grave. Like the others, Gregg imagined her as well. He pictured her reclining against her stone, slim feminine legs crossed at the ankle, dark hair cascading over her shoulders, a sly cool smile.

"Goodnight Frankie," Gregg whispered aloud.

As Gregg turned to go, a bright falling star streaked across the night sky before him, leaving a flicker of a tail in its wake, and in the distance, the dog resumed its bark.

CHAPTER FOUR
WE'RE LIVE ONE

SEPTEMBER 1, 2013

Gregg was pacing a ditch through his bedroom. He'd never done anything like this. With his cell phone clutched in his left hand, he listened to his family's distant murmured rise and fall dialogue further through the house. He stopped pacing. He stepped over to a window and split the blinds with two fingers of his right hand. He leaned down to look outside just as the phone in his hand lit and rang. He nervously swiped the screen and answered, "Hello."

"Hello, Gregg?" A jovial, warm, male voice asked from Little Rock, Arkansas.

"Yes," Gregg responded, trying to sound calm.

"Hey, Gregg this is Tony. How are you feeling tonight?"

"Oh, I'm fine Tony, a little bit nervous to tell you the truth."

"Oh, you'll be fine; nothin' to it. We'll go live in five minutes, just like I told you before. You'll hear our jingle, and then Dale and me we'll ham it up a minute or so. Then we'll introduce you. We've had a lot of interest in you tonight. Never know if we'll have callers or not, but sometimes it's best not to. We'll run live for three hours. Like I told you a couple of weeks ago, we've been lookin' at your website and Facebook page, so we have several questions pre-prepared. Gregg, you just hold still. We've got a few knobs to turn and things to click."

Gregg waited patiently on the other end. He could hear both men talking to one another, giving directions he didn't understand. Once he heard Tony comically curse at his partner.

"Ok, I'm back. I'm back." Tony said, sounding winded.

"I hope I'm what you guys are lookin' for. I'm more of a historian than anything."

"You're just fine, just fine. We've got a lot of questions for you, one Dale's dyin' to ask about."

"What's that?" Gregg asked as he stopped the pacing he'd resumed upon answering the phone.

"THREE MINUTES!" Tony shouted. "Dale, what's her name?" Tony asked his partner.

Gregg, for the first time, could clearly hear Tony's partner's voice on the other end. His voice was louder and sounded older than Tony's.

"Frances Bullock," Dale responded as if he'd leaned in close to say it. Gregg imagined Dale seated, twisting knobs, pressing lit buttons and taking a curt drink of coffee after he'd spoken. For several seconds there was near silence from Little Rock.

"TWO MINUTES!" Tony yelped again. "Yeah, Dale's been talking about that one all evening Gregg. He read a short synopsis you wrote about a storytelling event you did on the fiftieth anniversary of her death a few weeks ago; then he Googled it and found several newspaper articles that had been written about it. He can't wait to hear about that one. I want to hear about that final surrender myself." Again, the air between North Carolina and Arkansas died for some time.

Gregg had no problem telling the Frances Bullock story again, but it was long and intricate, and he'd hoped to squeeze several stories into the three hours he'd be allotted on the show. Ever since Tony had called Gregg two weeks earlier asking him to be a part of their late-night online radio show, Beyond the

Veil, Gregg had been mentally combing his catalog for the scariest stories, the wildest tales. Like Tony had suggested, Gregg
had made a list of such stories that lay unfolded on his wife's
dark makeup table beneath a pull-chain lamp he'd neglected to
turn on, as the light was a bit abrasive in the dark room.

"THIRTY SECONDS!" Tony again split the silence with his
abrupt proclamation. "But you talk about anything you want to
Gregg," the DJ more or less mumbled, picking up right where
he'd left off. "Dale's a big boy. He can handle not getting his
candy." Gregg could hear Dale in the background pretending to
cry with vociferous, gulping exaggerated sobs. Gregg couldn't
help thinking there was shortness in what Tony had said. He
feared it had been due in part to his own unintentional silence
on the other end when Frances Bullock had been mentioned.

Maybe they think I don't want to talk about her, Gregg all but
said out loud.

"Sure!" Gregg chimed in a bit too eager, trying to re-lighten
the mood, a mood that most likely didn't need re-lightening, for
most likely Tony's seemingly terse response was nothing more
than his knowing seconds were quickly passing and was most
likely merely the fruit of his professionalism.

"What's that?" Gregg heard Tony ask yet not wait for the reply. "FIVE, FOUR, THREE, TWO, ONE and we're live! Weeellll,
we are back with you all, all our little spiders and creepers and
shadow people out there in radio land. As always, thank you for
staying up late with us. I am Tony Driscoll, and you all know the
King Pin, the Prince of Darkness, the one that goes bump in the
night, Dale Morales. Say hello Dale."

"Hello, Dale!" Dale responded in a voice that Gregg imagined must have distorted his lips in order to reach such pronun-
ciation.

"Oh, that never gets old!" Tony, in his rich radio voice, slathered in Southland, replied.

"Hello, you ghouls and goblins and eye-less dolls!!!" Dale joined in.

"Speaking of dolls," Tony jumped in with a tone that likened itself to office water cooler banter as if he were oblivious to the sound bite of a creaking door swinging open for effect behind them. "I saw a doll the other day in an antique shop with my wife that damn near made me soil myself. I swear it was a cross between Chucky, a constipated circus clown and Eunice from Momma's Family. Do you remember Eunice on Momma's Family Dale?"

"Do I remember Eunice from Momma's Family? Who are you talking to?" Dale gruffly, if comedically responded. "If it's an egregious waste of time or a disgusting display of poor taste or an ass-backward opportunity I've done it, displayed it and taken it, and you know that. A creepy clown Eunice doll would be tough to beat, but how about a doll that was a cross between Ester from Sanford and Son, just after she's called Fred a fish-eyed fool and a burned Pillsbury Dough Boy or maybe one with the long horse face of Bentley from The Jeffersons nestled beneath a ragged, little girl's 1880s bonnet with gangly ill-proportioned limbs?"

Gregg listened with a grin as the two late-night talk show hosts attempted to one-up each other, hearing in their voices, though they were separated from him by the long black miles of Tennessee, a true friendship, a real camaraderie. After each man had successfully painted for the other and simultaneously multiple thousands of listeners, dolls, carefully culled from ancient TV Land reruns and classic horror films, and after they'd self-deprecated and accosted each other multiple times for having streaks of insanity, slothfulness and for having made frail life choices, they finally got to the business at hand. Gregg couldn't help but start, ever-so-gently inside, when Tony spoke his name.

"Gregg is probably going gray out there waiting for his turn to talk! He's going to die from old age and turn into a ghost on his own tour if we don't clam up and let him talk. He's got the real stories, so let's cut out this tomfoolery and let the man speak."

Gregg took a deep breath. "All the way from the mystic Great Smoky Mountains of Western North Carolina, we are honored tonight on Beyond the Veil to have Gregg Clark ladies and gentlemen. He's an eighth grade History and English Teacher, and he and his wife, Pauletta, own and operate Where Shadows Walk, Historic Ghost Tours in beautiful Franklin, North Carolina."

As Tony continued his introduction, Gregg's mind, seeing no difference between a live radio broadcast and mundane table talk, led him away as if on a leash, and the miles between them melted.

"Gregg, are you with us?"

"I'm here," Gregg responded as if he'd just physically run into the room.

"Good, thought we'd lost you there. Afraid Dale was going to have to sing to fill the time again."

"No, I'm here." Gregg, calmly and intentionally duskily answered.

"Well, where to begin?" Tony spoke, with what seemed to Gregg to be unfeigned anticipation; however, he was sure, being a professional radio personality, Tony could pull the same earnest eagerness from his vocal cords if he were discussing lighting fixtures or ink cartridges.

"Well," Gregg jumped in head first, knowing if he didn't, he'd sound unprepared, maybe even timid. "Guys I could talk all night! My wife, Pauletta and I, we created Where Shadows Walk, Historic Ghost Tours out of purely personal interest. We've both always loved mysteries and ghost stories, strange beasts, bloody tales and things that go bump in the night. It's really preservation through presentation as we see it. It's a win-win. We present the tales on tours or during speaking engagements, and in turn the history, the real, gritty, dark history is preserved."

"Man!" Tony jumped back in. "I was telling Gregg a couple of weeks ago that one of our last guests on Beyond the Veil talked about real, documented exorcisms, and that was great, but pouring over the list Dale just handed me, man oh man, I really don't know where to start. We pulled lots of these story topics from Gregg and Pauletta's Where Shadows Walk website and their Facebook page. Some we pulled from newspaper interviews of the two. So the final surrender of the American Civil War happened on their main street in 1865. They've got multiple tales of hangings, mass convict death, massacres, murder, and more ghosts than I can count. Where do we want to begin?" Tony asked, after blowing through his lips, the universal signal for having finished a daunting task.

"I did some deeper digging this morning," Dale informed his co-host, blocking Gregg's response in the process. "Listen to this—the Trail of Tears came right through Gregg's hometown in 1838, and the Indian mound there is considered by the entire Cherokee people to be the spiritual center of the Cherokee Nation, and listen to the names of the communities in Gregg's county, all Indian: Cullasaja, Cartoogechaye, Burningtown, Nantahala, Cowee, Tellico, Ellijay, Otto, Skeenah, Iotla, and the ones that aren't native sound like they'd be part of Winnie the Pooh's

Hundred Acre Wood: Oak Grove, Rose Creek, Holly Springs, Windy Gap. Don't they sound cozy?" Dale finished.

"They do at that my friend. Maybe we'll get there one day."

"Maybe we will."

"But for now, where do you want to begin Gregg?" Tony asked, in his smooth Arkansas drawl.

"Frances Bullock! Frances Bullock! Frances Bullock! Frances Bullock!" Dale, like a child, shouted over and over again.

"We know what Dale wants to hear about," Tony said, a bit fainter. Gregg imagined Tony had turned to place the paper he'd been reading from on a counter.

"Frances Bullock," Gregg said, quieter than he should have. He then with haste, said the dead woman's name again, much louder this time. "Frances Bullock."

"Yeah, let's go! Let's go!!" Dale was clapping his hands.

"Calm down boy!" Tony said. "So, she was murdered fifty years ago, right?"

"Yes," Gregg replied, "fifty years ago. July 26th, 1963 was the last night anyone ever saw her alive. Boy, this is the one story even I don't really know where to start, so many suspects, so much cover-up, never solved, dangerous case." Gregg paused long enough for Dale this time to leap into the saddle.

"Dangerous why?" Dale asked with a youthful exuberance that made Gregg rethink his initial assumption of his being older than Tony.

"Well, something about the case seemed to kill everybody," Gregg said, uncertain of where he'd go from there.

Upon completion of Gregg's strange comment, his bedroom took on a chill, and he, at least for the moment, decided not to pull the chain that would have bathed his pre-prepared list of stories in the light. Instead, he moved to a chair that sat alone in a dark corner of the room. Gregg could tell by the silence in Little Rock that the night would belong to Frances Bullock.

"I suppose that's where I'll start," Gregg said, "how dangerous the case has always been. I'll tell you about the game." Little Rock listened. "Pauletta and I decided last year that we would attempt to host our first Frances Bullock murder mystery presentation on the fiftieth anniversary of her death, which was this past July 26th. We had blown up black and white pictures. I'd written a novella of sorts that took about three hours to read, and we themed the night mid-century modern with finger foods and decorations of the era. We even made a recording of a woman who would have been similar in age to Ms. Bullock when she died to address the crowd at the end of the evening. It was great, and to sweeten the pot, among the last stragglers to leave the more than a century old historical museum we'd chosen to house the event, was a middle-aged lady who just kept lingering near the door, easing away then coming back. Finally, I suppose when she thought the crowd had thinned to her liking, she made her move. She whispered to me that she'd like to talk with me privately about the cold case, and guys, my heart felt like it was going to push out of my chest. We arranged a meeting place for the next day, a small diner, and she came loaded for bear: notebooks, folders, pictures; the lady had it all. She said, after situating herself in the booth, "I've been waiting twenty-seven years for this."

"Her eyes, as she wrapped her lips around the straw she'd just pushed into her soda, darted back and forth to all three entryways into the building then beyond me through the window before she began her story.

"It was 1986," she said. "that's when the late-night phone calls started."

CHAPTER FIVE
GAME ON

There was a movie I seen one time, I think I sat through it twice
I don't remember who I was or where I was bound
All I remember about it was it starred Gregory Peck
He wore a gun and he was shot in the back

From "Brownsville Girl" by Bob Dylan and Sam Shepard

JANUARY 28, 1986

66 Now don't you hang up! You listen to me! My cousin is Dover McCoy, the Sheriff of Macon County! This is getting pretty old! Say what you have to say, or stop calling huffin' and puffin' like a damned ole wolf! Do you hear me? Now stop it!"

Feeling she'd made her point and hoping the caller, a caller she'd sadly grown accustomed to over the past three weeks, had stayed on the line long enough to hear her threat, Maggie slammed the receiver down onto its cradle. Then, just like the times before, Maggie wandered into each dark room of her home, peered nervously from each window and then, sheepishly walked down the dimly-lit hallway to her bedroom. "If that's Dave, I swear to God." Her whispered-threat trailed off as she tossed her decorative pillows into a nearby chair, flung her blankets and soft purple comforter angrily to the side, removed her earrings and crashed down upon her waiting bed.

Maggie and her ex-husband Dave, a local police officer in their hometown of Franklin, North Carolina, had been playing a dismal ping-pong match of he said, she said, for months, and the heavy breathing phone calls at all hours of the night were breaking the back of the camel, one damn ring at a time. The divorce had been rough, and living alone, Maggie felt that any and all noises she heard after dark, from the loudest car horn in the distance to the silkiest hint of a footstep on the stairs was Dave just taunting her, trying to scare her. Soon enough though, her thoughts turned inward, and she drifted off to sleep thinking of a dead woman, something others might find macabre, but it was all part of the game.

"Knock Knock," Maggie said with a smile, as she rapped the knuckles of her right hand against the left-hand side of Sheriff Dover McCoy's office door. "I figured I'd miss you since it was after five. I wanted to...?" Sheriff McCoy, lifting the thick index finger of his left hand to his lips and motioning, with his right hand for Maggie to come in was engrossed in something President Ronald Reagan was saying on a minuscule, flickering, television set that rested on two, red, plastic milk crates beside his desk. Maggie, seeing her cousin was deeply invested in the speech, took a seat in a chipped and somewhat wobbly wooden chair that sat solely before his desk.

"Oh Lord, what's happened?" Maggie asked, bending the corners of her mouth toward the floor.

"Listen." The Sheriff replied, without tearing his eyes away from the tiny color television set. The President was talking about Sir Frances Drake having his body cast into the sea. Maggie couldn't make heads or tails of what the President was talking about; then, with the mention, name by name, of the Challenger's crew, a crew she'd been watching on the news of late, a crew Maggie knew was to enter space at some point earlier in the day, Maggie placed the closed fingers of her right hand over her gaping mouth and asked again. "What happened?"

The Sheriff, still tight-lipped, didn't respond to Maggie's breathy fear-filled question; however, within seconds President Reagan, whom Maggie was fond of and respected, spoke of how the Challenger crew had slipped the surly bonds of Earth to touch the face of God. Maggie's eyes filled up with tears, and when the Sheriff cut off the television and looked Maggie's way, he too had tears pooled upon his lower lids. Maggie had been at work since 8:00 o'clock that morning. She hadn't heard of the disaster.

"What happened?" Maggie asked her damp-eyed cousin for a third and final time.

"Damn space shuttle blew up. Killed em' all." The Sheriff said with an undertone of anger as if someone had orchestrated their deaths. "Beats anything I've ever seen. I watched it! Right before lunch it went off, and damn if it didn't blow all to Hell. Never seen the beat!" As the Sheriff was better adjusting himself in his black swivel chair, Maggie, after showing just the right amount of concern so as not to appear callous or self-centered, paused then spoke.

"Dover, I've been getting the phone calls again." Maggie sat up straight to say.

"Thought they'd stopped." The small-town Sheriff said while pulling a leaf-green pocket knife from the front left pocket of his pants and placing, ever so gingerly, the well-honed blade to his fingernails.

"They had for about two weeks, but about three weeks ago they started back. I've been meaning to get out here, but I got busy. The one last night was just like all the others, same thing, heavy breathing, won't say a word."

"Well," the Sheriff said, putting two strong syllables into the single-syllable word. "Let's put a trace on it. Next time you get a call, you come on in and we'll find out where the call came from. That sound good?" The Sheriff asked in a lethargic manner, due, Maggie assumed in part at least, to the sad dealings of the day.

As the Sheriff picked up the phone to arrange the trace, Maggie's eyes took a self-guided tour of his office. Right behind the high-Sheriff's head hung a Bryant Funeral Home calendar. It read 1986 in big red letters. Maggie could see that the 3rd and the 19th of January were circled. She, of course, had no idea why. The room boasted a handful of family pictures, shotguns leaned up in corners, stacks of papers, orange road cones and filing cabinets so archaic they looked like old men, chipped and scratched, dented and standing just shy of straight. Two old grey men filled with secrets, Maggie thought to herself.

"Ok, we've got her," Sheriff McCoy spoke quick and loud, hanging up the phone within the phrase. "Let's get home Maggie." The Sheriff said with a smile, standing up as he spoke and pulling his arms into his heavy, black, official Sheriff's Department coat that he'd had draped over the back of his seat.

"So now what?" Maggie queried her cousin.

"Now you wait and see if they call back. If they do, you come down here, and we'll get ahold of the phone company, and they'll be able to tell you where the calls are coming from."

This made Maggie feel a little better; however, she was still nervous about the whole scene.

"You reckon it's Dave, Maggie?" The Sheriff quizzed his nervous young cousin while tugging at the zipper of his freshly-donned coat.

"I don't know. I thought it most likely was, but he swears it ain't, and I can't for the life of me figure why he'd do it no way."

"Let's think a minute," Sheriff McCoy said, this time placing both of his palms on his desk. "You ain't got no enemies to speak of, do you?" The Sheriff asked his young cousin.

"None that I know of." Maggie came back.

"Ain't wronged nobody." The Sheriff said this next part to himself. "Huh," the Sheriff mumbled. "Well, let's just see if they call back," the tired-eyed lawman spoke with an audible labored inhale while straightening himself into a stand. He motioned for Maggie to precede him toward the open door of his office. He followed, grabbing a pair of gloves whose fingers had been draped over a file cabinet by the door, flicking the lights off as he went. He made his way behind his cousin, both aiming their strides at the fast-fading light pouring in through the door that stood at the end of the hall directly beneath a crisp glowing exit sign. As the two cousins walked from the Sherriff's office down the dismal hallway that led outside, a neatly framed picture on the wall to Maggie's left caught her eye. She stopped.

"Is that Bryce Ingram?" Maggie asked with almost no recognizable expression or tone to the inquiry save a hint of curiosity.

"That's Bryce." Sheriff McCoy exclaimed. "Young wasn't he?"

"I've never seen that picture of him." Maggie quickly came back, this time exhibiting a touch of nostalgia wrapped up in just a hint of suspense.

Sheriff McCoy, tapping the glass of the eye-level photograph as he moved on down the hallway said, got old quick didn't he?"

As Maggie and the Sheriff pushed open the door into the face of the grinning January wind, both of their breaths braided and broke like smoke signals. Across the near-empty parking lot jogged Rick Henderson, a heavy-set Sheriff's Department dispatcher with a scowl of disgust upon his face and a tall paper sack cradled in the crook of his left arm.

"Run Rick!" Sheriff McCoy called out to the large man at-tempting to outrun the winter wind.

"Screw you, Dover!" The dispatcher panted as he passed the High Sheriff and Maggie near the Sheriff's Department's en-trance. The Sheriff laughed.

The day was as gray as stone, and passing cars were already burning their headlights. Officers Gene Southards and Sonny Welch were walking up from where they'd parked their cruiser some twenty feet behind them. Both men, coats zipped up un-der their chins and hair-bearing the brunt of the wind in the most comedic manner, weren't speaking to one another. Both men were staring at different things in different directions.

Maggie, as she grabbed ahold of her cousin's arm for one last bit of assurance, thought the actions of both lawmen unusual. Either they were angry with one another or both men were hy-per-observant she decided.

Just as Maggie's cousin was lifting the door handle of his squad car he jumped just a bit, startled by the pinching grasp his cousin had placed upon his arm. Sheriff McCoy, ready to end his arduous day that found its climax in a national tragedy, turned again to his cousin who stood biting her bottom lip in the late-day winter wind. *"We have been playing a game Dover,"* Maggie spoke, closer to a whisper. "We've been playing a game."

The Sheriff, exhibiting just a slice of disdain in his eyes said, "Run around and sit down Maggie." As he said this, he motioned, with a light sideways nod of his head that told Maggie he meant go sit in the passenger seat of his car cause it's too cold to stand and talk out here. Maggie scurried along in front of the car that roared to life just before she reached the door. She settled her-self a bit, then with the customary confirmation of the cold, she blew through her lips a whooshing sound.

CHAPTER FIVE

"Now what about a game?" The Sheriff asked his cousin while fingering knobs and buttons that, upon his touch, erupted in a gush of luke-warm air from the dashboard and around their feet.

Having never connected the late-night phone calls with the game she and three other ladies had begun playing for a few weeks, she'd never mentioned it to her cousin or anyone else for that matter; however, standing in the icy, winter wind and seeing officer Gene Southards, a puzzle piece in the game himself, opened a window in the young lady's mind. A light came on.

Commanding the Sheriff's complete attention, Maggie began to speak. "Me and Abbie and Sarah and Dee, you know Abbie, Dave's cousin, and you know Sarah and Dee." Maggie, speaking fast, as was her custom, and with wide eyes full as a harvest moon continued. "They all work down at the store with me. We got to talkin' a few weeks ago about the Frances Bullock murder." As if the Sheriff had just received word that his wife had died, he cut his eyes, switchblade quick in his cousin's direction.

"What now?" He asked angrily. "What kind of game?"

The sky grew dark, and the police car, though filling with warm air, felt cold as Maggie explained to her cousin the Sheriff how she and the other ladies thought it might be fun to try and solve the Frances Bullock murder, a cold case that had locked the doors and barred the windows of their small mountain town twenty-three years earlier, a case that had never been solved, a taboo case. The rules of the game were simple. She laid them out to the Sheriff, whose eyes, no longer saddened, now looked anywhere but into the face of his young cousin. In one way it was his way of listening, but in a greater part, his reluctance to make eye contact was a calming method. He had words pushing out of his throat best not spoken.

"We all have one month to solve the murder," Maggie explained. "We can get newspaper clippings, do personal interviews, get into locations if permissible and really do anything that might help our angles or theories." As the Sheriff listened, he began flipping, with his right thumb, the thin silver lid of his car's ashtray, his heartsick at the rules of the game and growing sicker still as he learned the lengths the young ladies had gone to in order to win.

Stepping from the warm Sheriff's Department back into the freezing wind, officers Southards and Welch, perplexed as to why the Sheriff and his cousin were still idling outside and further vexed by the cold steel look the Sheriff's eyes wore, walked with haste toward their own cruiser.

Inside the Sheriff's car, the dashboard was lit up like Christmas. Sheriff McCoy cast quick glances to his left and to his right and into his rearview mirror every sixty seconds or so, and his mind, as his cousin spoke, painted the pictures. Finally, finished with all of her and her friend's theories, suspected killers, motives and drives, Maggie, after a purposely subdued reprimand on the part of the Sheriff to cease the game immediately due to the danger of dealing with cold cases, exited her cousin's car with a promise on her lips to end the game immediately.

The Sheriff then watched as his cousin got into her own car and turned on her headlights. He never broke his stare till her taillights too had become one with the night.

Nervous and concerned, and praying the phone calls had been pure coincidence, Sheriff McCoy, rather than drive home as he'd planned over two hours prior, decided to ease through town.

He turned on his headlamps. He pulled from the Sheriff's Department parking lot situated neatly behind the Macon County Courthouse and turned right onto Church Street. At Marshal Henson's tire shop he turned right again. He threw up his hand to Larry Stewart, Marshall's tire man, who was leaning with his arms draped over the tailgate of his truck like fleshy pendulums. He drove slow and deliberate as if he were looking for something, for someone. The Sheriff passed Franklin's town square fountain empty and dry for the season on his left and the Christmas Nativity on his right, in its last days before being dismantled for the year. He made the light. He made the next light and turned left in front of Shorty Mason's Market. It was dark inside as it was in Frankie's Barber Shop to his left. He drove past Stiles Exxon, Duncan and Simpson Oil. He passed Riverside Gulf. He raised his hand to Rocky, a jailbird artist of sorts as he passed him walking in front of the Direct Station. He pulled into the City Restaurant parking lot where Dink Love was walking around the building with a bag of trash. The Sheriff raised his hand to him as well. Sheriff McCoy then exited the City Restaurant parking lot and reentered the street. He turned right and headed out toward Franklin's skating rink and bowling alley. He pulled in there as well.

Two trucks and one car were parked nearest the entrance to the bowling alley. Old man McDonald was coming out the front door. The whole town called him Lightning, a gray-headed black man who, though he walked slowly, hence the facetious moniker of *Lightning* was looked upon with a sort of reverence in the small mountain town. Some say he could bi-locate, be in two places at once.

"Damn I wish I could." Sheriff McCoy mumbled to himself, for he'd hoped to be home three hours earlier; however, he couldn't silence the whistle the winter wind played through his bones like a reed flute, a damn lonesome song. He waved at Lightning and pulled away.

Back at the highway, the Sheriff turned right and then took the next left back toward Franklin's downtown. He retraced his path yet paused at the bottom of town hill. Should he take a right past Mountain Respiratory Services or go straight up the hill? He paused, as there was no one behind him, then chose to go straight.

As the Sheriff crested the hill of Franklin's Main Street, his eyes were pulled to the right and deep into the sad dark windows of the Macon Movie Theater. Gone were the gleaming red rope lights, and gone was the warm inviting golden glow of the open door. The marquee, showing its age, still held a death grip on a letter H and two letter Os. The Sheriff's mind, as he slowed to a crawl in front of the derelict theater, raced back to hot summer nights and cool autumn evenings standing in line at the old theater.

For reasons the Sheriff couldn't pinpoint, he specifically recalled waiting in line for Gregory Peck's, The Gunfighter. A girl was most likely at the heart of that memory. Which girl, in particular, was lost to the mists of time.

Sheriff McCoy could still see the smoke rising in a belly-dancing column from old Vernon Stile's cigarette on the window sill inside. The old man would always put his cigarette down to tear the tickets. He could smell the popcorn and see the laughing faces behind the well-lit counter.

John Wayne, Vivian Lee, Clint Eastwood, Audrey Hepburn, Henry Fonda, and Marilyn Monroe movie posters slid, as if on the flatbeds of slow-rolling train cars, just behind the Sheriff's mind's eye. Then, rolling fast from beneath the old memory train like a hobo on the run, the Sheriff woke again to the present. The old movie house had been silent and dark for two years and was soon to have her ribs, one by one, ripped from her sides.

As the Sheriff drove on through the last gray slush of snow the old timers said was lying in wait of the next, his mind filled up to the spilling point. Every face he passed on the dark sidewalk seemed to wear a crafty grin. They all seemed to have shifty eyes. The old man on the corner, had he looked back when the Sheriff passed him? Had his look lingered a bit too long? The Sheriff asked himself, paranoid since pairing the idea of his cousin's late-night threatening phone calls to the Bullock murder of nearly a quarter of a century before.

All of the buildings seemed to be sleeping or graveyard dead. The night was adorned with street lamps still clinging to their gently swinging glistening harps, bells, stars and wreaths, reluctant to let another Christmas pass.

The Sheriff passed Dryman's Men Shop on his left and Peoples Department Store on his right. The red light caught the Sheriff at the square, and he lifted his eyes to the Confederate statue that loomed to his left, barely visible due to its height. When the light changed, he drove straight. He passed the courthouse on his right and the Pendergrass Building on his left. He passed the Bryant Funeral Home as well. Everything was still and cold and void of life. He turned left down past the Police Department and raised his hand to Officer Keith Doster who was walking to his squad car. At the bottom of the hill, the Sheriff turned right. Upon seeing the bright A&P sign, the Sheriff recalled that his wife had asked him to pick up a jug of milk before coming home. He swung into the parking lot. He kindly greeted David, Louetta and Davitta Dills as they too were walking across the parking lot with a buggy filled with groceries, but he didn't stop to speak in length, just a head nod and a how are ya'.

David, a city police officer, was a friend, but the Sheriff's mind was far too heavy and full for a conversation. In fact, a conversation sounded like poison to the Sheriff at the moment. The Sheriff did grin though after they passed him, because it hadn't gone unnoticed by the Sherriff that David and Louetta's teenage daughter, Davitta, had shyly smiled at Mike Henry, a bagboy who had conveniently pushed a set of three carts closer to her then was altogether necessary, and his grin remained as he recalled stories of Louetta and Davitta.

Louetta, David's wife, was famous in Franklin for her practical jokes on her husband and his coworkers. She'd nearly killed one of them with Exlax once, and she was constantly hiding their cars. Davitta, much like her mother the Sheriff supposed, had just three months earlier been brought in by city police officer Gerald Roper for throwing eggs on Halloween night. He jokingly replayed for everyone at the Police and the Sheriff's Departments the encounter.

"I had my flashlight right in her eyes. She was hiding behind a low wall. The minute I realized who it was I asked, Ms. Dills, what are you doing back there?"

"Praying you wouldn't see me," she said."

As the Sheriff entered the grocery store, he could tell by the way Mike leaned cool and self-assured against his Orange Toyota Tacoma pick up truck in the parking lot, ignoring the cold and his buggy duties, and the way, in turn, that Davitta eyed him over, that they had other things on their minds.

With as little banter as possible, the Sheriff paid for his milk and walked back to his car. After leaving the parking lot, the Sheriff turned left up the hill toward the old Ingles grocery store where Alan Mashburn, a bagboy, appeared to be teaching Raymond Dowdle, a local mentally handicapped man, how to make a flying toy out of a corncob and Hawk feathers in the parking lot. After passing the grocery store, Sheriff McCoy then turned left at Saint Francis Catholic Church upon the hill, drove a few hundred feet and turned right into the entrance to the Franklin High School. He drove slowly, looking right and left. Nothing stirred. Once he could see the Panther Pit, Franklin High School's football field, the Sheriff stopped his car. He looked to his left. The old slaughterhouse was still standing. With his left hand gripping the wheel, the Sheriff actually lifted his right hand to scrutinize the top of it. He remembered like it was yesterday being green-handed. He remembered the ritual, the fear.

They'd blindfolded him, the other boys, the AG Boys. Said they were going to raise him up on this pulley system they'd concocted in that slaughterhouse. Said they were going to raise him to the roof and let him fall. Here again, the Sheriff smiled a half-hearted smile. They acted for all the world like they were raising him higher and higher in the harness they'd fastened him into, and he was certain he'd fall to his death. They let him drop! He fell. He fell about six inches. Those boys laughed and laughed. Then they painted the top of his hand with green paint. In turn and in time, as they'd done to him, he'd done the same to others after him.

The Sheriff turned his car around. The marque at the school's front entrance hadn't been changed since it's last event, a wrestling exhibition that featured Abdullah the Butcher, but it wasn't the gargantuan, Goliath of a man sporting fake blood all over his fat sweat-drenched face that would bring the last gentle smile of the night to the Sheriff's face, it was his memory of Guy Taylor and the bear. Guy Taylor, a wild swath of local color on Franklin's canvas, beloved by all, singer with the Country Gospel group, The Firemen Four, coach, father, grandfather, and all around good person, loved dressing in drag for comic relief, and it was his madcap performance at the wrestling event's halftime show that was etched into the Sheriff's memory.

Taylor had arrived to thunderous applause. The old high school gymnasium was throbbing with excitement, for caged in the dead center of the ring that moved up and down with every animated footfall of the dancing Taylor, was a huge black bear. Everyone stood to their feet when the cage was opened by two local men. Though the crowd didn't actually get to see Taylor lock arms and legs with the bruin, his hasty and comical exits and reentry attempts kept the capacity crowd in stitches.

"Crazy son of a bitch, high damn heels and all," The Sheriff mumbled to himself as he sat at the lip of the street, his left turn signal dinging. No one was behind him, so he didn't move. He stared at the marque a little longer remembering a past event recently held at the Franklin High School, a womanless wedding that saw Franklin's local Pediatrician, Dr. Fred Burger, tied up and forced at shotgun point into marriage to a big bearded man in drag while another Franklin legend, coach, teacher, principal and Franklin Panther Football MC, Tom Raby, the mother of the bride and dressed to the gills in drag, wailed and moaned and boohooed at losing her only daughter in marriage to the lank sawbones. The memory faded, and the Sheriff turned left.

He passed the Sky City shopping center on his right and continued down the Georgia Road. Still holding onto a handful of memories from the ghosts of Main Street's Macon Movie Theater, Sheriff McCoy decided to ride out to the new movie theater on the outskirts of town.

The new Ruby Twin Theater boasted two screens, and her parking lot was teeming with people. The Sheriff lifted his eyes to the marquee he believed must be visible from space and recognized the reason. Rocky Four had made it to town. The movie had been out for a couple of weeks; however, small Appalachian towns waited a while longer for most movies. Some movies never found their way over the smoky blue peaks. On the other screen, Out of Africa.

While turning around in the Ruby Twin parking lot, Sheriff McCoy saw the new owners, Jim and Harvey, standing on the sidewalk outside. Jim was smoking and Harvey was talking with his hands. They didn't see him. The Sheriff pointed his car back toward Franklin and turned left. Within a couple of minutes, he was easing his cruiser left again onto Golf Course Road. He then backed into a driveway and turned around. Just as he'd done at the slaughterhouse above the Panther Pit on Franklin High School's campus, the Sheriff stopped to think. This time though he didn't think of green handing or being green-handed. This time he thought of her.

With his headlights aimed across the street at the old Frances Bullock house, a house he was all too familiar with due to the routine calls concerning ghost hunting kids, the Sheriff lost the old movie house spirits completely, and the Ruby Twin faded as well. The Sheriff lost the Challenger and Reagan's big, serene eyes of earlier in the evening when a light kiss of snow swirled through his headlamp beans like so many dancing fairies entering into and out of a tunnel of light. He then, after sweeping his windshield one sole time clear of melting flakes with his wiper blades, allowed his mind to drift back to the conversation he'd had earlier with his cousin, and line by line and stroke by stroke, the Sheriff sketched and then painted on his mind's canvas the theories, the faces of the suspects and the speculations his cousin had dealt out to him like a winning hand of Black Jack....

"He said we had to stop," Maggie said quietly to the other three ladies seated with her at the table. "When I saw him last week, Dover said we had to stop. He said it wasn't safe."

"Oh, what did you have to go and tell him for?" Dee, who was sitting beside Maggie in the booth at the Hickory Ranch Restaurant, their favorite meeting place, loudly proclaimed while shaking a sugar packet.

"I was telling him about the phone calls, that by the way haven't stopped. I didn't go to talk about this. I didn't even connect the two until I was about to leave." Maggie said apologetically to the other three ladies who sat with disappointed eyes all around her.

"What do you mean haven't stopped?" Abbie asked as she opened her slick, washable menu.

"Night before last, heavy breathing. I went to him yesterday to let him know, and he called the phone company to see where the call was coming from as he'd said. Well, his eyes got big as golf balls. They couldn't trace it. Said somebody had called and canceled the trace. You believe that?" Maggie said, while still attempting to stuff her coat at the far end of the bench seat she and Dee were sharing.

"Who would do that? Who *could* do that?" Sarah asked, taking her eyes from the menu and gazing, with a squint over at Maggie.

"He's crazy!" Abbie, sitting across from Maggie in the tight booth with a furrowed brow, blurted out. "Maybe he did it wrong. There's no telling."

"The murder was twenty-three years ago. It's ancient history. Nobody cares anymore." Dee said before wrapping her lips around the straw she'd had to comically chase around the rim of her soda to the great delight of her girlfriends.

"Really, who cares if we try to look into that old murder? I've stayed up so many nights working on this. I almost got bit by a dog, and Mrs. Watkins, when I tried to ask her questions, all but pushed me out the door. I swear I think she wanted to hit me square in the face. We're finishing this up, ladies!" Sarah said while pushing her hair behind her right ear and pulling, from an oversized purse she fished up from the seat between her and Abbie, a yellow file-folder, tightly bound with rubber bands. "We'll stop, *for the Sheriff*," she said with mockery in her voice, "tomorrow, but as for tonight, we're gonna see who solved this thing girls." All four ladies laughed, and as they finished their meals, their drinks, and their desserts, they one by one, huddled together like school girls, built their cases and revealed their findings.

By night's end, the young ladies had left no stone unturned. There were multiple motives, scores of theories, countless suspects and shifting settings, plot twists and subplots racy enough to make a sailor blush.

The 1960s the ladies so colorfully painted was one of swingers, loud and rowdy parties, secret rendezvous, well-kept secrets, and well-worn paths. Their conclusions, all completely unique and filled with flavor, pinned the murder on a wide range of suspects from an even wider range of demographics, from financially-imprisoned housewives to town drunks, from love-sick wannabees to best friends, from cold-eyed, jealous neighbors to spurned lovers.

One of the young friends pointed the finger of accusation at Mary Spindale, the daughter of Flora Spindale, the last lady to see Frankie alive and ironically the first to find her body. She cast out the accusation due in part to the fact that Frankie had come home and changed into a blue Bobby Brooks dress when she should have changed into clothing suited for bed, at least in the young lady's opinion. The young sleuth reasoned that Frankie and Mary were planning to go out again but had gotten into a fight.

Another of the four friends though was certain it was a web of swingers gone terribly wrong, while still another believed Frankie hadn't even known her killer. All of their theories, presumptions, and speculations were dripping with sweat. They were all filled with arched backs, drugs, sex scenes, and scandal. Each one was rife with deceit, lies, and corruption ranging from speculated webs of aristocratic cover up to bad luck and pure coincidence.

The young ladies, eyes weak from attempting to read barely-legible jotted notes and small print and exhausted from laughing at each other's suppositions when they got just plain crazy and far-fetched, left their favorite haunt feeling on top of the world.

They'd completed their task. Though the Frances Bullock murder remained just as completely unsolved as it had been before their youthful and compulsive venture, they had completed their task, and they left laughing.

Abbie, Sarah, and Dee pushed open the door and were right away assaulted by the early February winds, while Maggie hung back. Something had tugged at Maggie's attention as she was walking toward the door.

Sitting, facing where Maggie stood at the door, was an old man Maggie hadn't seen in many years. He'd been sitting at the next booth up from the ladies the entire evening. Maggie remembered thinking when she saw the back of his head that she hoped she and her friends wouldn't disturb him too much.

Maggie had to look past the dirty clothes and ragged, torn, leather jacket. She had to look beyond the watery eyes and the way his hand trembled when he lifted the light blue coffee mug to his parted lips. It was C.D. Baines. She knew he'd been Franklin's Chief of Police from the 1930s well into the 1960s, and she knew well that he'd been Chief during the time of the Frances Bullock murder.

"He had to have heard us," Maggie mumbled to herself. Then, as if for the first time all night she'd become aware of her group's volume, Maggie cast quick questioning looks across the room. An old woman sitting at a table with what appeared to be her son, looked Maggie's way as she lifted a fork to her thin lips. A middle-aged man in overalls sitting behind and slightly to the left of where Maggie and her friends had been whiling away the night was also looking her way, and finally, as Maggie held the top of her coat together, bracing for the winter wind to come, the old Chief lifted up his gaze. His look though was impenetrable, indecipherable. Maggie couldn't read it. Had they made a mistake?

CHAPTER SIX
WE'RE LIVE TWO

SEPTEMBER 1, 2013

"Gregg, you wouldn't believe how much Dale's wrote down in his notebook already," Tony said with a laugh.

"Gonna solve it!" Dale shouted in the background. "This one gets solved TONIGHT!" He followed up, all but screaming.

"That's all it took Gregg," Tony came back. You didn't know all you needed was Dale Morales out of Little Rock, Arkansas all hopped up on Red Bull and potted meat to finally put this one to bed did you?" Tony laughed.

"No, but let's do it, Dale." Gregg played along. "Let's close the book on this cold case."

"Ok, OK." Dale broke in the second time with thicker resolve. "Now, Sheriff Dover McCoy did not actually ever work the Frances Bullock case; it was before his time, right Gregg?"

"Right."

"Chief of Police C.D. Baines, who the young ladies were sitting behind at the restaurant did work the case, right?"

"Right."

"But he's dead now for sure," Tony said, jumping back into the conversation.

"Yeah, he died in the 1990s," Gregg replied.

"Gregg were there any law enforcement officers that worked Ms. Bullock's murder still living when you were researching all this or were they all gone?" Dale asked.

"There was one, Gene Southards," Gregg said.

"Did you get to talk to him?" Dale and Tony asked in unison.

"I did. I had a nice long talk with him. Great guy. And, I got a world of information from him. He remembered things no one else did, and his suspects were different too, two brothers and a screen from the window."

"Slow down, slow down," Tony laughed. "Dale's gettin' bum-fuzzled, gonna hurt his hand."

"Sorry," Gregg said with a chuckle as well. "Let me start at the beginning. I met Gene at his deceased mother's home. It was a hot day. We never went inside the house, just sat in rocking chairs on the porch. He had the calm and cool self-assuredness of a much younger man, and his words were deliberate and succinct. He wasn't John Rambo curt. I could just tell that he chose his words carefully...."

CHAPTER SEVEN
TWO IN THE RAIN

You know, it's funny how things never turn out the way you had 'em planned

From "Brownsville Girl" by Bob Dylan and Sam Shepard

JULY 26, 1963

G ene turned the car radio off after hearing of an earthquake in Yugoslavia and about a speech President Kennedy was poised to deliver within the hour, and for a while, he and Sonny rode in silence.

"You think he'll get it next time?" The young officer in the neatly-pressed uniform asked while squinting through the breaks of clarity the windshield wipers begrudgingly offered he and his partner on their nightly rounds.

"Think who'll get what?" The officer's partner slowly responded between sips of coffee from a paper cup he held in his right hand, as he was driving with his left.

"Kennedy," the first officer said, without making eye contact with his partner. "Do you reckon he'll get the office again next year?

"Hell, I don't know Sonny. You know what they say, I'd rather have a sister in the whore house as a brother in the White House. They're all the same. All come out kissin' babies and wavin' the flag with a King James in one hand and a jug of sweet tea in the other, the Star Spangled Banner lightly playing behind their every damn footfall." A crooked smile crossed Sonny's face for a moment, one Gene, his partner, would never see due to the darkness in their old squad car, but he heard the smile in his partner's response.

"My daddy used to say that whore house thing. Yeah, I guess they are all bout alike, but you messed some of that up hotshot."

Gene, stoic to a fault, cut his eyes over to where his partner was sitting in the darkness beside him. "What did I mess up?" He asked without real anger, but without a smile either.

"The King James part," Sonny replied, a bit quieter than before. "Kennedy's Catholic. He don't go by the King James." For a moment, as the wipers swept the dark rain from the glass before the two lawmen, neither man spoke, then, after one more deep swallow of coffee, Gene replied.

"You know what I meant."

The rain had been falling in buckets since dusk, and the two city police officers on duty, Gene Southards, and Sonny Welch had just begun yet another drive through of their small town of Franklin, North Carolina. Earlier in the evening they'd stood and talked in front of the Franklin Police Department with Johnny Gregory, a young local man, about baseball. Neither Gene nor Sony was huge followers of baseball; however, they listened and nodded kindly as Johnny went on and on about a home run hit by Willie Mays in the sixteenth inning against the Milwaukee Braves at Candlestick Park earlier in the month. After leaving the young baseball fan, the two lawmen drove up to the Sheriff's Department. As they'd walked in, the Sheriff, Bryce Ingram put his left index finger across his lips. Several men were gathered around a snowy, flickering round-screened television set someone had brought in and sat on the Sheriff's cluttered desk. Before they'd even seen the screen, the two young officers could tell it was Kennedy that had their cohorts so enrapt. After waiting around a few minutes, shifting their feet and leaning over a shoulder or two to listen and better see, Gene and Sonny left the Sheriff's Department, realizing Kennedy wasn't anywhere near finished talking about some Nuclear tests or whatnot.

The two officers had then ridden out to the Woodlawn Cemetery, looking for parkers. The local kids liked to park out there. As Gene and Sonny gracefully and slowly swung their flashlight wands onto the faces of hundreds of crooked and shining gravestones, the rain began to lighten and then fade, and then rising mist, as if on celestial cue, grabbed the baton and took off running.

It wasn't uncommon for Gene and Sonny to ride in silence. They knew each other so well it wasn't important that they constantly talk or even acknowledge each other for longs spells of time, and after the King James comment it was fifteen minutes before either man spoke and oddly, it was Gene who broke the stalemate.

"You ever know why they put Woodlawn out there?"

"Not a clue," Sonny replied quick, almost startled, lifting his head from a doze.

"Old Baptist Church was built in the 1820s, been gone for years, but she sat out there where all them chicken coops used to set." This was all the description Sonny needed to know exactly where his partner was setting his tale. "Well, it set smack dab in the middle of the graveyard. Most of them graves is rocks, ain't no names or nothin' on em. Really it was a pioneer graveyard. Ones that do have writing have died spelled dide, Scots-Irish you know." Gene then attempted to pronounce it the way it was spelled, *dide*. This made Sonny grin, but he quickly thought better of his reaction and lowered the edges of his mouth. "Well that graveyard was filled up," Gene continued. "The Presbyterian across the street as well, and over by Bryant's Funeral Home, the graveyard behind the big Methodist church was bustin' at the seams too. So not a handful of years ago, they decided they'd better make some room or the water in town might get contaminated. Don't know how many graves they dug up and put over there at Woodlawn. Some famous. Old Nathanial Rankin and his wife fought in the Civil War and started them schools in Franklin, they moved them.

Tom, lives right next to the old Baptist graveyard, said his boy had nightmares after watchin', from his bedroom window, all them old wooden caskets and bodies comin' up. Said some of em' fell apart as they were raisin' em', skulls rollin' out on the grass. They put a bunch of them out there at Woodlawn. Some of em' probably Catholic."

Sonny cut his eyes over at his partner, and both men grinned. The rain began to fall hard again and Sonny shared a tale about a hunting trip with his father that had gone terribly wrong when he was a boy due to the same kind of hard rain, and Gene, feeling unusually talkative after his little comedic turn-around, jerked their old cruiser into a parking space on Main Street, killed the lights and the engine.

Theirs was the only car parked on Franklin's Main Street, and with the absence of windshield wiper blades cutting the water and headlights cutting the night, both officers felt as if they were hunkered inside a dark cave behind a waterfall. With the ambiance set, Gene took his last hit of coffee from the paper cup and lifted his left arm higher on the door. Sonny repositioned his left foot nearer the gear stick. It was story time, and both men knew it. The tales started off anecdotal, but, as the rain fell harder and the minutes ticked away, they evolved to better suit their setting. Gene began by telling Sonny of his first day on the job at the Franklin, Police Department.

"Chief Baines handed me a gun by God, told me to check all the doors in town, make sure they was locked up good, and he told me to keep the peace. That's every word the man said. I walked into the station and the older lawman I was to ride with was starin' out the window. I said hello. He never said a word one, never looked my way. I thought, God what have I done here? I was just out of the service and here I was not even worthy of a damn hello. About thirty seconds passed and the older fellow said, never turnin' from the window, said,

"I told them boys to leave." He then turned and looked at me, said, "Come on if your comin'."

"I followed him out to the car, and he hit that siren, scared everybody to death. What it was, they was a bunch of young guys drunk up there, and he'd told em' to leave a little while back, and they hadn't gone. Well, just me and him and at least nine of them. The ones that would fit in the back of the car he squeezed in, and the rest he made walk in front of the car. Locked all of em' up. I'd never seen the beat." Gene finished with a chuckle.

"You ever hear the Chief talk much about the Civil War?" Sonny asked, abruptly switching stations in the conversation.

"Sonny, you know talkin' to you is like talkin' to a damn young'un half the time. Here I am tellin' you about my first day on the job, and damn if you don't follow it up with the friggin' Civil War. Why not pancakes or Daffy friggin' Duck?" Gene asked, swiftly wiping his mouth with his large open hand, an overt display of irritation. Sonny laughed and punched Gene in his right shoulder.

"I was listenin' damn it. The rain just got me thinkin'.

"About the Civil War?"

"Yeah, about a story the Chief told me last year. You ever heard tell of Andersonville Prison, down in Georgia?" Sonny asked his brooding partner holed up with him in the rain.

"No." Gene's response was curt but not conclusive. It had an edge of curiosity, but just an edge. Sonny knew there was an unseen and unspoken stopwatch running. He knew his story had better be good.

"Confederates built a big prison for captured Union Soldiers during the war down in Georgia, called it Andersonville." Sonny elaborated. "It wasn't anything but a big fenced in area really. It wasn't an actual prison; didn't have a roof or nothin'. The men that didn't die of exposure or starve to death actually rotted alive. Hell of a story. Anyway, the only water available to the men was a little creek that run through the middle of the prison, and it dried up in a drought. The men were beggin' and prayin' for rain. Weeks into the drought, thunder started to roll. Dark clouds covered up the sky, and the rain started to fall, but then the rain fell like it is tonight, hard and just wouldn't stop. A big part of the lower wall fell down, cause the ground turned to puddin' basically. In the middle of the storm, lightnin' struck inside the prison, and chunks of dirt went flyin'. A geyser, like they've got out west, erupted about a hundred foot in the air, and it never has stopped. Chief said he went down there a few years back, and the water's still comin' up pretty as you please. Don't know why I thought of that, I guess the rain tonight. Chief said they call it Providence Spring. I'd like to take the wife and kids down there."

"Chief's full of them wild tales," Gene said, flicking the keys hanging in the car's ignition with his right hand.

"It ain't a tale. It's true. They're all true."

For the next hour, Gene and Sonny took turns telling tales. Some were funny. Some were not. Gene told a story about Pan

Handle Pete, the one-man band who always made his way to Franklin for celebrations and events. Sonny told about Riley Henry digging up a human skeleton down by the old Indian Mound while attempting to dig a septic tank line for the Sinclair Service Station in 1955. Both men shared high school stories of girls, green handing and teachers, and both men agreed that old Mrs. Winstead, Stewart, and Mathews were the meanest educators they'd ever locked eyes with.

"Twenty-five lines of poetry, memorized, every two days by God," Gene growled. "Twenty-five!" Talk of teachers led to talk of locals both men knew, and Bill Fuller came up.

"Wouldn't take a bite of food in the house, and it was always, 'Naw sir, naw sir, naw sir.' If a man could get him to set down and eat anything it was in the yard," Gene said.

"Worked for Furd Burrell didn't he?" Sonny asked.

"Long as I can remember," Gene responded.

Over the hour, the two lawmen discussed the Manassas trees, the two trees Dr. Samuel Harley Lyle brought back as saplings from the first Battle of Manassas in Virginia and of old Buck, the town dog who hardly ever left the side of the old doctor's son, Dr. Harley Lyle Jr. Old Buck had been given a funeral and an obituary in the Franklin Press some twenty-three years prior. Just as Gene was placing his fingers upon the keys, Sonny asked a question that darkened the tone of the night.

"Is that elevator still haunted down at Burrell's?"

Burrell's Motor Company sat down past the Macon Movie Theatre on Main Street, and it was common knowledge that the employees, especially the owner, was terrified of the elevator. It had a mind of its own and often rose and fell at will.

"Last I heard anyhow," Gene replied, letting the keys alone.

"Did I ever tell you the story about my Great Uncle Randal?" Sonny asked while cocking his head to the right.

75

"Don't reckon," Gene replied, feigning a total absence of concern.

"Lord, he's been dead for years. He was born in 1857. He froze to death up in Little Canada over in Jackson County."

"Froze to death?"

"Yeah, died of exposure, a life-long drunk. He'd been about eighty or so when I was seven or eight. He told me a story one time that kept me up for weeks. I still think about it. The night he met the Devil."

"*The Devil?*" Gene repeated mockingly.

"The one and only," Sonny assured him. "Uncle Randall said he got in the habit of walkin' to his momma's grave late at night." As Sonny went on, the drone of the falling rain, the darkness, the close quarters and the macabre story wove themselves tightly together, and it wasn't long till both men were mentally walking along-side the old drunk in the night...........

The moon was full, so full in fact, the weaving drunk could make his way up the old logging road without lantern, flashlight or lamp, so full, the trees, stripped bare for the dying time in the Southern Appalachians, glowed like lank angels, looming above the death-dark Laurel, so full, he could already see the tombstone tops softly lit upon the hilltop, as if painted in warm, Autumnal hues on a gloomy nightscape canvas.

The old drunk stopped walking when he saw the tree. A giant tree had fallen across his well-worn, ritualistic path that led to the cemetery, a tree that hadn't been there on his New Moon trek just days before. Each Full and New moon, the panting toothless drunk filled himself with warm Corn Liquor and made his way along the crooked, steep, oft-canopied logging trail that wound its way up to his family's cemetery. By three o'clock in the morning, he'd be there. Depending on the time of year, he'd ease his geriatric frame down into the tall, warm, cool, cold, soaking wet, frost or snow-covered grass beside his mother's grave, and by three-thirty in the morning the old sot would be either weeping, a mouth-wide-open bawl with thin strings of whiskey spit hanging like spider's webs to the grass, or he'd be laughing, laughing with such rattling-ferocity, the night sounds dissolved around him and a rainbow of stars danced dizzyingly behind his eyes.

The novel fallen tree didn't send the old drunk sailing away crestfallen. It didn't deter him in any way. In fact, it offered up a challenge. The challenge wasn't in crossing the fallen tree. The challenge lie in not spilling a single, solitary drop of his Smoky Mountain Moonshine Whiskey while doing so. The wrinkled, old Shine sponge, eyes gleaming, rimmed in gold like a coyote shocked in the lamplight, slung one fat leg across the mammoth Oak blocking the trail he could have walked blindfolded. Holding his jar high, still half-full, the drunk straddled the fallen tree. It was then that he heard the high-pitched squeak of the bats. Foregoing slinging his other leg across the tree, the gassed mountaineer began pawing the underside of the freshly-toppled Oak with his one free hand. The other was raised up in the air like Lady Liberty so as not to spill his White Lightnin'.

The old drunk laughed as he ripped two, small brown bats from beneath the fallen tree's trunk with his long filthy fingers, and he laughed harder as he poured, drop by precious drop, of Moonshine Whiskey down their squalling pink throats.

Tossing the furry corn-whiskey-soaked bats off into the darkness, after having had his fun, the old drunk carried on with his pre-dawn stroll up to the boneyard. He stumbled after crossing the tree, and again, using a lit tombstone top as his North Star, he ambled on, mumbling and sipping and cursing and laughing and mumbling and sipping again.

A Screech Owl, warming up its chords in the nearby low-leaning limbs brought another sin-licked grin to the grizzled drunk's face just as a cold gust of wind blew up the hillside.

As fast as the old man's smile was nearing completion upon hearing the blue moan of the owl and the rare wind, it fell. It fell due to laughter, loud, raspy, high-pitched laughter ringing out from behind where the old man stood on the trail. Spinning around, ice cold inside with fear, the drunk saw a dark form leaning against the tree he'd just seconds before straddled and crossed. The old drunk's eyes grew as wide as goose eggs when the realization hit that the dark form was that of a tall slim man and that the wild, cripplingly-hideous laughter was spilling from the stranger's gaping mouth. The strange man's laughter heightened and rose with the intrusive wind to a piercing peal, a deafening and putrid roll of

*noise that somehow sounded like smoke smelled. The strang-
er, lit wonderfully and terribly by the full mountain moon,
wore a tall stovepipe hat and to the old drunk's shock, was
spinning what appeared to be a walking cane in his fingers
like a showman, like a sideshow carny.*

"Knock, knock!" A voice called out from beyond Gene's
rolled up and rain-drenched window, accompanied by two loud
raps upon the glass.

"Mother --- !!!" Gene jumped and shouted. Sonny jumped as
well. Standing in the rain beneath a large black umbrella rapping on Gene's window was the Mayor. With burning embers
in his eyes, Gene rolled his window down.

"Scare ya?" The Mayor asked.

"Little bit," Gene remarked, as his heart slammed so hard it
hurt.

"Don't forget to check all the doors on Main Street tonight fel-
las. Fred said there's been a stranger hangin' round the square."
The Mayor, upon completion of his genial order, turned and
bled into the dark rain.

Gene jerked his hand toward the keys and started the car.
"Son of a Bitch scared me to death," Gene said with a snarl.

"Me too." Sonny laughed.

Gene flicked on his lights and backed out of the parking spot
the two lawmen had called home for the past hour and a half
just as the rain faded and stopped. A thick mist, heavier than
earlier, began rising from the road before the two officers, and
Gene cut his windshield wipers off. The mist was rising up the
walls of the Bryant Funeral Home as they passed, and Gene,
even though he wasn't at all certain he could be seen doing so,
threw up his hand to George Norman, the coroner, whom he

saw standing in an upstairs window. Norman, as usual, had a bottle in his hand and was watching the night.

"Sleeps up there sometimes." Sonny blurted out. "Sleeps right up there with them corpses and caskets by God. Sheriff swears he stepped up there one mornin' early lookin' for Harry Neil and that crazy sombitch was layin' thire asleep in a baby blue casket, sleepin' sound as Mary's Little Lamb. He said they was a bone-dry bottle of Old Grand Dad tucked in the crook of his arm. Crazy sombitch." Sonny repeated while unzipping his dark Franklin Police raincoat as Gene eased the old cruiser to a complete stop in front of the old Tourist House Inn. "Guess the President's said goodnight by now," Sonny said while repositioning himself in his seat and rolling down his window simultaneously. Gene waited a solid minute before he rolled his own window down, solely to ensure that his partner wouldn't think that he had given him the idea.

The night was mild, and the audible sound of the squad car's tires ripping the puddles apart cast both officers into a sort of reverie, not unlike the story of the Devil and the drunk had done just moments before. They circled town twice and then headed out toward the Georgia Road.

"Wonder whose little TV that was up at the Sheriff's department." Sonny rhetorically asked. "You ever wonder who had the first TV in Franklin?" This question, by the way, Sonny turned toward Gene as he asked it, needed at least a nod. Sonny was surprised when he received more.

"J.C. Jacobs said that Charlie Blaine had the first TV in town."

"Is that a fact?" Sonny retorted. Just then, amid the mundane banter and the sound of water spraying the side of their squad car, their CB radio squawked to life. Gene teasingly slapped Sonny's extended hand away and quickly spoke into the grid. The calm voice at dispatch on the other end informed the two lawmen that some teenage girls had apparently jumped the fence at the golf course and were skinny-dipping in the pool. Gene, in an even calmer tone, assured the voice on the other end they'd check it out. He hung up the CB radio and sped up just a bit.

The Franklin High School principal, Harry Corbin, was parked down at the Tasty Freeze. He was looking intently at his front right tire. Gene slowed to a crawl and called out through his open window.

"You alright Harry?"

"Oh yeah, I'm fine. Run over a stick or something up yonder at the school. Just checkin' her."

"Alright, goodnight." Gene offered, and Sonny waved. Gene crept along till the principal's headlamps burned.

"What do we have here now?" Gene asked as he swung the front end of their old squad car onto Golf Course Road not sixty seconds later. About twenty feet ahead of the two lawmen, acting blinded by their burning headlights, on the side of the highway, dripping wet, stood two teen boys. As the two lawmen approached they recognized the boys as brothers that lived away on down the Georgia Road. They were standing in the road that led to the Franklin Golf Course yet looking across the road.

"You boys bout soaked through?" Sonny asked through the previously rolled-down window, as they were on his side.

"Bout," One of the brothers responded straight-faced and distant. The other brother, the younger of the two, with both hands stuffed into the pockets of his jeans locked eyes with Gene and nodded.

"You boys headed home?" This time it was Gene who resumed the inquisition.

"Yeah, headed home." The older brother spoke again.

"Well, most time people walkin' is walkin'. Looks like you two are gettin' nowhere pretty fast."

"We just stopped to catch our breath." The older brother spoke. "Have a good night." The two brothers then began to slowly walk away, and Gene, casting a wary eye on both boys, continued on out to the golf course. There were no girls in the pool when Gene and Sonny arrived. They'd already scaled the fence and hightailed it home. When the two lawmen passed where the two wet siblings had been standing no more than five minutes prior, they found them to be gone as well. Thunder rolled in the distance, and for the first time all night, the big white moon slipped out from under the wispy smoke-grey clouds. "So, you're sayin' the man in the top hat was the Devil. Is that right?" Gene asked, without looking at his partner.

CHAPTER EIGHT
WE'RE LIVE THREE

SEPTEMBER 1, 2013

66 Don't do it, Dale! Dale! Dale!" Tony comically demanded.

"I can't help myself!" Dale called out like a child. "Tell us more about the skinny-dipping girls!" Both men laughed.

"Well, as that was fifty years ago, there's not much I can do in the explanation department; however, in researching the case, I actually did come across one of the girls from that night. She was so funny. She told me all about it but said I'd better not mention her name in any of our presentations, so I'd better not say it on here it either."

"Dale will be fine," Tony said.

Gregg could almost imagine Tony patting his friend's head, not unlike a big-eyed dog being reassured after a harsh scolding.

"So these two boys," Tony rejoined the conversation as serious as he had previously been playful. "Were they the prime suspects? They were there. They looked suspicious. What did they say when they were brought in?" Tony asked.

"They were never brought in," Gregg quickly replied.

"Never questioned." This time it was Dale with disbelief in his tone that spoke. "Never questioned? Why?"

"That's a good question," Gregg replied.

"Gregg," Tony jumped in. "When we got the green light that we'd be interviewing you two weeks ago me and Dale searched you up online like we do with all our guests. We found your website, your Facebook page, newspapers articles where you'd been interviewed, and over and over this case came up affiliated with you. That's when both of us got so intrigued with it, but there's another name tied to almost every newspaper article, Janice Crane, Frankie's cousin. From what we've read she's put years into the solving of her cousin's murder. Have you spoken with her about the case?"

"Oh yes, many times. Mrs. Crane is a wealth of information. Nobody knows the case like Janice." Gregg assured Little Rock. "I owe her a huge debt of gratitude for her being so forthcoming with the information she's garnered over the years concerning her cousin's case."

"Does Janice think the two boys in the rain did it?" Dale asked.

"No," Gregg replied. "Though she would be quick to tell you that she can never be certain who killed her cousin, she is very vocal about her suspect of choice, and she'll happily offer up her time to explain her theories as to why if you don't catch her at a bad time. The first time I caught her at a bad time. She had music on her mind."

CHAPTER NINE
BLUE VELVET

You know there was somethin' about you baby that I liked that was always too good for this world.

From "Brownsville Girl" by Bob Dylan and Sam Shepard

APRIL 30, 2013

It was Gregg's 37th birthday, and it had been a good day. He was hoping to end the day on a good note as well. Earlier in the week, Gregg had seen a flier on Franklin's Main Street saying that Janice Crane would be performing at the Rathskeller Pub on his birthday, and Gregg was hoping to gain at least a brief audience with the older troubadour so as to schedule a time to meet with her privately to discuss her cousin's life, murder and the mystery that had eclipsed it.

Before even entering the door of the Rathskeller, a warm semi-dimly-lit pub and coffee house squeezed neatly below a quaint bookstore and beside an eclectic flower shop on the backside of Franklin's Main Street, Gregg could hear the flawless piercing notes of George Gershwin's "Summertime" oozing from within.

Pausing but a breath, Gregg passed the bottle tree, an old African good luck charm of sorts that stood tall and jagged to the right of the door, whose rusted metal trunk sported brown, purple and blue bottles aimed at warding off evil spirits.

As Gregg walked down the carpeted ramp from the Rathskeller's door to the main floor below, a necessity, as the pub was situated below street level, he held to the thin metal railing on his left while his eyes caught the wall to his right, a wall peppered with vibrant posters, brochures, business cards and the like that boasted, begged, and promoted upcoming concerts, lawn maintenance, piano lessons, pet sitting, Yoga, hiker hostels, his own ghost tours and more.

Just over the railing sat Janice Crane, the woman Gregg had come to see. On a stage raised a few inches off the floor, a stage large enough to accommodate a full band yet intimate enough not to make a lone performer appear as a single bowling pin left standing at the end of an alley, Mrs. Crane sat erect on a small squat stool—her fingers were deftly careening across the well-worn keys of a bright red electric piano.

As Gregg's feet found the main floor, he ping-ponged in his mind about the piano player's style—was her style more Norah Jones or slow and sultry Jerry Lee Lewis?

Warm applause broke out throughout the little pub upon Mrs. Crane's finale of Gershwin's Porgy and Bess classic. Mrs. Crane then, without the benefit of banter or even facial acknowledgment of the packed house's gracious response, strode softly into Kris Kristofferson's "For the Good Times."

"Well good evening Captain." Gregg loudly addressed a man seated near the ramp's end. He'd had to almost shout as the little bar was thick with laughter, words, and song. The man, John deVille, was not a real captain; however, since Gregg's having met him years before, for reasons unknown to either man, that's the nickname Gregg had given him, and it had stuck.

"Good evening to you sir. You have a tour tonight?" John asked, lightly lowering the cell phone he'd been engrossed in from his direct line of sight.

"No, I came to see if I couldn't catch Mrs. Crane for a few minutes. Need to set up a research date."

"Well pull up a seat," John said in a warm, inviting way.

"I was just leaving anyway Gregg," a tall thin man Gregg had met several times before but couldn't for his life recall his name quickly stood to his feet. "You can have my seat."

Gregg thanked him, and with an animated grunt that he felt certain no one else heard, squeezed by the man in passing as the place was packed.

John deVille was the most intelligent man Gregg had ever met. There were no close seconds. A self-professed information junkie, John knew it all. He could have worked for NASA, Harvard, Yale. He could have been a Robert Ballard if he'd desired. He could have found a Titanic of his own. Hell, he could have built one; however, it pleased him to teach history, civics, and when the state budget allowed, philosophy at Franklin's high school. He was perfectly content to frequent local watering holes and metaphorically solve the world's problems from a tiny forested corner of it.

A big man with thick greying hair, matching goatee and the haunting eyes of a Romantic-era poet, deVille was a true asset to Western North Carolina, because though his setting suited him fine, his ambition did not run parallel to old drawn-out, sluggish Southern Appalachian stereotypes that still shrouded the region.

When he wasn't in the classroom, he could often be found lobbying politicians in Raleigh and Washington DC for better pay, benefits, and fighting the loss of tenure for teachers.

"Buy you a beer?" John asked above the drone of the crowd.

"No, I'm good. Thanks though." Gregg replied, turning to look over his shoulder at the night's entertainer who was behind him due to the placement of the seat that had come available at John's table.

"She's damn good," John spoke, staring deep into his phone, always learning something.

"Used to play on TV, played with many of the Grand Ole Opry stars, Tony Bennet once," Gregg said while looking over his shoulder at the woman tenderly touching the ivories as if they were friable.

She was deep inside of "For the Good Times" when Gregg's eyes started working the room. Gregg and John were so comfortable with one another they didn't feel the need to entertain each other, so while John was silently devouring some new nugget of information online that would most likely elicit cursing or laughter upon completion of his having learned it, Gregg scanned the crowd of faces and forms before him.

"Israeli airstrike kills suspected Palestinian militant," John said, still looking at his phone.

From the stage, having finished "For the Good Times" to gracious applause just moments before, Mrs. Crane was beautifully knocking out Hoagy Carmichael's "Stardust."

"Walpurgis Night," John said louder this time, lowering his phone. "It's Walpurgis Night."

"It sure is," Gregg replied. "The Devil will be out tonight, won't he? Witches sailing through the air, ghosts on the wind!" Gregg curled his lips and raised his eyebrows as he spoke.

"Hundreds of years ago babies born on Walpurgis Night had to be watched by the entire village till after midnight, till it was safely the first day of May. They believed demons and witches would take them if not," John explained.

"Well, I don't know if I was watched or not. Time will tell I guess." Gregg replied to John's comment, while once again looking over his shoulder at the piano player.

"It was only babies born on April 30th," John said, picking up his phone again.

"That's me. Just call me a Walpurgis baby." Gregg grinned.

"Shit, is today your birthday?" John again lowed his phone.

"All day," Gregg replied.

"Well, Happy Birthday you crazy son of a bitch."

"Thank you very much," Gregg replied while placing both of his hands, palms down, on the wooden table and rapping his fingers to a punctuating beat.

For the first time since Gregg had arrived, the music stopped. He spun his head around. Janice was fingering the cord that led from the wall outlet to her piano.

After having never spoken a word as to her abrupt pause in playing, no apology or explanation, the first few notes of Sinatra's "In the Wee Wee Hours" filled the overly-warm room.

Janice's long slim fingers again found their muse, and again rich applause filled the space—also for the first time since he'd arrived, Gregg took the time to really look at the piano player.

Janice Crane was a woman of about sixty-five-years Gregg guessed, lean and of medium height, she wore her smoke-gray hair beyond her shoulders and a long-sleeved white shirt beneath a black vest and shiny, black, dress shoes. After combing the entertainer with a journalistic eye, Gregg picked up right where he'd left off before, surveying the place and watching people.

The brick walls, entire chunks missing in places, were decked with abstract art. The bellies of flags from foreign countries suspended at their corners sagged over the heads of bustling patrons who Gregg watched laughing, talking, playing cards, drinking and checking their phones.

There was a line of four people at the bar. A young AT hiker, Gregg assumed, with dreaded hair that hung like gallow's rope over his shoulders was coming out of the bathroom. He made eye contact with Gregg before climbing the carpeted ramp and stepping outside the pub.

Prior to Gregg's having entered the pub earlier, the crowd outside had been thick, but even though the hour was growing late, through the wide picture window behind where Mrs. Crane was tickling the ivories, Gregg could tell that the horde had grown in size.

When entering, as Gregg had been doing inside the bar, he'd carefully taken mental pictures of the people happily lingering outside in the dusk of day. He'd seen men and women with dreads, long beards and long colorful dresses, fanny packs, tall psychedelic socks, light-as-air Chacos, and clumsy Birkenstock sandals.

Gregg assumed it was Janice's song choices that kept the hiker's party outside. Deep cuts from Neil Young's Tonight's The Night, The Grateful Dead's Live Dead or Phish's debut album would have most likely pulled them all inside with cheers and praise, he thought, but he knew he could be wrong.

"Walpurgis Night," John said again. Redirecting Gregg's attention back to his immediate vicinity.

"It's always Walpurgis Night in Franklin Captain. We even talk about this place on the tours.

"I know, I know," John said before taking a long drink from the beer in front of him, a beer that Gregg hadn't seen him touch since he'd arrived.

"That's warm isn't it?" Gregg queried.

"It's fine."

"That urn up there is my favorite part of this place, as far as the stories go. When the previous owners bought it in two thousand, they found multiple urns in the back filled with human remains, ... ashes. Nobody has a clue where they came from, so they went up to the funeral home and got that big urn. They put em' it in, and it's still sittin' up there." Gregg finished.

"Sick as shit ain't it?" John replied with his eyes closed while shaking his head.

Having left Sinatra behind, Janice was working her way through Cindy Walker's "You Don't Know Me" when Gregg remembered when he'd first learned about Walpurgis Night.

He'd been in college. An English professor, Bob Harris, had asked him his date of birth. When Gregg replied, April 30th, 1976, the grey-bearded professor tugged at his beard, leaned back in his chair and drawled, "Walpurgis Night." He then went on to explain to his young student the ins and outs of the ancient dark holiday, and Gregg had been rather proud of it ever since.

"You go to Silas McDowell's grave on your tour don't you?" John asked, again waist deep in his phone.

"I do."

"Have you ever read his poetry?"

"I have not Captain. Read me some."

"Read it your own damn self," John mumbled as he was obviously reading it from his phone.

Silas McDowell, Gregg knew, had been a legend in Franklin, North Carolina in the 1800s. He was a scout, a scientist, a great writer, and thinker. It was Silas McDowell who gave the information to Robert Strange about the great Cherokee Chief Yunaguska, John Welch and the blood chase, which resulted in the first North Carolina novel ever written, and it was Silas McDowell's reluctance to participate in a duel between two feuding senators that brought Davy Crocket down from the hills to take his place, but Gregg had never read his poetry.

All of a sudden the room erupted in loud applause, and several people rose from their seats. While lost in thoughts of gunpowder and Cherokee Chiefs, Gregg hadn't realized that Janice had completed the last song of her set.

She stood up, pushed her stool away from her and stepped from the stage into the crowd.

"How are you?" Janice asked Gregg with a smile as Gregg and John's table was closest to the stage and impossible to pass without recognition, feigned or genuine.

"Great, and you were great as well. I swear you're the best I've ever heard."

"Oh, I'm a learner." The piano player sheepishly and humbly replied.

Within the last half hour, a couple of tables had opened up in the back of the bar and eased in between other thoughts, Gregg had been carefully monitoring them, hoping they'd remain free.

"Are you taking a break?" Gregg asked.

"About fifteen minutes maybe," Janice replied.

"Could I steal about three or four of those fifteen minutes?" Gregg asked, tilting his head the way one does who hates to ask something of someone.

"Sure, just let me hit the little girl's room," Janice whispered.

"I'll be back there." Gregg pointed to the two empty tables in the back. Janice shook her head and walked away.

"Ok Captain, It's been nice," Gregg said as he rose from his chair.

"Happy Birthday again," John said, barely looking from his phone. "I'll see you soon."

After taking a seat in the back of the bar, Gregg realized, as his perspective had changed, that there were probably thirty young hikers outside.

The Appalachian Trail ran through Franklin, and locals offered hostels, shuttle services and more to the hundreds of hikers that wandered into Franklin monthly. They were good for the economy, and Gregg believed they brought an eclectic-cool to the small mountain town even if they didn't much care to come inside.

"Whew!" Janice said with a smile, as she sat down beside Gregg at the little table in the back of the bar. "Got hot up there."

"I'll bet," Gregg replied.

"Can I get you a drink?" Gregg asked the glistening piano player.

"No, no, I'm fine. I have water bottles up there." Janice politely replied to Gregg's offer. "So, you're doing the first presentation on Frances in July right?" Janice asked.

"That's right," Gregg replied. "July 26th. I know now is not the time or the place to discuss any of this," Gregg said. "I was hoping to set up a time though if you wouldn't mind."

"We need to get a room out at the library Gregg because I've got more stuff to show you and tell you about than you'll believe. I've been working on this for years Gregg, especially since I retired, and with the fiftieth anniversary of Frankie's death coming up in July, it's all I've been thinking about."

"You will be at our presentation on the 26th won't you?" Gregg asked the piano player who had begun casting glances back to the stage.

"I wouldn't miss it. In fact, let's make sure and meet out at the library soon because I have lots of old pictures of Frances, family pictures and such you might want to use. I'll burn them on a CD and bring em', how about that? Then, you can use them how you see fit."

"That would be perfect. Thank you so much. Oh, and guess who else is coming?" Gregg didn't give Janice time to answer. "Gene Southards and Harold Cloer."

"Well, won't that be a night?" Janice said, this time more wistfully as if her emotions had neared the surface. "She'd be ninety now," Janice continued, and Gregg was certain he detected just a hint of melancholy in her voice. "Sad, sad," Janice finally said as she stood up.

Just before she walked back to the stage to begin her next set of songs, Janice once more looked at Gregg. "She lost so much, and you know what I remember about her most? I was fifteen-years-old when she died. I remember how she shined. The rest of us were country as Cornbread. We were dull you might say, but Frankie—Frankie had a shine about her. She walked into a room—it was like a light came on, like a Christmas tree. Sometimes I think she was too good for this world." Janice finished and walked away.

She repositioned her stool and microphone, and for the first time all evening, she didn't smile as she began playing. The smile would come within the minute, but it was sleeping late. It was lost in the dark for just a moment. The song Janice began to play ever-so-softly to a gracious wave of applause was "Blue Velvet."

Gregg couldn't help but wonder if Janice had decided upon that particular number in the short span of time it had taken her to reach the stage in front of the packed house, for it had been such a popular song the year her cousin had died.

With each perfectly placed finger calling forth notes that somehow stung like a bee, unlike the previous songs she'd performed earlier in the evening, the musician's face twitched with emotion, moved with the music.

As Gregg watched the hikers mutely laugh, smoke and converse through the glass of the front window behind Janice's head, as he listened to the gentle rumblings of the patrons inside the bar, as he smelled the tart beer that hung in the air and felt a slim creek of sweat meander down his spine, he couldn't help but imagine her, Frances Bullock, with the grace of a spring breeze swaying in time to the rhythm her cousin was creating with her fingers. Gregg couldn't stop himself from mentally integrating the long-dead woman into the scene, a phantom waltzing in the ether between worlds.

CHAPTER TEN
WE'RE LIVE FOUR

SEPTEMBER 1, 2013

66 Well, we'll have to get you back on here sometime just to talk about this Walpurgis Night stuff Gregg." Tony broke in. "I want to know more."

"I want to go to the Rathskeller! Urns of ashes and bottle trees sounds like our kind of place." Dale added.

"It's a neat place," Gregg confirmed.

"So you didn't get much that night from Mrs. Crane, but I assume due to your deep knowledge of the case that you did end up meeting up with her later," Tony said, with what Gregg audibly perceived as a drop in confidence in Gregg's actually having a deep knowledge of the case at all. The way he'd phrased the word deep, had told on him, so Gregg quickly leaped forward into the online conversation that seemed to be quickly losing steam in order to reassure Tony and Dale of his prowess with the case.

"I did meet with Mrs. Crane twice after that night, before the July 26th presentation, and as I said, she was a wealth of information, but remember I had lived with the Frances Bullock murder my entire life," Gregg said.

"What do you mean?" This time it was Dale who asked. "What do you mean you lived with it?" He repeated, placing this time more heat on the word lived.

"My father was a Franklin police officer. The last twelve years of his career he was the Assistant Chief, and though he didn't put on the uniform until 1976, the Chief of Police in 1976 was Ernie Caswell. If Dale's taking good notes..."

"I've got him!" Dale shouted.

"You'll recall then that Chief Caswell, a brand new officer in 1963, was one of the first officers on the porch that day awaiting SBI Agent Nathaniel Cole. Chief Caswell was on the scene, in the home, and that murder haunted him to his grave.

"So he's dead," Tony said.

"Died a few years back," Gregg retorted, "and Frances Bullock's murder was somehow part of that."

"What do you mean?" Both Tony and Dale blurted out simultaneously.

"I mean her shadow fell across his casket. I'm not insinuating that he had anything to do with her murder, not in any way. He was a fine man. I'm saying her murder haunted him. It wore on him, wore him down. My dad said he and Chief Caswell used to ride around for hours in the Seventies and Eighties discussing the case. Chief Caswell would share with my father his every thought, his every suspicion, even took my father into the murder house a time or two to verbally reconstruct for my father what he'd seen on that day, how it had all gone down. Chief Caswell had filled notebooks with his thoughts and suppositions, and from his death bed, he asked his family to burn it all after he was gone. He knew the cold case was still so dangerous, he didn't want anything with the name Frances Bullock on it in his home after his passing. That's what I meant by Frances Bullock's murder was part of his death in some way," Gregg concluded.

"Wow!" Tony followed up with a gasp.

"So that tells us how your father became an expert on the case via his Chief, but how did you soak it all up?" Dale asked.

"Well, I'd heard her name dropped around our house from time to time since I was a little boy, and then in 1987 I heard some old men in a barbershop bring up her name. I asked my dad that night more about her, but I don't recall him going into too much detail. It would be six years before I'd get the whole bloody mess in story form, but when I did it never left me," Gregg trailed off.

"So," Dale said, "If I'm getting my math right here...."

"And trust me, Gregg, there is smoke coming out of his ears, and his eyes are crossed," Tony said with a laugh.

"You were a teenager when you learned everything," Dale said.

"Well, I'd never say everything, but I learned a lot because I had plenty of time to listen," Gregg said, placing a strong emphasis on the word plenty.

"What do you mean?" Tony chimed in. "Were you grounded?" Both men laughed.

"Everybody was grounded!" Gregg lowered his voice as he went on.

CHAPTER ELEVEN
BLOOD IN THE SNOW

Well, I keep seeing this stuff, and it just comes a-rolling in, and you know
it blows right through me like a ball and chain

From "Brownsville Girl" by Bob Dylan and Sam Shepard

MARCH 12, 1993

The mountains disappeared. The newsman had called for snow, but nobody had anticipated the gravity of what was to come, and when it started everyone believed somewhere in their hearts that it would never stop. When the snow finally did let up, Franklin and the surrounding region was cut off. Living seven hard crooked miles from the small town of Franklin, Gregg and his family had been excommunicated from any semblance of society or humanity. The hum of electricity that most believe to be silent, ended, proving to many in the region that it isn't silent at all. In the wake of the snowstorm, a stillness filled the hills and valleys that very few had ever experienced.

"Oh, thank God!" Audrey said when her snow-covered husband opened the door. "I think we'd have died." She said much quieter, dusting snow from her husband's thick Franklin Police Department coat. "Who brought you?" She asked, knowing there was no way his police cruiser could have made it through the snow.

"Vernon Stiles got me part of the way in his truck," Jimmy answered. "I walked the rest. Damn, I'm froze through. They told us with family outside the city limits to go on home. I'd have come whether they had or not." Jimmy curtly said while placing his hands over the kerosene heater that stood like a glowing tree stump in the middle of the room.

"Where are the boys?" Jimmy asked.

"Already outside, and Scott's been screamin' at Gregg already. Already fightin' out there." Audrey said while looking out of the lofty, large picture window that offered a broad view of their back yard. Below, both boys were attempting to force snow down each other's thick coat collars.

"God a mighty Audi, you would not believe what town looks like. They ain't nobody ever seen nothin' like this." Jimmy said, taking his coat off in the process.

"They were callin' it the storm of the century on the news before the power went out," Audrey added.

"God I reckon!" Jimmy popped off.

The day grew dark, and when night closed in, Gregg and his family huddled close, still and quiet in their living room dimly illuminated by a single oil lamp and the warm glow of a short, stout kerosene heater.

Gregg was lying on his belly in the floor drawing cartoon birds in a sketchbook while his little brother Scott was silently mouthing the imagined screams and groans cascading from George the Animal Steele and Ricky the Dragon Steamboat, two, large rubber WWF Wrestler figures as mentally they attempted to kill each other in his small pale fingers.

"Ernie told me something new this morning," Jimmy said, shaking free of the binding calm the early darkness had bound the room up in. "Said when he'd gone back to Frankie's house a couple of days later he thought to get a better look at the stairs leading down to the garage, cause they'd found that bloody rag down there. He said there was absolutely no blood on the stairs, but there were tiny specks of blood all down the wall beside the stairs." Jimmy then lifted his left arm above where it had been resting on the couch's arm. "Ernie seems to think the pattern fits a swinging arm. He thinks somebody had her by the shoulders, and somebody had her by the feet. He believed her hands were swinging like pendulums, hitting and missing and hitting and missing like a swing set."

"That makes sense," Audrey responded.

"What are you talking about?" Gregg asked, lifting his eyes to his father.

"Oh, just an old tale," his father replied.

"Was Ernie talking about the house where that ghost jumped on you?" Gregg asked with a slanted grin. Jimmy had forgotten how much he had talked about the Frances Bullock case at home. He quickly cut his eyes in his son's direction, remembering that he'd been present the morning he'd come home after that awful night several years ago, remembering that both of his boys had heard it all.

"Yeah same house, the Frances Bullock house. Ole Ernie ain't never let it go. He told me when he closes his eyes to go to bed, he keeps seein' it all rollin' in. You stay out of there! You hear me! Those kids are gonna get hurt always messin' around out there." Jimmy then leaned his head back as if to settle into sleep.

"What do you think happened that night dad?" Gregg asked while curving a dark line that would become an animated River Crane smoking a cigar. Scott looked up from his toys. Though it was only seven o'clock at night, outside it was as dark as pitch. There was a lot of night left before them. Huddled by a heater, in what, if one were to blur their eyes, could have just as easily been the year 1800, Jimmy took them all back in time. Word by carefully-chosen, delicate word, he pulled back Frances Bullock's living room curtain. He broke and entered her privacy. He stole scenes not his to steal, and as voyeurs, via his tale, the small weather-trapped family collectively went back to three days in 1963.

CHAPTER TWELVE
GOODNIGHT FRANKIE

I don't have any regrets. They can talk about me plenty when I'm gone.

From "Brownsville Girl" by Bob Dylan and Sam Shepard

JULY 26, 1963

66 You almost had a Smother's Brother's scene right here in the yard," Frankie called back to her dear friend, silhouetted in the front porch light.

"Did you about fall?" The lovely young widow's elder friend's response was cloaked in laughter.

"I almost hit the ground," Frankie replied. Her own comment wrapped in the same laughter.

"Well be careful, and watch for snakes. You know they crawl after a good rain."

"Oh, now I'll have bad dreams," Frankie spoke into the darkness, not bothering to turn her head. The metallic squeak of Frankie's car door, as she swung it open, fractured the calm of the night, and as she placed the bag of onions her elder friend had given her to take home on her car seat, she could hear the television inside her friend's front room replaying the commercial for that night's Jack Parr show they'd been talking about earlier.

"Comedian Jackie Mason and the Smothers Brothers tonight," a loud and bouncy voice called out from inside the house. The moment Frankie had heard the music that accompanied the commercial she called out. "There Flora, what time did it say it was coming on?"

Flora Spindale, a nurse at Angel Hospital some twenty years Frankie's senior was leaning over her front porch banister attempting to light a cigarette. She then pulled back her screen door and leaned inside. "It said it was coming on next Frankie, so you better get home or you'll miss it."

"Oh, I don't live that far away," Frankie called out as she sat down on her car seat and shut the door. "I could just about walk and not miss it."

"You walk?" Flora piped up joyously. "Hope you've gotten better at it," Flora called out laughing while Frankie, sitting in her dark car, mocked her laughter, sounding like a cross between Santa Clause and the Mad Hatter.

"Goodnight Flora. It's not enough you made me sit through the President, you have to hope I fall as well. Don't I have the best of friends?" Frankie rhetorically quipped as she turned the key and shook the tight shoulders of the night awake with her engine. Flora was still laughing when Frankie clicked on her headlights and begun to ease her newly purchased tan 1962 Mercury Monterey out onto the quiet rain-soaked street.

Not four hundred feet from the happy home filled with laughter and innocent irreverence, the neatly dressed young widow found herself, like so many times before, staring into the night at the old First Baptist Church graveyard. The church, which had stood nearby in the 1820s had long since been gone, given way to a large new Baptist Church just up the road, but the ancient tombstones were still visible, leaning into the past, sunken and broken and just dripping with what-ifs and I wonders.

Frankie always drove slowly home, and due to the many visits to her friend Flora's home, the old graveyard had become a usual, though unusual, point of interest. Frankie always almost stopped as she drove past the graveyard. It was a lonesome feeling it gave her, but there was also a thrill in easing so close and so slow. What might run out of the darkness from amid the bending markers? Upon completion of her macabre private game, Frankie would smile and press her foot, always clad in the finest of shoe, onto the gas pedal, leaving the boneyard in her wake till the next time.

As Frankie stopped at the stop sign in front of the large, new First Baptist Church, she ran her left index finger along the upholstery at the top of her car door and began humming a melody that had plagued her all day. Her mind drifted back to the all Mozart concert she'd attended at the Methodist Church the night before and how the gentleman she'd gone with, Lewis Clayton, hadn't stopped humming the opening piece for the rest of the evening. Cursed by the melody, she too had hummed it all day. Normally Frankie would have only come to a rolling stop at this particular stop sign, especially after dark, but there was another car coming slowly down the street. From inside the oncoming car, through the open windows, Frankie could hear a song playing on the radio. The song slid like thin wind into the open window of Frankie's car smooth and clean, the singer singing something about blue velvet, then the song fast became static and then another song, static and then another.

The young man driving the car had one hand on the wheel and one arm draped around a lovely young girl wearing a letterman jacket that fit her like a car cover. She was leaned forward, obviously attempting to find a station or a particular song on the radio. Realizing the couple was not going to move for a moment, Frankie pulled the wheel to the right and turned onto Church Street. She couldn't help herself. As she drove slowly past the two young lovers, she called out.

"WNOX" out of Knoxville is good and WLS out of Chicago."

The young man smiled, and the young lady, feverishly fingering the dial never acknowledged Frankie's assistance, but before Frankie was ten feet beyond the couple she could hear the smooth voice of Sam Cooke pouring like warm milk from their open windows. As Frankie moved on, the voice faded with their taillights into the darkness like a dying echo.

As Frankie continued slowly up Church Street, her headlights warmly lit a sign on the side of the road that read, St. Agnes Episcopal Church. The momentary glint of the word saint cast impromptu memories upon Frankie's mind's canvas, and without warning, she found herself adding to the mental painting, stroke by bold stroke, a creation that in reality was begun and finished in a blink, but to Frankie felt like an hour. As her car crawled along through the wet summer night, Frankie, with all the vibrancy of a million rainbows, remembered Norah. She could see her weak, broken smile and hear her laugh that always begun and concluded with a cough. Norah had lain in the bed next to Frankie's on that cold sanatorium porch in 1940 breathing icy air. It was believed the cool mountain air was medicinal, so the residents slept outside upon large long porches. It was Norah who kept Frankie's spirits up night after night as both girls fought for their lives so many years ago in Black Mountain, North Carolina.

Tuberculosis. Frankie's father, who had valiantly survived trench warfare in World War One, had withered away in the cold grasp of the disease at the Veteran's Hospital in Asheville, North Carolina. Images of her strong father wasting away weighed on Frankie's mind, but Norah, a constant ray of sunlight, wouldn't allow Frankie to even dream that anything worse than their miserable porch might possibly happen to her. It was Norah that taught Frankie so much about boys, art and animals.

She loved all three and not necessarily in that order. It was her late-night whispered stories, always riddled with strained giggles that Frankie truly believed kept them both alive, and it was Norah who taught her about saints.

Norah, a devout Catholic from Boston, Massachusetts had been sent to the Black Mountain TB sanatorium as a last-ditch effort to save her life. Each night Norah would pray her rosary, and each night Frankie would watch in awe at the reverence her sick young friend demonstrated as she fingered the red beads of each Hail Mary. After the Hail Holy Queen, Norah would always look at Frankie, smile and say, "Ok, saint time." Norah would then teach Frankie about a new saint. Frankie couldn't remember the last saint's name Norah had taught her about, but she did recall that he was homeless and died in Rome.

Frankie woke one cold September morning. Seeing her own breath hanging before her like a phantom, she pulled the covers tightly over her face in an attempt to seal out all of the colds: the cold weather, the cold reality of having one lung and the cold reality of having a life-threatening illness.

Through the thin blankets, Frankie heard murmurs hushed and methodical. She heard what sounded like holy words being whispered. Frankie gently eased one edge of the blanket down in order to ascertain the speaker and his purpose. Her heart, like her one decent lung, seized inside of her. A priest was pulling, ever so gingerly, a white sheet over Norah's face.

Frankie's stomach tightened. A horn was barely tapped behind her.

"Sorry," Frankie mouthed, without really speaking, in response to the lightly irritated driver behind her. How quickly the church sign had taken her back. She'd all but stopped in the road. Frankie then sped up and turned left onto Harrison Avenue. She past Bryant Funeral Home, and as always, purposely averted her eyes so as not to lock them on the place, but for some reason that night a chill ran up her spine as she drove past.

Though the Franklin High School Frankie had attended had been located on Harrison Avenue, as she passed the newer and more modern Franklin High School that sat on the hill just above the Tasty Freeze, a deluge of memories from her own high school years spilled over like a jostled cup of tea. She smiled remembering how her history teacher one year had come to school falling down drunk and how all the students laughed when he fell into the blackboard. She remembered warm stolen kisses, funny friends and rich laughter.

As her old high school memories melted into the darkness behind her, Frankie raised her hand in a gentle wave to Officers Gene Southards and Sonny Welch passing in their squad car. She could see they were talking and wasn't offended when they didn't wave back.

As Frankie neared her home, she quietly hummed the new song the DJs were overplaying on the radio, Blue Velvet, then turned left onto the short road that would in seconds bring her to her neat, two-story brick house nestled amid the tall trees.

Frankie could hear the gravel crunching beneath her tires as she pulled into her driveway, and her headlights shone brightly upon her garage door. She turned off her engine and quickly snapped the keys from the ignition. The reflected headlights had made a mosaic of multi-colored stars that gaily danced behind Frankie's eyelids.

Grabbing the slick, brown bone handles of her black, patent leather purse, Frankie got out of her car and shut the door. Usually she put very little thought into how she opened or shut her car door, but that night, for reasons she couldn't explain, Frankie eased the car door shut, and with her usual poise and confident stride, the lovely young widow, swinging her purse, and still humming the novel melody, strode across her dark lawn, up her sopping wet back steps, and onto her porch.

"I'll get the onions when I put the car in the garage," Frankie thought to herself. She didn't want to miss the beginning of the Jack Parr show. She'd joked earlier with her friend about how her near fall in the yard was like the Smothers Brothers who were known for their off the wall antics. She liked them quite a bit and didn't want to miss them.

At her door, Frankie pushed her hand into her purse to retrieve her keys. Out of pure habit, Frankie had dropped her keys into her purse when she got out of her car. She'd forgotten, like she did most times, that she would need them for the door. Feeling around in her purse, Frankie felt the thin leather holster that housed the small pistol she carried for protection. She felt a special stone, smooth and cool in her hand, and it made her grimace. Gordon Morrison's voice flooded her mind.

"You keep this stone; I'll take the other one. I know a jeweler. I'll have it put in white gold, a Tiffany setting. How does that sound?" He'd asked Frankie just weeks before.

"It sounds like a lie," Frankie mumbled to herself, recalling their near marriage.

Not finding the keys right away, Frankie placed her bag on her porch, knelt down and used both hands. She then scooped up her broach watch with her keys. Seeing she was holding both of them, Frankie shot a quick glance at the time, visible due to the moon. It read three minutes after ten o'clock.

"*Late, late, late, late, late,*" Frankie repeated, in a whisper, over and over again as she fumbled with her keys. Then, with a swift series of movements, Frankie had opened her door, turned on her living room light, turned on her television, on which Jack Parr was already laughing heartily at something and placed her keys next to her purse on the counter by her stove in the kitchen. She then stood before the television set for a moment as the flickering lights lit and darkened the crisp, blue and white dress she was wearing.

At the first commercial break, Frankie decided to put on something more comfortable. As she turned, she saw, lying on her dining room table, the beautiful violin she'd recently brought home from New York City, but it didn't make her smile, because just as quick she recalled how her brother, Willie, had almost lost it. Then, just like that, Willie was on her mind. She hadn't seen him in about four days, ever since she'd told him she was cutting him off, no more money. He'd gambled away too much already; however, she expected him tomorrow. He would come sulking around, quiet, then after a few minutes, he'd act as nothing had ever happened. It was always the same.

As Frankie climbed the stairs to her bedroom, she thought about something her mother had told her earlier in the day, something about Willie. Her mother had broken out the cliched adage, blood is thicker than water, and she'd said it in a way that made Frankie feel guilty, but Frankie entertained that thought for no longer than a second. Willie had to be cut off, she reminded herself. He wasn't dependable, and he blew through money like grain through a goose.

Frankie could hear the television set from her bedroom as she gently placed her blue and white striped dress upon the bed and quickly donned her favorite Bobby Brooks pink house dress. She then slipped on some comfortable Italian sandals. Just before Frankie left her bedroom, she lifted the novel she'd been reading off of her nightstand and thumbed through it. She found the dog-eared page from the night before, opened the book and read about two sentences before the Jack Parr audience laughter from downstairs pulled her from the conflict and scene she'd already started rebuilding in her mind. Also on her nightstand was a new magazine she'd barely cracked. Frankie, in one hurried motion, tossed the magazine and novel onto her bed then jogged down the stairs so as not to miss the remaining minutes of the show she'd been waiting to watch.

Frankie made herself comfortable on the couch and illuminated by the flicker of her black and white television, she laughed. When the show again went to commercial, Frankie suddenly felt hungry. She remembered a Cantaloupe on her counter that was soon to go bad if it wasn't eaten. While she listened to adds about the finest soaps, cars and stain removers, Frankie quickly sliced the cantaloupe in half, then into fourths, then into thin pieces. She placed three slim portions of the juicy fruit onto a yellow plate and walked back into her living room, licking the tips of her fingers as she went.

As the Jack Parr show was ending, Frankie leaned down and turned off her television. Her home grew absurdly quiet, then all of a sudden Mary Lou's dogs went crazy across the street.

"Oh, please don't bark all night," Frankie spoke as if the dogs could hear her. Frankie then stepped over to the window situated beside her backdoor. From where she stood she could see her old goat house just barely lit by the little splinter of moonlight the canopied trees would allow. She sighed gently and then leaned down to lift her plate from the small table that sat between her couch and her television. She took her plate and placed it in the sink, looked over at the mess of cantaloupe and then remembering the onions on her seat and that her car wasn't in the garage decided, though tired, to go get them and pull the car in, but that meant changing clothes. For a brief moment, Frankie thought she'd slip out in her house dress to get her onions and pull the car in, but her raising wouldn't allow it. She couldn't go out in her house dress.

CHAPTER TWELVE

Frustrated with herself for not pulling her car into the garage when she got home, Frankie cut the remaining good fruit from the rinds in a hurry, placed the cleaned rinds in the sink, placed the knife on the edge of the sink and trod quickly upstairs to don the dress she'd recently removed, but before Frankie could reach her bedroom door, a loud knock rang out from downstairs. Frankie eased to the bottom of the stairs. She slyly peered around the wall then breathed a sigh of relief. Ever since she'd lost her husband, Ebb, three years prior, Frankie had felt a bit uneasy at night, living alone as she did, but this was no stranger. She smiled and walked to the door to open it.

CHAPTER THIRTEEN
WE'RE LIVE FIVE

SEPTEMBER 1, 2013

66 God, I'd have loved to have heard your daddy tell that story like that by lamplight!" Dale erupted.

"Me too." Tony agreed. "Dale's turning the page Gregg," Tony said.

"Ok, so she was in for the night, house dress and all," Dale said. Gregg could tell Dale was writing as he spoke.

"Whoa! Don't write that down!" Gregg slipped in. "That was my dad's understanding back in 1993. We've since learned the pink Bobby Brooks house dress Frankie came home and changed into was not in any way a housecoat. It was simply another dress and a rather stylish one at that."

"So she came home and changed clothes before bed?" Tony asked.

"Maybe she was going back out." Dale followed up. "Well, what does your dad think now?" Dale asked.

"We lost my dad in 2005—Heart Attack. I was never able to update him on the multiple new pieces of information that we've unearthed in the last few years concerning the case."

"We're so sorry!" Both men again spoke together.

"Thanks, but it's not the dress issue that I'd run to tell him first if I could. It kills me that I can't share the fifty-year-old secret we just uncovered in the case. The secret would have blown his mind.

"Tell, telllll!!" Dale loudly interjected then repeated with a long drawl.

"July 17th of this year I scored a private audience with Harold Cloer, the last living civilian to have been onsite at Frances Bullock's murder scene and to have participated in her autopsy as a witness. We met for breakfast at a restaurant in Franklin called the Sunset. Man did he take me back in time! I swear my heart beat loud enough to have been heard across the room when he lowered his coffee cup from his lips and whispered, *"I've sat on this for fifty years son. Somethin' the coroner said that day never set well with me."*

CHAPTER FOURTEEN
STABBED TO DEATH IN THERE

*I can still see the day that you came to me on the painted desert
in your busted down Ford and your platform heels.*

From "Brownsville Girl" by Bob Dylan and Sam Shepard

JULY 29, 1963

Sheriff Bryce Ingram was leaned back in his chair, his legs crossed upon his desk. He swirled half a cup of luke-warm coffee with his left hand as he listened to his friend, both personal and political, imitate what Barney Fife had said on the most recent episode of the Andy Griffith show.

"They bout got us nailed ain't they Harold," Sheriff Ingram crowed about the Andy Griffith show.

"That Barney makes the show, and that's a fact. God a mighty when Gomer dropped that gun off the roof, I thought my sides would split wide open." Harold said laughing.

"How about his boots stickin' out over the roof's edge and the Christmas lights?" The Sheriff added. Both men took a deep breath and sighed, then finished with a final, behind the breath chuckle. Sheriff Ingram placed his coffee mug to his lips and loudly finished the last of his lunch-time coffee.

"I do believe Ed filtered this coffee through his damn socks this mornin', Harold," the Sheriff said with a slight grimace as he swallowed the last mouthful—"Whooo!"

CHAPTER FOURTEEN

Harold just grinned and looked up at the Bryant Funeral Home calendar hanging somehow slightly crooked behind the Sheriff's head. A small metal fan aimed at the Sheriff's sweat-slick neck rattled away, lightly turning up the corners of the calendar.

"Twenty-ninth, we've about got July licked ain't we Sheriff?" Harold rhetorically asked while putting his hands behind his head, leaning his chair back and closing his eyes. Harold continued his inquisition. "Have you had the meatloaf down at the Dixie Grill?"

"No, heard from CD that it's good though." The Sheriff answered, his eyes closed as well.

"Hell yeah, it's good. The cheeseburger down at Bower's snack bar's good too. Course the Chicken and Dumplings down at H and J's ain't bad either."

"Damn Harold, go eat." The Sheriff grumbled lethargically.

"I may here in a minute. Did you hear Harold and Joanne got into it the other day down at the restaurant? Hell of a fight they said. Young'un run outside and pulled officer Fred Dillard in off the street."

"Fred set em' straight?" Sheriff Ingram asked, never breaking his pose.

"Fred, Hell! Yeah, said he set straight down and ordered a grilled cheese."

"Sounds about right." The Sheriff replied, void of any discernable expression.

"Oh, I've got to get up from here," Harold said with an exaggerated exhale. "I've got to run down to Macon County Supply—said the ole man's boy, Lyman's, got a key cut for me, and Dr. Killian asked me to come by and sign a birthday card for his momma. The wife's asked me to pick up something down at S and L, and what else—what else?" Harold grew silent.

With the exception of the rackety metal fan, the room became as quiet as a stillborn calf for the next ten minutes as both men slept.

"There he goes." Sheriff Ingram mumbled awake. Outside, a man's voice busted a hole in the balloon of tranquility both men had allowed to encompass them.

"And Jesus said, AAAAHHHHH! Lest a man be born again AAAAHHHHH!" The Sheriff swung his legs off his desk and walked to the window that offered up a view of the town square.

"Thought he was done for the day," Harold spoke, still seated, eyes still closed.

"Probably just went to get him a bite to eat," the Sheriff replied.

Franklin was known for its soapbox or sidewalk preachers, and in the summertime, it was rare to ease through a weekend without hearing one or two.

"Are the boys listening to him?" Harold asked the Sheriff as he lowered his arms and opened his eyes.

"They Hell no. Ain't an empty bench out there, and they ain't a one lookin' at him. Settin' out there tellin' dirty jokes and swappin' knives, all their doin'." Sheriff Ingram grumbled.

"Leaves will be turnin' for you know it. I even heard Wayne talking to JC about the fair this mornin'." Harold said.

Once more both men grew still. As the Sheriff gazed out upon the sleepy Southern town he'd sworn to protect and serve, only the metallic hum of the old metal fan that was stirring the calendar pages could be heard.

Sheriff Bryce Ingram was Franklin, North Carolina's very first Republican Sheriff, and it was due in part to the tireless, behind the scenes work of Harold Cloer. Cloer, a dedicated Republican, was pleased with the outcome of the recent election and visited the new Sheriff almost daily.

"Well," the Sheriff said, "believe I'll head up to Conley's Barbershop for a trim, see what's going on in town. I don't need to pick up the paper anymore; five minutes up at Conley's and you get it all. If he don't know it his wife does and damn if she won't put it in the newspaper."

Mrs. Conley was the closest thing to a reporter Franklin, North Carolina had. She specialized in social events, weddings and such. Just as the Sheriff was turning from the window, the phone on his paper-stacked desk screamed out, splitting the calm late-summer day like an ax thrust into a jagged piece of stove wood.

"Sheriff Ingram," the Sheriff answered genial and quick—"What?" He responded. The Sheriff's face blanched, and his eyes took on an earnestness Harold had yet to see in his friend. His lips pinched to a white slit as he stood soaking in the contents of the phone call.

Harold turned toward the Sheriff.

"Damn!" The Sheriff said, muffled, through gritted teeth. "We're on our way! Come on Harold!" Sheriff Ingram commanded as he tightened his gun belt and scooped up his hat. "There's a body been found out on the Georgia Road."

Harold jumped to his feet and swallowed hard. "A body?" He repeated.

"Body, just what I said. Let's go!"

The Sheriff hit the lights and the siren, loud and uncommon on Franklin's generally serene streets. The spectacle tugged at everyone's attention. The sidewalk preacher didn't miss a beat though. From every window and parking lot people watched. Sheriff Ingram and Cloer passed a packed house at the Dixie Grill, faces pressed against the glass. A handful of men gathered on the sidewalk behind the Bryant Funeral Home lowered their pipes and lifted the brims of their fedoras as the squalling car sped past. The Sheriff ran the red light between Henry's Motel and the B and D Restaurant. He sped past an ample crowd of teens gathered at the Tasty Freeze below the high school. Within sixty seconds of passing the Tasty Freeze, the two men were pulling up to the house where neighbors claimed they could see the dead body of Frances Bullock inside. Several neighbors, family members, and friends were already on the scene.

Moments later, as the two men were scaling the steps of the home to see what neighbors were already convinced was a dead body; City Police Officer Ernie Caswell arrived with his siren wailing like a Banshee as well. Caswell, a tall, lanky young man, fresh from the Navy joined the two men on the porch. All three men cupped their hands around the edges of their eyes and stared through the warm glass of the front door's window to ensure a clearer picture. What they saw inside was indeed and without a doubt, Frances Bullock, a well-known resident of the town, lying on her back with her legs crossed and her hands folded neatly upon her midsection. Officer Caswell began ordering people away from the windows and porch. He tried to no avail to push back the onlookers.

The next vehicle on the scene was an ambulance driven by George Norman. Norman held many titles in the small Appalachian town, ambulance driver, coroner, and mortician. As Norman jumped from the ambulance and started walking quickly toward the house, several onlookers began quizzing him right away about what was going on. The coroner, without hesitation, whirled on his heels and shouted, "That lady's been stabbed to death in there! You all need to back up!"

Sheriff Ingram and Harold Cloer exchanged looks of confusion.

"George," The Sheriff asked, after he'd joined them on the small porch, "how do you know she's been stabbed?" The coroner busied himself and feigned ignorance.

"I said she's been killed." The coroner hastily corrected.

All four men, the Sheriff, Officer Caswell, Cloer and Norman stood quiet for a moment, then the rush of inquiries and cold reality hit them in the face. Sheriff Ingram was a small town Sheriff. He'd never had to deal with anything even remotely similar to the seriousness of a murder, and he was convinced he was ill prepared to do so.

"I'm calling the SBI." Sheriff Ingram blurted out. Nobody goes in there till the SBI arrive, is that clear?" The Sheriff, using an unusually authoritative tone, told the other lawmen and onlookers. Sheriff Ingram radioed in for the State Bureau of Investigation to be called. For what felt like a week, they all waited for the agent to arrive.

While the lawmen waited they were bombarded with questions from the onlookers.

"Who did it, Sheriff?"

"How's she layin'?"

"Can you all see a weapon?"

"Should we block off the road?"

"Should I call her momma?" "I have her number."

"Where's CD?"

"Ain't this CD's jurisdiction?"

CD Baines was Franklin's Chief of Police, a small, wiry man who took nothing from no one. He had a reputation as a man who finished fights. He rode a motorcycle everywhere he went and he was passionate about law enforcement. Chief Baines could only boast an eighth-grade education, yet he'd made history championing the cause of retirement benefits for police officers in the state of North Carolina. It's due to Chief CD Baines that all police officers in the nation have retirement benefits to-day; however, that particular evening the well-respected Chief had taken his son to a dentist in a neighboring town. It was an absence that would haunt him for the remainder of his days.

"Hell, I don't know where CD's at." Sheriff Ingram erupted! "Ernie, where the Hell's CD?" Sheriff Ingram had only been Sheriff for a very few months. Previously, he'd been a city officer under Chief Baines.

Well over an hour later, having driven from Waynesville, North Carolina, The State Bureau of Investigation officer Nathaniel Cole arrived on the scene. With his arrival, the floodgates opened, and the next half hour was an amalgamation of neighbors, friends, and family crying and begging for answers and blinding flashes from both the Franklin Press photographer's and Agent Cole's cameras, both men snapping picture after picture in and outside of Ms. Bullock's home.

"Here's your murder weapon!" One old man in bib overalls called out, lifting from the kitchen sink, a long knife still clinging to cantaloupe peels. Friends and family were parked in the yard. Neighbors roamed the halls freely as if children on a field trip. Family and friends leaned over the dead lady's body raining salty tears upon her already stiff frame. The entire crime scene was destroyed inside and out.

When Chief of Police, CD Baines, finally made it back to town, he was disgusted. He refused to even go the crime scene, because the whole mess had been so completely compromised, and he couldn't understand why, why a seasoned SBI agent would allow such slipshod police work.

A forty-year-old widow, many would say in the prime of her life, had been brutally stabbed to death. Her body, which should have remained right where it had been discovered for several hours for investigative purposes was removed after merely forty-five minutes. All expectation of retrievable physical evidence both inside the dwelling and around was crushed and crumbled like dry cookies in strong hands due to the absurd amount of civilian foot traffic allowed inside and outside the residence of the deceased.

Fingerprints were lifted from the home, but shockingly few. Other than a scant number belonging to the deceased, far fewer than should have been found, two partial prints were discovered, one on the back side of Ms. Bullock's television set, the other near the top of a kitchen cabinet's door. The first belonged to Ms. Bullock's brother, Willie, the later, found on the cabinet, belonged to Bill Triplet, a former boyfriend of the deceased.

As the body was being removed, Officer Gene Southards, who was freshly on duty, arrived at the scene of the crime. Before entering the home he noticed footprints near the edge of the back porch and promptly pointed them out to Agent Cole who, waving his hand scoffingly, dismissed the young officer's observation, stating that he himself had made the tracks a few minutes prior. Inside the home, Officer Southards found a three-ring circus in full swing. Neighbors, friends and family members of the deceased were going through every dresser drawer and cabinet in the house. Nothing was cordoned off.

Knowing already that Mrs. Bullock had been stabbed multiple times, via cross conversation rising from officers within and outside of the home, Southards was shocked to hear the agent making comments that leaned in the direction of self-infliction—suicide. After a brief time, Southards, disgusted at the scene before him, was instructed to go about his rounds as usual. He was asked to leave.

The day was quickly waning, and the night was coming on fast. In every kitchen, on every street corner, at every diner counter, buzzing through every telephone line and on everyone's lips was the name, Frances Bullock. Everyone had a suspect. Everyone swore by their choice and was angered when bombarded with contrasting views.

"It's her brother, Willie! That's who's killed her!" some said.

"It was one of her girlfriends that done it. You see how they all dress, wearin' them tiny little short skirts and platform heels. It ain't Christian!" old women whispered.

"It's her neighbor, Mrs. Nelson. You know her husband Jeb had been flirting around with Frankie, and you know what kind of man he is. They say he was caught just last week with a gal in one of the rooms at his motel, and how many tellers has he lost at the bank due to his roaming hands?" others stated.

"I believe it's that man she had working in her yard, Charlie McFalls; he's bad to drink you know."

"Everybody knows it was the coroner. That's why her body was moved so fast, why there weren't hardly a fingerprint one. He'd done and wiped it all down."

"No, it was Danny Cochran that worked out at the mill."

"You're all wrong; Frankie had been sneakin' around with some IRS man. Kate saw her waitin' for him at the golf course several times lately, settin' there reading a book as pretty as you please."

"Frankie Bullock was killed by the mob; it was a hit man!"

"She was killed by a doctor. I heard she was runnin' around with a doctor."

As the summer cicadas sang and the streets grew quiet, the good folks of Franklin, North Carolina made their way home, but not everyone would sleep that night. The Franklin Police officers and the Macon County Sheriff's Department deputies eagerly awaiting the autopsy findings and photographs paced the floors and interviewed multiple suspects.

Several local men had been called in to witness the gruesome ordeal inside the home of the deceased, while others had been asked to gather around the cold metal table beneath the hot morgue lights to witness the autopsy. When the results were finally released early the following morning, the lawmen listened like small children at the foot of an old storyteller....

Frances Bullock, age forty years, had died due to multiple stab wounds to the torso. Her intestines and her lone lung had been deeply punctured. Her left wrist was broken. She had defense wounds inside her hand, and she had a small knick in the center of her chest where the SBI coroner, Jake Stockton, who'd been called in special due to the sensitive nature, seriousness and severity of the crime, believed whoever had done this to the young widow had held the knife in a threatening manner prior to the actual slaying.

Early the next morning, the Franklin Police Department was abuzz with activity. Neighbors and friends and many who barely knew the young widow were calling with theories and suppositions. Notes and numbers were being jotted down with the quickness of hummingbird wings. Coffee was being poured. Cigarette smoke hung on the ceiling like translucent cotton candy. What-ifs filled the room and the officers kept their hands closer to their guns than usual. The lawmen were on edge, yet tried hard to be kind to every old lady who called knowing the killer, knowing the why the when and the how. It was in the midst of the havoc of the morning when the Franklin Press photographer stepped inside the building.

"Hey Paul," Officer Caswell called out to the young press man. "Let's see them pictures. Lay em' out on this table."

Paul Slagle, the twenty-six-year-old photographer for the Franklin Press stood in the doorway of the Franklin Police Department awkwardly. He was noticeably wan, pale as powder, and he stuffed his hands quickly into the tight pockets of the same jeans he'd worn the day before as Officer Caswell spoke, an obvious attempt to conceal their trembling.

"I forgot to load film in the camera," Slagle said in a terrified voice. All the lawmen stopped what they were doing and stood silent.

"You what?" Chief Baines asked with his left index finger pointed at the trembling cameraman.

"I forgot to load film Chief. I was nervous. I had never seen a dead body before," the newspaper man sheepishly responded.

"You had three cameras, Paul," Officer Caswell reminded Slagle. "You forgot to load film in all three cameras?"

"I was nervous." The newsman replied again, this time looking at the ground and grinding the toe of his right shoe into the hardwood flooring. "I'm sorry," Slagle said quieter this time. He then turned, walked down the hall, and, as if escaping from a sinking ship, pushed his way through the door into the hot July morning.

No one spoke for a moment inside the small town police station. No one knew what to say. Caswell was certain, he told the others, he'd watched Slagle snap what seemed like a hundred photos. He'd even watched him switch cameras twice.

"Didn't the SBI man take pictures?" Chief Baines queried with a furrowed brow.

"He did,"Officer Caswell responded.

"His will probably be better anyway." The Chief said, sitting down at his desk to thumb through the autopsy report again. Just then the phone rang.

CHAPTER FOURTEEN

"Ernie get that." The Chief said. "I'm sure another old lady has it all figured out."

Officer Caswell rolled his eyes as he answered the phone. "Franklin PD."

"What?— Chief!— Chief!" The young officer was holding the phone to his chest and motioning with his available hand for Chief Baines to hurry over to the phone.

The Chief took the phone from the wide-eyed deputy and spoke deliberately and strong. "Chief Baines." The Chief, after a look of disgust, washed over his face, actually broke

a smile. "OK, I see." The Chief said, soundly for all the world like he'd just received word of a loved one's passing.

"That was the SBI wasn't it?" Officer Caswell quizzed the Chief who, after hanging up the phone, was sinking down into his desk chair. "What did he say?" Caswell begged.

"SBI man said his camera malfunctioned," Chief Baines spelled out to the glowering awe-struck room—"Got no pictures." The old Chief then raised his right hand and ever-so-slowly rubbed his right index finger up and down the thumb of his right hand, the universal gesture for big money. The rattle of the fan was the only sound to be heard for several seconds inside the Franklin Police Department.

Meanwhile, at the Sheriff's Department, Sheriff Ingram and his deputy, Floyd Coffey, were fussing over several stacks of paper. Some were typed. Some were handwritten. All were about the murder. The Sheriff had not gotten a wink of sleep. The puzzle wasn't fitting together. There were so many suspects, so many alibis, so many twists and turns.

"Let's try to piece this together Floyd," the Sheriff said with both palms over his eyes. He then allowed his open hands to slide down his face, tugging his eyes open till the red under lids were grotesquely exposed in the process.

Finally, the Sheriff took a long deep breath and began reading aloud from the notes he'd typed out over the seemingly endless and sleepless night—

Frances Bullock, forty years of age, recently widowed.

Her husband Ebb had been electrocuted at the Nantahala Power Plant three years prior. Husband had been down in his back for several days, but work called and he insisted he was up for the job against his wife's, Frankie's, better judgment. He was electrocuted and taken right away to Andrews' hospital. Frankie sat by his side for three days before he finally succumbed in a burn unit downstate. Frankie had been hunting for rocks with her aunt, a favorite hobby of hers, at the Corundum mine area on the Highlands Road when her husband was hurt. The family had to go find her. Upon the death of her husband, due to negligence on the part of the power company; however, multiple onlookers said it looked more like a suicide than an accident. Frances was given an ample monetary settlement, making it possible for her to start an antique shop, which she ran out of her home with her brother Willie as her business partner.

Frankie had been to visit her mother earlier in the day on July twenty-sixth. She had then spent the evening with Vivian Spindale and her daughter Mary. Looks like they went to a produce stand at which Frankie purchased a bag of Vidalia Onions. She left the Spindale residence at around 9:50 pm. We can only assume she drove straight home. If so, she should have arrived sometime around 10:00 pm, and that's where we lose her. The next day when Frankie didn't call or visit her mother, her mother got worried and called her son, Frankie's brother Willie. Willie adamantly refused to check on Frankie. Bad blood it seems. Neighbors grew concerned when they saw her car parked outside the garage. Said she never left her car outside the garage. On Saturday two neighbors, the Wallers, walking in the evening, noticed Frankie's car windows were down and rolled them up since it looked like it might rain again. Two neighborhood boys mowed her yard. Charlie McFalls was seen banging on her door late Saturday evening, seemingly trying to receive payment for prior work. On Sunday, after church, a friend, with whom Frankie was supposed to attend church with that day, came to check on her. He says he was concerned that her car was there, but she didn't appear to be on the premises. Said he looked through the windows and couldn't see a thing. He'd told her he would fill in some holes in her yard the last time he'd seen her, and while he was there he and a friend who'd ridden with him, filled in the holes. He then left a note on her door asking her to call him when she arrived back home. Late Sunday evening, terrified that something was wrong, Frankie's mother finally twisted Willie's arm enough. He went to her home but wouldn't even go on the porches. He walked the perimeter of her home, calling her name, and when he got no response, got in his car and left. Monday, the same thing, neighbors nervous and worried because a hallway light had been burning all Friday, Saturday and Sunday night. Finally about midday Monday, Vivian and Mary Spindale went to the home of Ms. Bullock. Standing on Frankie's back porch they looked into the home through a window that peered into the dining room. It was there that the two ladies saw the body of Frances Bullock lying behind her dining room table. A neighbor called the police. I was the first law officer on the scene. Harold Cloer had ridden with me there. Officer Ernie Caswell was the second law officer on the scene, followed by the coroner George Norman. We arrived finding all Hell breaking loose. I decided to cordon off the home until an SBI agent could arrive. Over an hour later Agent Nathan Cole arrived, and we all entered the home together, having to force entry, as all doors were locked from the inside. Inside the home, there was no visible sign of a struggle. Though the home was filled with extremely expensive and fragile antiques, nothing was broken or out of place. There was a thin trail of blood leading from the kitchen to the body. There was a small blotch of blood along the bottom of the stove near the floor. There was another small swipe of blood at the top of a kitchen cabinet, and underneath the body of the deceased was a small pool of blood as well. Two wine glasses sat upon her dining room table, and two chairs had been pulled out as if she'd been casually sitting with her assailant. There was some question about the position of the body right away. Deputy Caswell was the first to notice the abnormality. The deceased's head was touching the wall. Her body was laid out flat. She was on her back. Her ankles were crossed, as if napping and her hands were placed upon her midsection, one upon the other. After Caswell brought it to our attention, we all recognized the awkwardness of the body. It appeared to all on site that the body had been placed post mortem in *the seemingly restful pose. The Franklin Press photographer arrived and begun taking crime scene photographs. Agent Cole began taking photos as well. The only item missing from the home among many very valuable items was the victim's purse, almost completely ruling out robbery. Before long the crime scene was compromised due to neighbors, friends, family, and onlookers walking the perimeter of the home and entering the home unbidden. Within forty-five minutes, at the insistence of the coroner, the body was removed from the scene of the crime. An autopsy followed.*

CHAPTER FIFTEEN
WE'RE LIVE SIX

SEPTEMBER 1, 2013

❝ Well, that's it then!" Dale called out. "Coroner did it! You don't have to be Ben Matlock to figure this one out. The house was locked. No one had been inside. He hadn't even gotten up to the house when he told the yard full of onlookers that Frankie had been stabbed to death. How else could he have known? Case closed!"

"That does seem to close the book Gregg," Tony said, agreeing with Dale.

"Maybe, maybe," Gregg replied, but that's just one secret to leave the time capsule with this case. There were others, and don't forget, at that particular time there was absolutely no reason to suspect the coroner. There were by far more suitable candidates, by far."

CHAPTER SIXTEEN
NEON PUZZLE PIECES

Turn him loose, let him go, let him say he outdrew me fair and square
I want him to feel what it's like to every moment face his death

From "Brownsville Girl" by Bob Dylan and Sam Shepard

JULY 1, 2013

Gregg arrived an hour early at the Macon County Library. He believed if you weren't early you were late. He checked his watch and stepped inside. He was to meet Janice Crane for what he hoped would be a lengthy and fruitful meeting shortly. Gregg stepped over to the checkout desk and tapped with his middle finger on its hard wooden surface so as to gain the attention of his aunt who was studiously scrutinizing the computer screen before her face. His father's baby sister, Tina, had arranged for a private meeting room for Mrs. Crane and her nephew so the two men could converse in private.

"Hey, hey," Gregg said, leaning his right elbow upon the desk. "How's your day?"

"It's fine," Gregg's aunt replied with an eye roll. Sometimes Gregg actually found it painful to look at his aunt's eyes as they so resembled his late father's.

"She's not here yet." Tina quietly said.

"Yeah, I'm early. Thought I'd go flip through the historical documents back there, the ones you can't check out!" Gregg accented the later part of his sentence with comical anger in his eyes and three sharp raps upon the desk to better ensure his librarian aunt received the message of his disdain at not being able to peruse the material at home.

"Well have fun with that." Gregg's aunt responded with a facetious grin. "You guys will be in room A-3 back there by the help desk. I'll send her back that way when she shows up."

"All right. See you in a bit." Gregg said, again tapping his finger upon the desk as he departed.

Gregg lifted three bound volumes from a shelf he was quite familiar with and walked them to one of many vacant tables. He pushed two to the side and opened the thickest of the three. Franklin, North Carolina, Her Past and Her People, the book's title read. Gregg began thumbing through the book. Though he knew much of the information already, he was never content that he'd gotten it all. He always believed there was a hidden gem amid the lines and old black and white pictures of the small Southern Appalachian town. The library was exceptionally quiet and void of people. In fact, there were only two people in sight. One old man, Gregg would gauge to be in his early eighties, sat at a computer donning large blue headphones, and Gregg could see the top of a young woman's head inside one of the private study rooms. She appeared to be reading and deep in thought.

"*Old Indian cabin,*" Gregg whispered to himself as he analyzed the black and white picture staring back at him from the open book. The image that had elicited Gregg's audible acknowledgment was that of a grand old mansion with tall white pillars three feet thick and twenty feet high. The caption below the image read: The Jesse Siler home. Though the photo was taken in the 1970s, Gregg knew from his research that the home had been standing like a fat white southern gentleman since its completion in 1828. The stories living in the dark corners of the old place had long since been abandoned ranging dramatically from tales of gun-wielding pioneers, shafted Indian chiefs and stagecoaches to Civil War Bushwhackers and headless slaves. As savory to the mind's pallet as dusty wagon wheels and the crack of six shooters were, it was the tale of the headless slave that won the bid on Gregg's full attention. Soon, Gregg's attention willingly left with its bidder. The quiet library with its scant occupants morphed into a dark and stormy night, a night that had been all too real. A night full of thunder, whiskey and dead bodies.

"Recon the old Rider'll come fer her tonight Jess?" Joseph Welch, *the oldest man in a pack of old men, blurted out before raising a nearly empty whiskey bottle to his lips. Four of the men were holding tight to rope ends, two on either side of the coffin. All four men huffing and wheezing as inch by inch they lowered the brand-new coffin down into the dark Earth. One rope was beneath the head, the other the feet. Since the grave had to be dug two feet deeper than the usual given the bizarre circumstances, the coffin had to be lowered down gingerly on the ropes. The ropes would then be thrown in on top and covered with worm-filled earth.*

"God above I hope so Welch. Hate to thank of that thang crawlin' out of there and hainten us all." Jesse Siler replied, completely understanding Welch's remark. Every man that night and every man, woman, and child in the vicinity for that matter knew of the Rider. It went back to the old country. The dark writhing souls from those bodies buried at the crossroads were believed to be gathered in the wee hours of night by the Dark Rider, a pitch-black specter of death on horseback whose sole mission for all of eternity was to gather damned souls as one might collect hand-fulls of wildflowers. "Yeah, by God I hope so Welch," Siler reiterated.

Joseph Welch, one of Franklin, North Carolina's founding fathers was a wild and woolly character. He'd been involved years before in a lawsuit with an old Indian named Euchella over disputed land that Welch claimed he'd purchased in the 1818 Waynesville, North Carolina land auction; however, Euchella, wouldn't leave the newly attained land. North Carolina's Supreme Court found in the old Indian's favor, only perpetuating the fued between the two men. Ironically, years later, Welch and Euchella became neighbors and friends, and it was Welch that fought for Euchella's being able to remain on the land when General Winfield Scott came through the region in 1838 with the Trail of Tears.

Welch's trial wasn't his last brush with fame though. He'd owned and operated a turnpike road in the Great Smoky Mountains. He'd owned one of the first taverns and voting stations in the mountains, and when General Scott did make his way through the mountains in 1838 it was Joseph Welch's home the General stayed at, as it was one of the finest around. The slice of history though that most hindered Welch's dreams concerned an old Indian by the name of Tsali. Tsali and his two sons were killed by firing squad in Welch's back yard before the General took his leave of the place, and what Joseph Welch and his family witnessed had not only become a local legend but fodder for nightmares. Just before the bullets ripped through the faces and chests of the three bound and blindfolded men, before a single shot had been fired, Tsali's blindfold, white as cotton snow, turned black and red with fresh blood. Where the blood had come from no one could ever tell, but it was after this that Joseph Welch aided in founding the Cowee Baptist Church and became a regular churchgoer. Some say Welch had compared Tsali's preemptive bleeding to Christ in the Garden at Gethsemane when he sweated blood. But, it wasn't Joseph Welch's night. In fact, Welch was all but broke on this night. Gone were the turnpikes, taverns and fine homes. Most he'd lost to the richest man in the region, Nimrod Jarrett. On this night, Welch was but a bystander, a ghost from the past himself. The night belonged to Jesse Siler.

Jesse Siler had arrived in Franklin, North Carolina in 1818. He and his three brothers had become very famous and wealthy men, and unlike Welch had been able to hold onto their fortunes. Jesse's father, Weimer, had been a drummer boy in the French and Indian War and a decorated soldier in the American Revolution. Jesse and his brothers had moved their elderly parents to Franklin years prior, and up until this night, though death was as common and as certain as Wednesday prayer meetings, nothing as grisly had occurred in connection to him or his community.

The year was 1853, and Jesse Siler was the richest slaveholder in Franklin, North Carolina. The previous night had offered up a rainstorm like hadn't been seen in a coon's age many of the men agreed, and it was in the storm that Jesse had lost his slaves.

For whatever reason, no man would ever know, Jesse's favorite slave and dear, personal friend, Alfred, had somehow lit a metaphorical fire beneath his little old wife, and sometime in the night, sometime in the storm, in her fury, she'd slit his throat open to the world with his own straight razor. As the razor had been rather dull, Alfred's little old wife had had to work the meat a while. When Alfred's wife was finally successful in reaching her husband's spinal cord with the razor, with sweat dripping from her nose, she allowed for an ax to finish the job.

After placing her husband's head, mouth agape and one eye open in the crook of his own arm, making the old man comically appear to be holding his own severed head like a freshly plucked melon, she then cut an old bed sheet to ribbons, fashioned a noose, braved the storm and went swinging from a crooked tree limb on the Siler family's back property.

The next morning, as the sun lifted the rain back up in the mist, she and Alfred had been discovered. Alfred was found on his bloody bed where his wife had left him, his big, dark, ham hands crossed over his belly button, his head, completely detached from his body and cradled in the bend of his own arm. His killer, eyes bloodshot and set in a saucy death stare, had been found hanging like salted meat on the hillside below the Methodist graveyard, a thick foam about her lips.

Alfred had been buried in the Methodist graveyard at four o'clock that afternoon with fine white preacher words spoken over him, but his little lady had been offered no such Christian luxury. In the Southern Appalachian Mountains, one couldn't bury a suicide or a murderer in the hallowed ground or even around decent folks. Those bodies had to go to the crossroads, and there were rules to follow, methods to ensure were administered.

Alfred's old wife had been put into her coffin exactly how she'd been found on the hillside. No pearl handled brush had gone through her briar patch of hair. There had been no borrowed gown or shined up shoes. She went down wet, swollen, foamy-mouthed and muddy. Her only adornment in her coffin was a two-foot piece of Hickory. In keeping with crossroad burial customs, the old killer had had a stake driven directly through her heart.

"Worshed that taste out yet Nathan?" Sheriff Bynum Bell asked with a grin no one could see in the dark night.

"Go to Hell Sheriff!" Nathan Smith, Franklin's coroner, replied just before spitting another warm swish of whiskey into the open grave. Old man laughter iced the night like a cake.

Smith had taken it upon himself, due to his position, to drive the stake, and he'd gotten a mouth-full of heart blood in the process.

"Mary'll not kiss you till the mistletoe comes out I'll wager Nathan." Will Higdon added, throwing yet another dry log onto the fire of good-natured ribbing at the coroner's expense.

"You can go to Hell too you son of a bitch!" Smith shouted back between gags and curses.

The candles that glowed on the window sills of the Bower's Boarding House down the hill and the hint of a moon that kept playing peek a boo with the wispy autumn clouds was their sole light, as tradition said a crossroad burial had to be done in abysmal darkness.

"Jess, reckon we ort to sang her a song or somethin?" Jacob Siler, Jesse's brother, asked while lighting his pipe, the glow of which brought into crisp focus his bushy and unruly grey eyebrows and mustache.

"Song Hell!" Jesse mumbled in the darkness.

The old man at the computer across the room coughed hard, breaking the spell Gregg had been under, and to his great chagrin, in a wink, the flickering candles in the Bower's House windows and the peek a boo moon had gone black. Back to their wet dark graves where tree roots most likely snaked through their rib cages and wriggling worms made a home of their eye sockets went the funeral party. As the fancied scene from the past dissipated, replaced by the mundane present, Gregg couldn't help but grab a hold of one last cool tree limb as he ever so reluctantly allowed his characters to slip through his fingers.

"You ready?" A soft voice from behind Gregg asked. Gregg spun his head to see Janice Crane, briefcase in hand, standing behind him.

"Yes, yes," Gregg replied. Just let me put these back. Gregg rather harshly slapped shut the book he'd been reading and scooped up all three together. As Gregg re-shelved the books, Mrs. Crane stood quietly behind him.

"Sorry about that," Gregg said. "I'm ready now. I just can't get enough of the shades of yesterday I guess." Gregg smiled.

"You're not telling me anything," Janice replied. "I've lost many a day in these stacks. They pull you in don't they?"

"That they do."

"Well, let's get started. I've got more to tell you than I could fit into a week," Janice said with a reserved smile.

"And I'm ready to listen," Gregg responded with a smile of his own.

Over the next three and a half hours, with all sound concealed inside the private meeting room Gregg had reserved, Janice couldn't have painted a more vivid picture of Franklin, North Carolina in 1963 had she broken out brushes and canvas. She couldn't have recreated the murder and subsequent mystery any finer had she summoned the souls of those involved from their crumbling tombs to tell their own tales. Gregg took notes fast and disjointed with zero concern for sequence, timeline or cohesion on site. He knew he'd glue it all together at a later time.

- Frances Stanfield had been born to Grover Cleveland and Odessa Louise Frady Stanfield....
- She had a childhood peppered with fun and frolic, a childhood of walking milk cows to pasture and close family ties but also of tragedy....
- As a young girl, Frances had been confined to Tuberculosis sanatoriums and had undergone painful operations.... She survived the dreaded disease, but not without losing one of her lungs....
- Her father was absent often due to illness and hard times....
- Frankie had been living in New Jersey when she met her first husband William Stark....
- Her second husband, Ebb, Ebion Richard Bullock, had been an orphan.
- Ebb was a Mason and a member of the Lion's Club. Both affiliations offered Frankie multiple opportunities to dress and act in a manner she'd

desired all of her young life....

- Frankie and Ebb had a dog named King.
- Frankie was allergic to cow's milk, so she and Ebb had a goat house behind their house. This ensured she could always have fresh goat's milk.
- Frankie's brother Willie was constantly plagued with financial problems.
- Frankie and her Aunt Mae loved to go hunting for Gems.
- Frankie took trips to Colorado to visit family.
- Ebb had been electrocuted while working for the Power Company in 1960, and Frankie had had to fight tooth and nail to receive widow's benefits.
- Ebb's last will and testament had left Frankie the beneficiary; however, if Frankie were to have died before him, the estate would go to Ebb's brother, John David Bullock and their nephew Paul Townsend. Frankie, one year after Ebb's passing, removed Ebb's brother's name from his will and placed the estate solely in the hands of Ebb's nephew should she pass....
- Frankie's temper was iron hot and had caused embarrassing scenes. She'd even been known to get down on the ground in public kicking and screaming to get her point across.
- Frankie had created within her home an antique shop. Some treasures within were, a 1791 German violin, a faceted Alexandrite gemstone and a gold Elgin ladies pendant watch.
- Frankie's neighbor, Frank West, housed many of her larger antique pieces in a basement beneath a shopping center he owned.
- Frankie's mother, Odessa, and brother, Willie, also got into the antique business with her.

Janice Crane talked and talked, sweeping every last granule of informative dust from the metaphorical dark corners of her cousin's short life. Many stories were accompanied by artifacts the amateur sleuth had amassed over the years: hand-drawn maps, letters written in her late cousin's hand that covered everything from mundane day to day sharing of news to telling past lovers to rot in Hell, newspaper clippings, photographs and more, but it was her murder, the mystery that chased it and the mile-long list of suspects that Gregg found most appealing, so as Janice laid out the list of men and women who'd raised even the slightest of eyebrow among law enforcement, Gregg took careful pains in his recording of the information both on paper and in mind.

• Frankie's brother, Willie, was the first real suspect. He'd refused to look for his sister when others believed her to be missing. He and his wife had both failed lie detector testing. They'd claimed to be at a drive-in movie, but neither could give the title of the movie or describe anything about it, and due to Frankie's brother's belligerence, he'd even been held in police custody during his sister's funeral.

• A local mail carrier, an Episcopalian Priest, an unknown telephone company employee, an insurance salesman, an IRS agent, several suitors, Ebb's brother, Johnny, wives of reported suitors, wealthy businessmen and doctors, Frankie's lawn man, female friends, respected city officials, coroners and more were suspects as well.

The list was exhausting, and there were so few common threads among the suspects. At the end of Janice's and Gregg's time together, Gregg was beyond words impressed with his elder. She'd done a masterful job of recreating, evaluating and objectively analyzing the life, murder, and mystery of her long-dead cousin Frances Bullock. So many new puzzle pieces had been spilled out before him. Some pieces fit. Some didn't, but in Gregg's mind, it was the burning neon pieces that vexed him most, the glowing pieces that looked like madness but weren't. The pieces that haunted him were pieces that seemed to fill empty slots in other puzzles, puzzles attempted by the masses. The gleaming odd pieces that seemed to fit nowhere in Frances' puzzle depicted secrets and lies.

• Frances had received a financial settlement upon the death of her husband in 1960; however, in many people's opinion she was living far beyond her means, and not just in goods and services but in travel, and it was on her many voyages to various places that her secrets and lies were born....

• Frances had begun telling select friends and family members of a mystery man she'd recently met. She said his name was John Peterson. To some, she claimed she'd met him on a plane bound for Denver, Colorado. She told others that Peterson was her nephew's Sunday school teacher. Still, to others, she claimed to have met him in Chicago, Philadelphia and Honolulu, Hawaii. And to a select few, Frankie allowed that Peterson was a General in the United States Army whom she'd met in New Orleans, Louisiana....

After thanking Janice repeatedly for her time spent with him, Gregg shook her hand and watched her gracefully exit the library, a briefcase full of mystery in tow. Gregg looked back at the bound volumes on the back wall and for a split second entertained the notion of a few more minutes of study but thought better of it. He'd leave the bones alone, for he had neon puzzle pieces to think about, and something more, something in the way Janice had looked at him prior to walking away, a look of passing something on, something dangerous.

CHAPTER SEVENTEEN
WE'RE LIVE SEVEN

SEPTEMBER 1, 2013

66 So let me get this straight," Dale said as one might after learning of some vile rumor his or her name had been attached to. "You have people buried in your little town with stakes through their hearts."

"That's where you go?" Tony all but shouted over the phone. "After all that, that's where you go?"

"That's exactly where I go! My God, I can't wait to visit this town, but I know already I'll need garlic and wolfbane and rosaries and wild roses—I've never heard the beat!"

"It's an unusual little town." Gregg joined in. We've definitely got a story or two to tell.

"Well," Tony eased back in, "Let's get back to the story at hand. So you have all these suspects. Dale just filled up another page."

"Gregg!" Dale called out.

"Yes, sir!"

"I'm going back a bit here, but you said that Officer Southards saw footprints outside that nobody seemed to want to talk about. Is that right?"

"It is. He said they all acted like it was nothing, acted like they'd seen them already, sent him on his way, but to this day he believes it was an integral part of the evidence that was completely overlooked. In fact, he went back."

"Went back?"

"Went back that night, he and his partner."

"Do tell my friend." Tony comically demanded, stretching, like warm taffy, the word "teeellllll" to its snapping point.

CHAPTER EIGHTEEN
LOUIS LOUIS

Well, there was this movie I seen one time
about a man riding cross the desert, and it starred Gregory Peck.
He was shot down by a hungry kid trying to make a name for himself.
The townspeople wanted to crush that kid down and string him up by the
neck

From "Brownsville Girl" by Bob Dylan and Sam Shepard

JULY 29, 1963

66 What in the Hell did that song even mean?" Officer Gene Southards rhetorically asked his partner Sonny Welch after snapping off the radio.

"Bout somebody named Louie, Louie I reckon. That's about all I got out of it." Sonny replied.

"Horse shit is what it was, pure horse shit."

"Yeah, it wasn't much was it?"

"Reckon we ort to roll over to the Police Department for a while, see if they've got anything." Sonny quizzed his partner whose face betrayed any attempt at conveying ease.

"They Hell no!" Gene growled back. "They done got this thing wrapped up. We'd just be in their damn way." Sonny sat silent. He'd had to hear at least three times since the two lawmen had stopped for dinner of how Gene's observation in the dead woman's yard earlier in the day had been so callously dismissed and probably ten times before that.

"Chief said to run out to the airport tonight; said them kids was parkin' out there again," Sonny mumbled before lifting a steaming cup of coffee in a dark, black mug to his lips.

"When'd he say that?"

"You was in the bathroom."

Gene mumbled something beneath his breath. He turned the key in the cruiser's ignition, jerked the car into gear and spun the steering wheel hard and fast to the right.

"Dammit!" Sonny shouted, lifting his coffee mug chest high and looking down at his crotch. "They ain't no fire. You made me spill my damn coffee." Gene didn't reply right away. As Sonny dabbed at the front of his pants with an old napkin that he'd found stuffed down into a nook in the console, Gene spoke.

"We ain't law enough to help with that damn murder, but if you need somebody to run off them naked damn young'uns twisted together out there at the airport, we're your men!" Gene all but shouted when the red light caught him across from the town square. Sonny decided to let it be. Gene turned his cruiser to the left in front of the A&P. The two lawmen, not speaking at all, passed Loganville Louis' antique shop, Downs and Dowdle feed store, and the Shell station. They turned right. Britches Poindexter was getting into his pickup truck to their left, and the lights were on at the Friendship Tabernacle on the hill.

"Did I ever tell you about the time me and Riley Henry got our asses busted for slippin' out of the tabernacle," Sonny asked, an obvious attempt to lighten the foreboding mood that was filling the cruiser like choking smoke.

"No," Gene quietly replied.

"Sure did. Went and got us a pack of stick gum from old Britches' gas station. When our mommas found out, God a mighty we wore a whoopin." The lawmen passed the Big Dollar Grocery on their right. Sonny lifted his hand to Warddie Young who was pushing buggies across the parking lot. Gene picked up speed. They passed Joe Henry's Rock Shop and Hall's Sign Company. Gene barely slowed the car at John Higdon's cabinet shop when he made a sharp right.

"You're gonna kill us tonight," Sonny said, swiftly grabbing the dashboard with his left hand. Like the golf course pool of four days prior, when the two lawmen arrived at the airport there wasn't a car in sight.

"Let's ride out there," Gene said in a hushed tone after he'd turned the cruiser around.

"Ride out where?"

"Out to Ms. Bullocks."

"What the Hell for?"

"I want to check something." Gene finished, expressionless. The two officers rode in silence to the dead woman's home some four miles away. They arrived a few minutes past 11:00 pm. When they reached the house, it was completely dark. Everyone had gone.

"Come on," Gene commanded.

"Come on Hell. I ain't goin' in there."

"The Hell you're not. Now come on." Sonny reluctantly opened his car door and stepped out into the humid night.

"You're crazy. You know that? What are you lookin' for anyhow, them damn footprints?" Sonny asked while pulling his hat on. Gene cut cold eyes over his shoulder at his partner.

"Nothin', and something—Come on!" Gene replied while fingering his flashlight. Sonny followed Gene through the darkness. Gene's flashlight, after a slew of garbled curse words and an animated shake, brought the night to life before the two young officers.

"There they are," Gene said, his wand of light illuminating the deep creases and clefts in the mud left behind by what appeared to be men's boots.

"Now look how close to the side of the house they are. Right under this window. Come on, let's see if that screen's been messed with."

"In the house?"

"Hell yeah in the house."

"And how pray tell, me amigo are we to gain this entrance you seek?"

"One of the deputies busted the garage door. It'll open." Gene assured his reluctant partner. "We won't stay but a minute." Gene lifted the garage door, and it slid audibly across the ceiling then stopped with a jolting CRASH. The two men went inside. With the aid of Gene's flashlight, the two lawmen quickly scaled the steps to the main room. They opened the door at the top of the stairs and soon found themselves in the very room the deceased had been discovered in just hours before. The still-lingering aroma of her dead flesh mingled with the humidity turned Sonny's stomach in an instant.

"*She was laying right here, pretty as you please, hands one atop the other, legs crossed at the ankle,*" Gene whispered to Sonny in the darkness.

"Is that blood?" Sonny queried his eager partner while pointing at an approximately one foot by one-foot stain on the hardwood floor.

"I reckon so," Gene replied. "Follow me." Guided by the light provided by his flashlight, Gene led Sonny to a window. He then shined his flashlight through the window and spoke.

"Right down there. This is the window has those prints below it." As Gene spun around to face Sonny, the wand of his light caught the corner of something metallic.

"Looky there!" This time it was Sonny who spoke first. "Look back there behind that nightstand." Gene's theory hadn't been wrong. It appeared someone had stood beneath Ms. Bullock's window, and thanks to Sonny's solid scrutiny, another leaf had been turned. The window's screen was tucked behind a nightstand just inside the next room as if it had been purposely hidden away.

"They Hell far, how in God's name did they miss that?" Gene again rhetorically spoke.

"I wonder if..." Sonny was cut short by the dispatcher.

"Southards! Welch!" The dispatcher called out from their squad car's radio. Gene had intentionally turned the volume up so as not to miss a call while he and his partner were inside. Gene turned and led the way back toward the stairs that led to the garage.

"Wait a minute," Sonny spoke, with a hand raised in the air.

"What?" Gene replied.

"Did you hear that?"

"Hear what—the radio?"

"Hell no, we both heard the radio. No, I could have sworn I just heard a woman talking."

"Screw you, Sonny!" Gene retorted and kept walking.

"I'm serious! I swear I heard..."

"Yeah, yeah, come on," Gene mumbled while descending the stairs. Sonny stopped for just a thought at the top of the stairs and listened.

"I heard something," Sonny thought to himself.

Both officers crossed through the dismal garage, shut the door back and strolled quickly to their squad car. Gene grabbed the CB radio.

"Southards, go ahead."

"Gene!" The dispatcher spoke. "They've got a young man over at Angel Hospital raisen' all kinds of Hell. Got a knife, scarin' the nurses. He's piss drunk."

"On our way," Gene assured the dispatcher. When Gene and Sonny arrived, an ER doctor and two nurses met them at the door.

"He's down there guys, settin' in the floor!" One nurse said while pointing down a long dim corridor.

"I KNOW ABOUT FRANCES BULLOCK!" The young man drunkenly shouted. "I KNOW ABOUT HER!" He sobbed.

"Come in here about thirty minutes ago just a bawlin'. Didn't take out the knife till just a few minutes ago; that's when he started talkin' bout Ms. Bullock." The nurse informed the officers. Leaning down to eye level with the young man, Officer Southards tried feverishly to elicit more from the intoxicated youth but to no avail. When they realized he wouldn't talk, Sonny wrenched the knife from the young man's hand and Gene lifted him to his feet.

The knife was several inches long and appeared, even upon brief inspection by both officers, to be coated in dried blood. As the officers carefully laid the nearly catatonic youth upon a bed inside the Macon County jail, their minds were racing like prize ponies, because both men had seen the boy before.

CHAPTER NINETEEN
WE'RE LIVE EIGHT

SEPTEMBER 1, 2013

"Dale's dancin' Gregg. God, you ought to see these moves. Never mind that. Nobody should ever see these moves." Gregg could hear both men laughing on the other end of the line.

"The boys in the rain that night, right? He was one of them, right? BOOM! Nailed it!" Dale shouted from Little Rock.

"He was," Gregg responded in a reserved manner.

"So," Tony broke in. "Was it the knife?"

"Don't know."

"What do you mean you don't know? Gregg, don't you make me drive to North Carolina tonight!" Dale comically shouted. "How can you not know?"

"It was never examined."

"Gregg, Dale's holding his head between his knees. Help me out over here." Tony said.

Gregg had been pacing back and forth across his bedroom floor up to this point; assuming at some juncture that the topic would shift, for he had a plethora of other stories to tell, but as the hour grew late, he resigned himself to the fact that the Frances Bullock murder would remain the main course, so he settled himself into a large soft chair, took a deep breath and went on.

"Gene and Sonny didn't sleep a wink that night. Stayed up all night discussing the case, driving around, waitin' for sun mostly. They were so excited about their catch. Yeah, it was one of the brothers from a few nights earlier. Yes he was wielding a bloody knife, and yes, he was ranting and raving about knowing about Frances Bullock. Open and shut you'd think. Question the young man, analyze the weapon, but it didn't work that way."

"What happened?" Tony asked.

"Well Gene and Sonny, red-eyed and beat, strolled into the Franklin Police Department that next mornin' knife in a little bag. Said the SBI agent, who was still in Franklin because he was supposedly still working the case, was sitting at a desk with a monocle on his eye, lookin' at coins. He was a coin collector and had several rare coins he'd taken from Mrs. Bullock's home. Gene said he held out the knife, told him about the boy and waited."

"What'd he say?" Dale blurted out.

"Said give it back to him."

"Said WHAT?"

"Said give it back to him. He wouldn't even touch it. Gene showed him the blood. He told Gene it was most likely deer blood. Wouldn't even the touch the knife."

"What happened to the kid?"

"Let him go."

"Nobody interviewed him?"

"Nobody said a word to him. That's when Gene and Sonny realized that the Frances Bullock case was different in some way. They knew that day that it wouldn't be solved. It wasn't just that kid and the knife. People were acting strange all over town, and not the usual fear strange, you know, locking up doors and windows that had never been locked before, but a guilty strange, a knowing strange."

153

"How?" Tony asked.

"Some of Frankie's neighbors flew to Europe. People left organizations they'd for years been a part of. Close friendships
dissolved, and then there was the incident at Woodlawn Cemetery."

"Ooooohhh, the cemetery, go on." Dale warbled from Little
Rock.

"It was a Saturday, our second presentation at the Historical
Museum. We did two nights, Friday and Saturday, this past July
26th and 27th. We had just wrapped up that last presentation,
and almost everyone had gone. Almost everyone."

CHAPTER TWENTY
HE DID SOMETHING BAD

The only thing we knew for sure about Henry Porter
is that his name wasn't Henry Porter.

From "Brownsville Girl" by Bob Dylan and Sam Shepard

JULY 27, 2013—LATE EVENING

❝Mr. Clark."

"Yes."

"Could I speak with you?"

"Of course. What can I do for you?"

"I can't talk here." The cryptic-acting woman hissed. "Could we meet another day?"

"Sure," Gregg replied. "Would you like to meet here tomorrow afternoon?"

"Yes, please."

"How about two o clock? Would that work?"

"Yes." The whispering woman agreed, looked over her shoulder then quickly made her exit, just barely nodding to Gregg's wife, Pauletta, as she passed.

"Who was that?" Pauletta asked while closing the door.

"I have no idea, but I guess we'll find out tomorrow."

CHAPTER TWENTY

JULY 28TH, 2013 – THE NEXT DAY

The old museum was too warm when Gregg arrived at around 1:45 the following day. He set the air conditioning to 68 degrees. He placed his bag upon a long ancient table that filled the museum's back room. He took from his bag a leather-bound notebook and a pen. He placed the pen atop the notebook so that the pen's ends were aimed at the top right and bottom left corner of the book. Gregg was meticulous when it came to details that most would deem unworthy of the effort, and nonchalant with matters of dire consequence or high importance universally recognized by others. He wore the world like a loose garment, tossing it off as he saw fit.

Gregg then strolled back to the front door, lifted the latch and looked outside. To his left and right, down and up Franklin's Main Street there was no sign of the mysterious woman from the previous night, but he was early. He stepped back inside and shut the door. Allowing his eyes to take in the museum's many colorful and authentic displays from a full frontal perspective, Gregg paused. Somehow it had previously evaded him how Robert had positioned the two rival pharmacy signs, both about ten feet high, one on either side of the room and facing each other. One read Angel's Drug Store, the other Perry's Drug Store. Like the signs now gracing the museum walls, both drug stores, both long gone, in their day had been situated directly across the street from one another, and the rivalry was epic. Beyond the signs, a whirlwind of history beckoned the viewer: Nazi flags snagged from France still clinging to grains of Normandy sand, Civil War weapons and amputation kits, old pianos and desks, hundreds of native Cherokee pieces, long antebellum gowns and uniforms representing many foreign conflicts draped over the plastic shoulders of headless men and women, and sundry other items of various purpose and use. The door opened behind Gregg.

"I'm here." The still-unknown woman spoke while pulling the door closed behind her.

"Welcome," Gregg said with a wide smile. The lady didn't return his hospitality with equal exuberance.

"Thanks for meeting with me Mr. Clark. I feel like a tick about to bust. I've sat on all of this for fifty years."

"Well, let's go bleed you then," Gregg spoke back, still smiling and leading the way toward the museum's back table.

THREE HOURS LATER—

Gregg sat alone at the table. He'd called Pauletta the moment the woman had left to tell her everything, as she'd been waiting on pins and needles too. He didn't know where to begin the construction. There was so much, so many names, theories, suppositions. Before him on the scared old table, spread out in neat piles were probably thirty sheets of yellowed notepaper, multiple sticky notes and carefully clipped newspaper excerpts, and articles that the lady had brought with her. Apparently, she thought nothing of leaving it all to Gregg, never to see any of it again, in fact, she insisted upon it. Alongside the piles of freshly garnered material was Gregg's own leather-bound book. Several pages boasted bulleted lists of information, dialect intact, Gregg had scratched out as the lady poured out her heart, her brain and by the way she left it all behind, her burdens.

Gregg opened his notebook and began reading to himself the multiple pieces of information the mysterious lady had blessed and plagued him with.

- The main thing I can say about the coroner is that he wasn't who people thought we was.
- I was a teenager in 1963.

157

- My father and the coroner, George Norman were close friends.
- I was always hearing around the house stories of George Norman.
- Dad had come home many times talking about how George wouldn't stop talking about Frances Bullock.
- Dad talked about how much George drank.
- The day Frances Bullock died George hadn't come in for work. I remember dad going to the phone that evening trying to call him. He hoped to be the first one to tell him about her murder because he knew how he felt about her.
- He said George acted like it was yesterday's news when he finally got to tell him the next day. Acted like he was just fine.
- Six months after Ms. Bullock had died, dad came home furious. I remember where I was sitting at the kitchen table. I remember dad going to the phone. I remember him slamming it down on its cradle too. Mamma wanted to know what was wrong. Daddy sat down and loosened his tie. He said George had showed up at Woodlawn Cemetery right in the middle of a funeral. He said he spun gravel he was driving so fast. He said everyone under the funeral tent stared at him. Daddy said George grabbed him by his lapels and started pulling him down the hill. He said people under the tent started bawlin'. "What the Hell are you doin'?" Daddy asked him. Said George was cryin', face was all swole up. "I've done something bad!" George hollered. "I've done something bad!" Daddy grabbed George by his lapels this time, told him to get his drunk ass home. Told him he'd call him when he got off work.

- I remember plain as day settin' there as daddy tried to call George.
- Never answered the phone.
- Daddy whipped that tie off, said, "Well, I reckon George and Helen have finally called it quits. Recon that's the bad thing he's done anyhow." I remember daddy said.
- He's killed her, Mr. Clark. He used to visit her all the time, nighttime too, cause from where we lived we could see her driveway, and he'd go in an out at all hours.
- She was missin' for three long days. It wasn't till the fourth mornin' did anybody see her and not before.
- He's pulled her down the stairs into the garage while he's cleaned the crime scene at night. He had all the chemicals to do it with. He was the only man in town who did have all the chemicals.
- There were hardly any fingerprints in Ms. Bullock's house at all. They'd all been wiped clean.
- Ms. Bullock I believe was living a loose lifestyle.
- I believe she and several other ladies in town were frequenting parties.
- I believe there was cocaine and pills and who knows what.
- It's not just me that thinks it. Lots of people were saying she was into that kind of stuff.
- She'd left Flora's house that night just before 10:00 on the 26th, but she didn't go home and put on night clothes. She went home and changed her dres altogether. Had on a blue dress when the police found her. Now, who does that but somebody who's heading right back out?
- I believe George showed up when she was heading

out. I believe because she was running around they
got into it. I believe he killed her.

• Even Dr. Trout said, years after Ms. Bullock had been
in the ground, the wounds on her body "looked more
like scalpel wounds than anything...."

The notes went on and on painting Frances Bullock as a
tramp and George Norman as her killer. Gregg was shocked
with the information the secretive woman had dished out like
hot mashed potatoes at a soup kitchen, but he wasn't convinced,
not by a long shot. He'd need more than fifty-year-old memories and postmortem slander, but they certainly were some of
the most vibrant puzzle pieces he'd been offered yet.

CHAPTER TWENTY-ONE
WE'RE LIVE NINE

SEPTEMBER 1, 2013

❝ So, this coroner drives up to a funeral in progress. He's acting drunk. In front of God and everybody he grabs ahold of the lapels of his friend, a coworker at the funeral home, and screams, "I've done something bad?" Tony theatrically summarizes.

"That's what happened."

"Then it's him! You've got your murderer! You said earlier he slept up with the caskets. He let it slip that Ms. Bullock had been stabbed when nobody had been in her house yet! That's it! Wrap it up! It's done! Solved!"

"Well, not really," Gregg replied.

"How not really? Don't tell us that the SBI Agent didn't interview him either."

"Well, he didn't, but it wasn't because of lack of concern or conspiracy in Norman's favor."

"Then why wasn't he interviewed?" Both men angrily asked.

"He died."

"Died, when?"

"He died that night."

"No, he did not! No, he did not!" Dale yelled from Little Rock.

"He did. Dr. Ed Angel's official autopsy said he died of heart failure." Gregg reassured the men on the other end of the line. The line grew silent. Seconds passed.

"Guys?" Gregg asked, thinking he'd lost the call.

"We're here," Tony spoke in a waver barley more than a whisper. "This is unbelievable Gregg. How old was he?"

"Late forties."

"I want to cuss, and Dale left the room. He can't take any more."

"It only gets worse. I had a long conversation one evening with an old man who had a puzzle piece he didn't know that he had."

CHAPTER TWENTY-TWO
PILLOW TALK

You know, I feel pretty good, but that ain't sayin' much
I could feel a whole lot better

From "Brownsville Girl" by Bob Dylan and Sam Shepard

JUNE 28, 2013

Gregg sat still in his car, seriously contemplating leaving. The home he'd just arrived at was beautiful, a mansion by Gregg's standards. Though he'd never had any trouble conversing with all manner of people regardless of their social status, it was the particular topic he knew he would be broaching at some point in the evening that allowed thoughts of a hasty retreat to clamber to the forefront of his mind.

Gregg lowered the sun visor in front of his face and lifted from its back the mirror cover. He checked his teeth in its reflection. He turned his face, ever so slightly to the right then to the left, looking at his beard, almost completely gray. With his face gently tilted left, the sunlight caught his left earring. He immediately tugged at the thick hoop then turned his head to remove the other. Gregg had worn hoop earrings since high school. He changed them often, but he rarely removed them for longer than it took to exchange them for another pair. But, today they'd stay in the console of his Jeep Patriot that idled just outside the fine home of the man he'd come to see. Gregg couldn't imagine that a 95-year-old Southern Appalachian man would think well of a 37-year-old man that wore two hoop earrings.

After resigning himself to the task at hand, Gregg cut off his engine and opened his car door. Sixty seconds later Gregg was inside the fine home. The doorbell had barely had time to finish reverberating once when the old man had swung open the door and welcomed his much younger guest inside.

Inside, the vestibule was bright and inviting. Thick carpet gave beneath Gregg's feet. Gregg followed the old man through the vestibule to a room to their left, a warm room filled with books and leather high-backed chairs.

The old man, Benjamin Elkins, a living legend in Gregg's small town, eased his thick short frame down into a seasoned chair while instructing his visitor to take a seat in a chair of similar size caddy cornered to his own that appeared never to have been used.

Whatever hesitancy Gregg had harbored prior while idling outside, had been almost instantly effaced within the borders of the old man's opening sentence, "So you want to talk about history?" And, whatever feeble proportion of angst Gregg had assumed he'd suffer due to his interviewee's age and social status had died as well when the old man leaned back in his chair and laughed a laugh so rich and true it seemed a net snaring the room and all its contents.

For nearly three hours, that felt more like ten minutes, Gregg played the part of the attentive audience mostly. He listened as the old man talked of his time serving in World War Two. He remained perfectly engaged as the old timer talked of his business ventures and his family. He barely batted an eye when the wintery old man in the hot seat talked of God, but it's when the sage old gentlemen's stories edged toward the macabre that

Gregg's elbows dug ditches into his thighs as he leaned hard in to listen.

"There's a great deal of dark history as well in this here town." The old man spoke as if reminding his listener. Gregg barely blinked.

"1833," The old man began while leaning far back in his chair—

"We had what was considered the trial of the century, at least for this region. Preacher man by the name of Reverend Evan Jones had moved into the Cowee village to minister to and aid the Cherokee who hadn't left in 1830. Well, his young healthy lookin' wife turned up dead, and it wasn't three weeks she'd been in the ground when the good reverend showed up to the village with another gal, all swole up with a baby. Them Indians knew what was goin' on; went to the Justice of the Peace here in Franklin, Jesse Siler at the time. Old Jesse wouldn't hear anything from an Indian, so he sent em' packen'.

About a year after the baby was born, Preacher Jones' wife sent for her sister Cynthia Cunningham. Claimed she needed help with the baby. Pretty young thing, Cynthia.

Well about six months into her stay at the village, Cynthia took to havin' awful headaches, took to stayin' in her room. Cynthia's sister was scared. She couldn't figure out what was wrong with her, and her husband, the good reverend wouldn't let her see her sister either.

All Hell broke loose when Jones came out of her room one day after an exceptionally long spell claiming that Cynthia had died. The preacher went outside to get the Indians on building her a coffin right away. His wife ran to her sister.

There she was rockin' her little sister's cold dead body back and forth when the preacher came into her room.

165

'Let her be!' He squalled. But she wouldn't let her go. The preacher forcibly unlaced his wife's arms from the corpse and pushed her toward the door. That's when she saw the blood. Just a hint of blood on Cynthia's ankle caught the light. About that time a big Indian man stepped inside the room. Distracted by the arrival of the Cherokee man, the preacher stepped toward him." Here the old man grinned.

"Yeah, he messed up leavin' his wife alone with her sister that a way. She hiked up her sister's dress and screamed like a wild cat."

"Why'd she scream?" Gregg caught himself asking, not unlike an inquisitive child.

"The baby—Reverend Jones had crushed every bone he could in that baby. Its head was nearly flat. He'd took his belt off, tied the murdered little girl to Cynthia's inner thigh with it.

Yeah! Nobody knows if he'd killed Cynthia before or after he'd killed their baby, but I don't reckon that matters does it. Yeah, we've got us a bunch of dark history here in this area son," The old man finished, "but, sometimes it's a trick ain't it?"

"What do you mean?" Gregg asked, actually from the edge of his seat. The old man smiled, and his eyes lit like two twinkling, dancing candles before he spoke.

"Sometimes it's a trick." He elaborated as he leaned back in his chair. "Sometimes things that seem dark or scary, evil even, are just the opposite. Ole Gretchen Ravens knew that didn't she?" The old man asked with a knowing smile.

From the way the old man paused and grinned at Gregg, he knew he expected him to know all about this Gretchen Ravens, and Gregg felt devastated as he racked his brain and came up empty. He had never heard of her, and he had to admit it.

"The name doesn't ring a bell Mr. Elkins," Gregg had to reluctantly admit. The old man never stopped smiling.

"I knew her well," The old man said, softer than anything else he'd said that evening. "They found her about six days later as I recall, 1994 I believe it was. She'd come back to Franklin from time to time. Her suicide letter in California ort to be made into a poem or short story or something. A perfect example of how something that seems dark ain't necessarily so here in these mountains."

Gregg was lost. He mentally tried to tie ends together, make some sense of what the old man was saying, but he couldn't. He couldn't until the story began, then, as the old man spun the yarn, the warm room that the two men sat in quickly became a rainy forest at a dark and lonesome twilight....

Gretchen stood outside of the cabin. Little ribbons of rain trickled from the umbrella she clutched tightly in her aging fingers. The door to the house stood halfway open, hanging on by a single bottom hinge concealed by vines. The house, with its crooked stone steps, leaning and twisted porch, spiderweb-broken window panes, and Poison Ivy-laced chimney stared back at her like an old Cherokee War Chief, sure and unblinking.

Since she had arrived three hours prior and parked her car at the foot of the mountain, Gretchen had walked to the cemetery in the woods. She had traced her great grandmother's moss-encrusted name with her finger and yanked up some brown bristle grass that was concealing the face of her great grandmother's tombstone. She'd been to the creek too, the good one, not the one by the church. She'd stood outside of Ida Lee's house cupping her hands to the dirty but still mostly intact window glass seeing nothing but the darkness within due to the sky being as murky as swamp water and the late hour. She'd strolled methodically alongside fields of dead corn stalks with grotesque and wicked looking skeletons of what once had been plump scarecrows eerily peering back at her through the breaks. She'd eased alongside the black river and down sinuous trails canopied dark and grown over, but now, standing in the cold drizzling rain that had been falling for two days and staring into the pitch black yawn of a door that invited her in as always, Gretchen paused to remember why she'd come in the first place, why she'd driven all the way from California at 64 years of age, why she'd left the paved roads for the gravel roads of Appalachia, why she'd rolled the dice to come back to the deepest holler, the longest road, the tallest mountain.

Somewhere from the fog-topped trees an early whippoorwill called, and Gretchen smiled. Not that she'd forgotten, but her reason for the arduous trek had become hazy and blurred with white lines and truck stops, fuzzy radio stations and state line greeting signs. With the bird's shrill and lonesome whistle, Gretchen's reason was once again crystal clear.

As the old woman scaled the crooked grey stone steps that had once led to the most magical place on Earth, she unconsciously held her breath and called out, "Grandma?" ....

"Are you about ready girl?" Gretchen's grandmother asked from the open doorway of her cabin. "Lord I've seen dead ponies get along quicker than you." She finished with a toothless grin.

It was the most beautiful summer day Gretchen had seen in her nine years on Earth. The sun was high overhead, and just a hint of wind ruffled the leaves on the crayon green trees visible through the gaps of light that outlined her grandmother like a whole body halo.

Though it was only ten o'clock in the morning, Gretchen was already tired. Her grandmother, who was actually her ninety-one-year-old great grandmother, with whom she always spent three weeks each summer, hadn't let up all day. To begin, Gretchen had been shaken awake at five o'clock in the morning for a breakfast of hot eggs and cold cornbread.

"Eat it fast now." Gretchen's grandmother had said with a loving scowl, *"They ain't but so much daylight."* Directly after eating and cleaning their space, Gretchen and her grandmother walked two miles of trails, fields, across a creek and through a briar patch in the mist and morning dew to reach a spindly stream that cascaded down the mountainside.

"I like the lizards from here a fer piece better than that creek over by the church," Gretchen's grandmother had said while straddling the stream and dipping her thick wrinkled fingers into the icy early morning water.

After both Gretchen and her grandmother had wrangled six fat, slick, black lizards and placed them squirming and flipping into a milk jug half filled with sloshing water that she'd later in the day exchange for money at Brendle's Store, they'd gone looking for roots.

"You mix just a smidge of this with Sang, and hit'll take down a fever by George." Gretchen's grandmother informed her while waving, like a pendulum too close to her granddaughter's eyes, a twisted, yellow, dirt-coated root she'd ripped from the soft earth beneath a crooked poplar tree.

Now, with the sun on high, roots already bagged and put away, lizards already sold, Gretchen struggled with a knot in her tennis shoe string while her grandmother waited, tapping her old foot impatiently in the doorway.

"If you hadn't traipsed that creek like I don't know what you wouldn't have had to clean them shoes." Gretchen's grandmother reprimanded.

After Gretchen finally leaped to her feet and joined her grandmother at the door, their day of adventure continued. By noon they'd picked wildflowers and snapped a white bucket full of green beans.

"I's gonna make Leather Britches, some folks call em' Shucky

Beans, but they take too long. They wouldn't be ready in time." Gretchen's grandmother had said when they'd finished.

By two o'clock in the afternoon, Gretchen and her grandmother had listened to the Bryant Funeral Home obituaries on the radio, a ritual cut in stone.

"I won't be able to hear it next week." Gretchen's grandmother had said with a furrowed brow.

By six o'clock in the evening, the two had eaten a supper of cornbread and milk.

"They, this milk'll go bad." Gretchen's grandmother had said, raising it up to the light so as to see the consistency through the glass.

With a full belly and tired feet, Gretchen finally found herself sitting in a lawn chair that had squealed like a stuck pig when she'd unfolded it beside her grandmother in the yard watching the lightning bugs perform a show both brilliant and soul-stirring.

"Grandma," Gretchen spoke, breaking the only spell of quiet the two had shared all day.

"Yes, Sweet Thang, what is it?"

"Grandma, you said some funny stuff today."

"I did. What'd I say?"

"You said you wouldn't get to hear the funeral home show next week. You said the milk would go bad. You said you didn't have time to make Leather Britches, said they wouldn't be ready in time. How come? You never go nowhere."

"Well young'un, I'm about to go somewhere." Gretchen's grandmother said without tearing her eyes away from the luminous little ballerinas dotting the night sky.

"Where you goin'?"

"Oh, don't you worry about where I'm going. I can't go no ways till you see my play perties, and after you see them they's other odds and ends you've got to learn."

"Play perties? What? What have I got to learn?"

"Oh, you got to learn about the bees and the mirrors and the clocks, a whole bunch of stuff. Now let's quit a jawin' and listen to the night. It talks to a body you know."

"It does."

"Sure it does. Sweet Thang. Lord, the night, the mornin' the firewood, the snow, the wind, the rain. They's a-talkin' all the time. A body's just got to sit still and listen."

For the next two hours, Gretchen and her grandmother listened to the night. Gretchen's grandmother would whisper from time to time when a new animal sound or bird call joined the concert.

"Hear that ole coyote? Here comes ole Screech Owl. Listen,.... that's a painter way off toward the river."

Gretchen woke with a start. Not only did she not remember falling asleep outside in the chair, she had absolutely no recollection of walking to bed, but she was there, snuggled up warm and tight beside her grandmother, and it was her grandmother's pleading hand on her shoulder that had woken her.

"Gretchen, Gretchen!" Gretchen's grandmother whispered and shook Gretchen's shoulder. "Looky yonder, a-comin' down the hall. My play perties are a-comin'!"

Gretchen stared in silent awe as, from her count, seven egg-sized balls of light glided down the pitch black hallway and right into their bedroom. Stopping at the foot of the bed, the strange lights whirled and leaped as if they were playing a spirited game of tag.

"What are they?" Gretchen asked her grandmother in her quietest voice.

"Them's my play perties, my corpse candles. Aint they somethin'?"

Gretchen watched the glowing balls of light bob and duck and whirl for a long spell, but they must have lulled her to sleep because *she woke to the summer sun falling warm across her face. Her grandmother was nowhere in sight.*

Gretchen found her grandmother dressed and sitting on her front porch with a basket at her feet.

"Why'd you let me sleep so long?" Gretchen asked, stretching a mile and yawning.

"Them ole lights kept you up. You needed to rest." Having completely forgotten about the lights, Gretchen's mouth went agape.

"What were those lights grandma?"

"No time to talk now." Grandma insisted. "We've got to get to Ida Lee's. Run get dressed."

All along the winding path that led to Ida Lee's, Gretchen's grandmother's only neighbor and best friend, Gretchen worried her grandmother to death about the lights.

"Pleeeeaaaase tell me about em'," Gretchen whined.

"In time, now come on. We've burned half the day as it is." Grandma said as she scurried along the rough, stony trail.

When Gretchen and her grandmother arrived at Ida Lee's house, the strangest thing happened. Ida Lee had tears running down her sunken wrinkled cheeks, and she grabbed Gretchen's grandmother and held her tight.

"You seen him, didn't you?" Gretchen's grandmother asked her friend with her toothless grin.

"Over yonder by the barn bout dark last night and just for you two come up I seen him over by the creek, smilin' to beat the band." Ida Lee replied. "Have ya seen em', seen the candles yit?" She went on.

Gretchen couldn't hear her grandmother's response to Ida Lee's question because she leaned in close to her friend's ear and whispered her response, but Ida Lee's eyes betrayed any attempt at concealment of emotion.

Gretchen and her grandmother were halfway home before Gretchen realized that her grandmother had left the basket she'd carried to Ida Lee's earlier with her friend.

"You left your basket grandma," Gretchen said while skipping over trail rocks like a hopscotch walk.

"Yeah," Gretchen's grandmother said ever so quietly, then remained perfectly mute the remainder of the way home.

Just like the night before, Gretchen fell asleep listening to night birds and watching lightning bugs, and just like the night before, she woke in her grandmother's bed to a start, but it wasn't her grandmother's nudging hand on her shoulder this time that woke her. This time it was a scream. A long and lonesome almost too awful to hear, female scream wailed from the nearby trees outside their open window.

"Grandma! Grandma!" Gretchen called, horrified and shaking. "Wake up! Did you hear that?" Again the slow blood-curdling scream filled the night air. "Grandma!" Gretchen shouted. "Grandma wake up!" She called while shaking her grandmother's soft body, but Gretchen's grandmother didn't budge. A final scream rocked the bleak hot night and Gretchen put her young hands over her ears and screamed, "NO!!!!!" There was just enough moonlight in the room for Gretchen to see that her grandmother's eyes were open and her mouth hung open crooked and long. She was dead.

Weeping and pulling on the same clothes and shoes she'd worn the day before, Gretchen raced from the cabin. There was ample moon to see the stony path to Ida Lee's house, but Gretchen didn't have to run the entire way. About halfway to Ida Lee's cabin, Gretchen saw that a swinging lantern was coming toward her on the trail. Frightened further, Gretchen screamed, but her screamed was stifled and stilled when Ida Lee raised the lantern to her own face.

"It's me, child! It's only me." Ida Lee cradled Gretchen at her *side and let her cry. She didn't have to ask why.*

Within minutes Gretchen and Ida Lee were walking into Gretchen's grandmother's bedroom. In all the horror and shock, Gretchen hadn't realized that Ida Lee was carrying the basket her grandmother had left with her friend. Ida Lee went to work. From the basket, Ida Lee pulled small black pieces of cloth. Gingerly, as Gretchen followed silently beside, she draped every mirror in her grandmother's house with the dark cloth.

"So her spirit won't stay in one of em'." Ida Lee whispered.

With that done, Ida Lee went around the house stopping each and every clock.

"Gotta record the time of death best we can." She whispered.

Ida Lee continued around the house doing all manner of odd things. Finally, she leaned toward Gretchen and whispered, as if she feared waking her cold dead friend.

"We need to go tell the bees."

Ida Lee then led Gretchen out the front door, down the bank behind her grandmother's house and to the edge of her grandmother's garden where her grandmother tended to a hive of bees.

"They'll ever one die if we don't tell em' she died." Ida Lee said. After whispering, like she had in the house, to the bees, Ida Lee turned to Gretchen and asked, "Did her candles come back? The lights?"

"No, but there was screamin'," Gretchen said, still wiping her eyes.

"Screamin'? .....Three screams? .....A woman's scream, come from outside?" Ida Lee's eyes pleaded as her mouth trembled at the edges.

"Yes, It was awful."

"Lord, that were the ole Banshee. I heard it once the night my oldest died in the war. You're lucky Gretchen. You're lucky." ....

As Gretchen stepped inside her grandmother's ancient cabin that nature had claimed years ago, leaving the rain outside, she folded her umbrella and again called out, "Grandma!"

Maybe it was the Cancer she couldn't beat, maybe it was something in the soil that had called her back, but standing in the pitch darkness where she'd made so many wonderful and hellish memories, Gretchen had come home.

Finding, after her eyes had better adjusted to the absence of light, a relic of a rocking chair perched by a paneless window in the corner, Gretchen sat down. She smiled in the darkness when she remembered summers filled with wildflowers and lizards, beans and moonbeams, and for some macabre reason, even to her, her smile spread wider when she thought of telling the bees, the lantern on the trail, the cloth draped mirrors the corpse candles and the screams.

As Gretchen rocked, eyes closed as the night sounds tickled her senses, she recalled a certain day. She didn't remember the day being important, just a day, but for some reason, the memory of it came flooding over her. She'd been about six–years–old. She was staying with her grandmother, and the two of them were heading in for the evening. She remembered her grandmother pointing at something alongside the trail. She remembered it looking like a gray potato.

"Looky here young'un." Gretchen's grandmother had said. "This here is the Devil's Snuffbox. Watch this." Gretchen then lucidly recalled her grandmother lifting her old foot and stomping the strange object. Billowing green smoke erupted from within, concealing Gretchen's grandmother's foot entirely, and both Gretchen and her grandmother laughed.

Gretchen had grown up and learned that the strange item, the Devil's Snuffbox, was a fungus, something that occurred naturally in nature, not the Devil's actual Snuffbox, but that was irrelevant.

It's what Gretchen's grandmother had said after the green fog had faded that had changed her life.

"That's what I want me someday. I want me a Devil's Snuffbox death, not beautiful, but magical."

Gretchen's Grandmother had never elaborated further, and after a while, Gretchen stopped asking her what she'd meant by her strange words, but when Gretchen's Oncologist spelled out her expiration date three weeks prior. Gretchen understood. That's when she planned her trip.....

Gretchen must have fallen asleep in the rocking chair, for she woke with a start. In the darkness of the hallway, Gretchen had once known so well, which, if she could have seen it clearer, was impassible in vine, a soft light manifested. Gretchen held her breath, and sure enough, within minutes several feather-soft lights were dancing down the hallway toward her. Gretchen smiled. Then, from her Grandmother's old bedroom to her left, Gretchen heard breathing, cool but familiar breathing.

As Gretchen rocked on, she knew she'd done wrong in her family's eyes. She knew her skeleton might someday be found in the rocking chair, vines threading her rids and eye sockets, a ragged umbrella tattered and faded on the porch. She knew her family would never understand, but as the lights brightened down the hallway, the breathing from the bedroom came closer, and outside in the darkness something began screaming.

Gretchen, just like her grandmother before her, died a Devil's Snuffbox death, not beautiful but magical.

"What about Ms. Frances Bullock?" Gregg accidentally interjected, startling the old man in the process, to Gregg's great dismay.

Unlike Gregg, who'd come with a red-hot purpose, the old man had been content with regaling his guest with local history, tales of murderous preachers and old friends who'd come home to die Appalachian Mountain deaths. He would have most likely cordially declined meeting all together had he known the taboo name of Frances Bullock was to be discussed. But, it had been brought up, and he was too much of a gentleman to excuse himself or request another topic of converstation.

Gregg had hoped against hope to ease into the topic of Frances Bullock with the old man, but something in his tale of a beautiful yet macabre death so contrasted that of Ms. Bullock that Gregg had to interject her name fast and furious, hoping to draw authentic emotion that didn't ride the wave of contemplation but of Wyatt Earp quick draw response. Gregg didn't get what he wanted.

Several seconds passed, and for the first time since Gregg had arrived, he grew cold and fearful. The ticking of the large ornate grandfather clock in the den's corner was audible, not just audible, but loud.

"Hadn't thought of her in years son." The old man mumbled. "I knew her, but not well."

"We'll be doing a presentation at the Historical Museum next month all about her, seeing as it will be the fiftieth anniversary of her death."

"Fifty years." The old man murmured.

"Been a while."

"Been a blink too."

"Mr. Elkins, what do you remember about that time—anything at all that would be helpful for our presentation?"

"I remember a pillow," the old man said while lifting his eyes to the ceiling as if recalling dark nostalgia. "I remember there was a pillow."

CHAPTER TWENTY-THREE
WE'RE LIVE TEN

SEPTEMBER 1, 2013

❝Oh my gosh, I want to talk about those death signs, rituals, BANSHEEEES!!!!!!, and what about that preacher huh??" Dale shouted from Little Rock. "Tony, we've got to have Gregg back on for those things alone."

"I agree," Tony said, with far less flavor, but no less sincerity, but let's stick with the dish we're cookin'. Tell us about the pillow Gregg."

"He went on to tell me in great detail everything he remembered about the time, the murder, the cover-up, but he said what had always bothered him had taken place six months after the murder. He told me that his wife and the coroner's wife had been best friends in the early Sixties. He told me of the morning, six months after Ms. Bullock's death, that his wife got a strange phone call. Helen, the coroner's wife, called his wife screaming and crying that she'd found her husband, George, dead. Mr. Elkins said he recalled his wife didn't even bother to dress but rather threw on a housecoat. He said she even went out in curlers. He said she was quite distraught by the time she made it home and not for the right reasons."

"What do you mean?" This time it was Dale that shattered the window of suspense.

"He said the coroner had been living in a small stone-walled guest house behind their main house due to his constant infidelity, and when his wife had pulled up, the door to the stone house was sitting wide open. He said his wife instinctively ran inside the guest house, assuming she'd be met by Helen, but that wasn't the case. What she saw was George alone in the room. She assumed it was George lying on his back upon the bed that filled most of the room."

"Assumed—Was it dark?"

"No, she could only see his body as his face was covered by a large pillow with fringe hanging from it."

"So is that the pillow he mentioned?"

"It is. He said just as his wife was about to remove the pillow, Helen came up from behind her and jerked her away so hard it hurt her arm. He said Helen screamed, 'Don't touch him!' He said his wife never understood. She'd been called, but when she arrived she was treated in such a way.

"Holy God, so he'd been murdered! He'd been shut up. Somebody knew he was about to spill the beans on the whole thing." Tony shouted.

"If he had killed her, nobody would have had any motive to kill him," Dale shouted, from what sounded like a distance.

"So someone knew he was about to talk, hence the pillow." Tony broke in just behind Dale's distant bellow.

"Maybe—Mr. Elkins said he and his wife had always wondered if Helen had covered his face with the pillow due to its grotesque appearance or discoloration maybe."

"Dale's literally taking his inhaler Gregg. Ladies and gentlemen out there on the airwaves, I know we're known here at Behind the Veil for tales of ghosts and demons and all things witchy, but have you ever heard such a tale?" Tony rhetorically asked the thousands of faceless listeners Gregg imagined sitting in dark rooms across the American Southland.

"This is going to kill me, Gregg." Dale weakly muttered before shouting—"I'M NEXT ON THIS HIT LIST! This case is going to KILL ME!" Gregg gently laughed.

"Ok, Ok, Ok," Tony puttered back in. "It's no wonder there are ghosts all over your little mountain town."

"Right, and we haven't even talked about ghosts proper yet," Gregg said this last with more gusto, as he was hoping to shift gears, for he had so many ghost stories he was aching to tell.

"Her house—Frankie's house, is it haunted?" Dale asked, on the tail end of Gregg's just having introduced the idea of ghosts. If Gregg hadn't been certain before, he was now. The life, death, and mystery of Frances Bullock would be the night's sole topic. Gregg would quit attempting any more rabbit trails. He couldn't whet their appetites for other flavors.

"You have no idea," Gregg said. "I could talk all night about what lives in that house."

Little Rock once again grew taciturn, and Gregg honestly felt a whiff of cool air tickle his fingertips and forearms.

CHAPTER TWENTY-FOUR
HALLOWEEN

How far are y'all going, Ruby asked us with a sigh? We're going all the way, 'til the wheels fall off and burn.

From "Brownsville Girl" by Bob Dylan and Sam Shepard

OCTOBER 31, 1983

"I thought I'd left Vietnam in the past." A gangly man whose indiscernible age could have been anywhere between twenty-eight and forty said before lifting an almost empty can of Pabst Blue Ribbon beer to his lips. He was seated on the tailgate of a rust red 1967 Ford pickup truck beside a noticeably younger girl whose hair draped across her chest in one thick dark braid.

"What?" The girl asked with a smile while reaching for the beer.

"Too late." The thin man said before sucking down the last few drops. You're too young anyway.

"Shut the Hell up Donnie. I've been drinking for years." The girl retorted.

"Not my beer you haven't." He said while crushing the can in his hand.

"What about Vietnam?" The girl asked again.

"I said I thought I'd left that place behind me."

"Well, haven't you?"

"Damn girl, look!" The rail-thin man said while pointing across the parking lot filled to capacity. Beyond the cars and trucks lit in patches and swathes by the giant drive-in movie screen behind them, police lights peppered and punctuated the night.

"Looks like a war zone to me." He said with a comfortable grin smeared across his beer-swollen face.

"David had better not get arrested this year. Daddy about killed him last year." The young lady remarked while reaching behind her skinny friend's back where she knew an unopened beer might be hiding.

"Back in seventy-seven me and Jake Sitton got arrested behind the high school. Jake had his daddy's old Army coat on, had big pockets. Damn coat full of eggs. Ole Ernie Caswell stood us up against his squad car, took out that damn blackjack and commenced to bust every egg old Jake had on him. I never laughed so hard. Threw us both in jail, and I believe it was for laughin' cause I knowed a hell of a lot of boys got their eggs busted like that, but none of them got throwed in the pokey.

"Last year..." The young lady broke in but was quickly silenced.

"Give me that damn beer." Donnie croaked. "You're slicker than duck shit girl." She grinned even after having the beer that she'd stolen several clandestine sips from yanked from her hand.

"Last year what?" The young man coaxed her back into the story he'd previously interrupted.

"Last year Judy almost drown in the river." The young lady continued after slugging Donnie in the arm. "We were all in Crystal's car, and we probably had twenty cartons of eggs in the back seat. We'd already nailed Chris Hall with at least six eggs out by the Direct and Crystal's car was covered. Crystal wanted to go wash her car. She said her daddy would kill her, so she let us out at the foot of town hill. Well Chris and the others had come down to the River Side Gulf, and they were watchin' for Crystal's car, so we decided, Einsteins that we were, to sneak up on em', to swim the river."

"We did that once. Bout froze to death." Donnie chimed in.

"Yeah, we got just a little way out and Judy started acting like she was going die of hypothermia, splashing about. We pulled her in and snuck over behind Stiles Exxon. We got in the back of Chad Welch's truck, and he took us down to the Robo Car Wash to find Crystal. We laid down in the back when we passed Chris and the others at Riverside Gulf."

"Well damn girl. You're a regular Dirty Harry." At that very moment, making them both break out into ribald laughter, Clint Eastwood cocked his pistol on the screen behind them before demanding someone on the receiving end of the firearm make his day. It was Halloween night in Franklin, North Carolina, and the Macon Drive In Movie Theatre was filled to bust. Donnie and his young cousin Gail had spent most of the day at Gail's house. They'd driven down to the state line package store in Rabun, Georgia earlier for beer and had at the last minute decided to catch the new Stephen King movie, The Dead Zone, at the drive-in. The previews were still rolling, one of which, Sudden Impact, which had ironically paired Donnie's previous comment to Eastwood's own famous one-liner.

"Yeah, I swear it's like a war zone out there. I can't do that anymore. Gettin' too old for Halloween nights in Franklin. I don't know how people ain't been killed." As the night wore on, Donnie and Gail paid far more attention to gathering crowds and stragglers than they did the movie. The air was cool with a waning crescent moon slipping in and out of the wispy veil-like clouds, and the air smelled of popcorn, cigarettes, and weed.

CHAPTER TWENTY-FOUR

"Trick or Treat Gaily Girl!" Melanie Houston shouted behind the old red truck.

"Melanie!" The young lady announced with a wide smile.

"What's up? Oh, my gosh, is that Donnie? Donnie Gibson, you get down from that truck and hug my neck." Melanie said while mockingly clapping her hands together. "I haven't seen you in years."

"Yeah, I've been out of pocket. Got back from Nam ten years ago, then I headed out west five years ago, worked with Gordon Jamison's older brother on a ranch out in Wyoming. Been back for a few months." Gail, Donnie's young cousin, and Melanie were both seniors at Franklin High School.

After a lengthy Anaconda hug, Melanie let Donnie go.

"Do you remember teaching me to blow bubbles? I was about eight years old."

"Vaguely," Donnie smiled. "I've slept since then."

"Still driving your brother's truck I see," Melanie said before gently biting her bottom lip, a gesture Gail notices and found to be a bit odd. "How long are you gonna drive that thing?"

"Till the wheels fall off and burn I reckon!" Donnie said with a sneaky grin.

"So what's up Melanie? What are you gettin' into tonight?" Gail asked while pushing her hands into the back pockets of her jeans.

"I'm supposed to meet Jay and Krissy here."

"Speak of the Devil," Gail said, pointing to a young couple, both clad in letter jackets coming their way through the dancing shadows created by the shifting movie scenes beyond them.

"You bout ready to go?" The young man called out to Melanie.

"Yeah, just sayin' hey to this old man." Melanie joked.

"Where yall goin'?" Gail asked Jay and Krissy, both she had known since the first grade.

"The MURDER house!" Jay said with arched eyebrows. "You all want to come?"

"Hell yeah!" Gail leaped forward. "Let's go! Oh, and it's Halloween! Donnie, let's go with em'!"

"You mean ole Frankie's house across from the golf course?" Donnie asked, slipping the tips of his slim fingers beneath his belt.

"Yes," Gail blurted out. "Let's go! Let's go!"

"Alright. Let me shut the tailgate. Who's ridin' with who?"........

CHAPTER TWENTY-FIVE
WE'RE LIVE ELEVEN

SEPTEMBER 1, 2013

66 Well, what happened?" Dale asked.

"Donnie ended up in the hospital, and the others went to jail that night."

"Back up, back up, back the hell up." Dale chanted from Little Rock. "Start at the beginning."

"Well, the beginning was the drive-in. They rode on out to Frankie's in Donnie's truck. Donnie drove while the other four rode in the back. They got there and did the normal teenage thing, walked the perimeter, looked in the doors and windows, called out her name. That's when it went south. They were all cupping their hands around their eyes, peering into the darkness of Frankie's house from her back porch when Melanie started screaming that she saw Frankie standing inside the house. All but Donnie jumped from the porch and ran back to the truck. Donnie just stood there like a stone.

"Why?" Dale asked.

"May never know. The others were screaming for him to come on, but he didn't budge until the tree limb fell."

"What?" Tony asked so quick, his question was merged with Gregg's last word.

"While he was standing there with his back to the others, a huge tree limb fell from a healthy tree at the edge of Frankie's yard, and it was a big limb." Dale joined in, almost shouting.

"That happened to Elvis! Damn if that didn't happen to Elvis Presley? When the pallbearers were hauling Elvis Presley out of Graceland in his casket, a giant, healthy tree limb just barely missed em' all. Everybody swore it was his ghost that did it. It's in lots of books, and I watched a documentary just last week about that happening."

"Gregg, don't get him started on Elvis, for God's sake." Tony comically demanded.

"Well, I can't say what caused the limb to fall that night, but when it did, Donnie turned around with as wild a look as anyone ever wears in their eyes. That's what the others said anyway. Said he slowly strolled down the steps, walked toward the trees that edged up against Frankie's yard, disappeared into the darkness and took off running. His uncle found him walkin' barefoot about a mile from his mother's house the next morning. He was hospitalized for several days afterward. They assumed it was PTSD from his time in Vietnam."

"Or was it?" Dale asked in the conspiratory tone Gregg had noticed rose up in his remarks from time to time.

"What do you think Gregg?" Tony asked. "Do you think he saw her in the house?"

"What about the other four?" Dale queried. "You say they went to jail?"

"Neighbors called the law because they were screaming and running around. When the police got there, they were all in a panic talking about Donnie running off, ghosts in the house and such. They took all of em' in for questioning—called all their parents."

"I want to go to the house, Tony! I want to go! I want to go!" Dale satirically whined like a child. Then both men broke out in nervous laughter, and not laughter based in comedy, but rather disbelief, laughter born of the factually insane.

"There are so many stories. People come to Pauletta and I all the time wanting to share their murder house tales, most of em' are at least twenty five years old."

"Tell us your favorite one!" Dale spouted.

"Well, I did get one the other day that was pretty good, but what made it so good was who it came from. The parents of a past student of mine saw me in a store recently, solid people, high school sweethearts. Got married right out of high school. Both are highly respected in the community, hard workers. They were asking about the tours. The topic of Frances Bullock came up, and their faces in unison sank, I mean visibly fell. They pulled me to a quiet corner and told me what had happened to them their Senior year in high school. It was around Halloween they said. Like all the other kids before and after them, they'd decided to go to the old murder house. A friend of theirs had purchased a Ouija Board. They said they all sat down on the back porch and started playing with it. They told me they didn't get a single response and that they'd only been seated there for about three or four minutes when they looked up and someone from inside the house was staring down at them through the glass of the back door. They went on to tell me they took off running across the yard back to their car, but here's where it gets good. They said they'd left the Ouija Board on the porch and that as they were about to drive off the friend that had brought it wanted to run back and get it. They said the moment the friend opened the back door of the car and placed one foot outside, the Ouija Board flew like a Frisbee off the porch and up into a tree."

"I WANT TO GO TO THIS HOUSE!" Again Dale shouted.

"We know, we've established that," Tony answered with a hint of irritability in his tone.

"Surely you've been to the house, Gregg. Do you have any stories to tell?" Tony asked, losing the glint of botheration he'd earlier exhibited to his partner.

"Oh yeah," Gregg shot back. "I've been there many times. There was this one night in 1993, I was a Senior in high school. I thought for sure I'd die that night. I felt for sure my heart would explode."

"We're listening!" Dale crooned like Tony Bennett from Little Rock.

"We'd been to the train and bus wreck earlier in the night. I'll explain that in a minute," Gregg reassured the two DJ's who he knew were just about to inquire further. "It was a bunch of us: Phil and Chris Davis, David Briggs, Brian Stuss, Shawn Joplin, Will Dills, AJ Bubacz, Nate Crawford, Mitch Gonzales and Lillian Booth.

Harrison Ford had just wrapped a film called The Fugitive. It had been filmed all around Franklin and the region. They'd actually wrecked a real train and a bus for the movie. The train and bus were both left to nature and cordoned off by high metal fences with razor wire on top. We, of course, found a way through that as all teenagers should. We went down and played all over the train and bus. The best part of that though was the tunnel. Right down the hill from the wreckage is the Cowee Tunnel. It's considered to be the most haunted railroad tunnel in America. Nineteen African American prisoners drown in the water below the tunnel in 1883. When their small boat capsized in rough turgid water, they all drown because they were all chained together. None of their relatives were ever contacted. They fished them out with big metal hooks and buried them in a mass grave above the tunnel. Books and plays have been written about it."

"Good God!" Tony drawled.

"Well, after we left the wreckage we all walked across the trestle into the tunnel. Man, it was like an Indiana Jones movie. You could see the water raging through the trestle's tracks. Really dumb lookin' back, but fun at the time."

"Let me squeeze in here a minute Gregg," Dale hurriedly said. "Funny you should mention Indiana Jones, and I bet Gregg knows where I'm going with this."

"I don't know where you're going with this you lunatic." Tony leaped into the conversation.

"Well listen and learn old boy. Says here online that the inspiration for the character of Indiana Jones actually comes from a Franklin, North Carolina native. Says he was a famous pilot. Says he discovered Angel Falls in Venezuela. Actually, it says the falls are named after him. His name was Jimmie Angel. Does that sound right Gregg?"

"It does. We talk about him on our tours. He was quite a colorful character."

"Alright, sorry for that rabbit trail, but I can't believe what I'm finding out about this little town. It's freakin' nuts man! Ok, sorry, go on Gregg."

"After we all got back that night from the train and the tunnel, we went our separate ways, all but Brian and myself. We decided the night was young."

CHAPTER TWENTY-SIX
3:16 IN THE WINDOW

Till the sun peels the paint and the seat covers fade and the water moccasin dies,
Ruby just smiled and said, ah, you know some babies never learn.

From "Brownsville Girl" by Bob Dylan and Sam Shepard

JULY 17, 1993

" Welcome to the Jungle!" Axl Rose, the lead singer of the rock band, Guns and Roses, screamed from Gregg's open car windows.

"There goes your dad," Brian said to Gregg as his squad car passed them in the night.

"He's got ole Charlie McFalls in the back seat. I don't envy him that. You ever smelled Charlie McFalls?" Gregg asked the young man who was lighting a cigarette in his passenger seat. "Smells like a Sky City bathroom." Brian cast out a knowing grin, as both boys were knowledgeable of the local department store's bathroom smell.

The flashing red letters and numbers on the Macon Bank sign read July 17, 1993. It had been raining since the boys had gotten back into Franklin from their escapade with the train and the tunnel, and their small hometown, nestled between the black mountain ranges of night lie solemn and still, like a soldier forgotten on some battlefield.

The banks, restaurants, and motels all seemed to be in bottomless slumber. The streetlights flickered off and on in the distance, and rolling thunder headed eastward was bidding the tiny town farewell.

While Gregg and his friend Brian were lazily cruising Franklin's streets, they were making fun of all the thirty and forty-something-year-old men who were parked strategically along the main strip. Every night those guys could be found there sitting in their low rider pickup trucks or little cars with ACDC or Hank Williams Jr. blaring from their souped-up stereo systems. The two boys always made sure to circle town every night at least once, just for a guaranteed hearty laugh at their elder's expense.

Gregg and Brian had just turned eighteen years of age within six days of one another, and in little mountain towns like Franklin there wasn't a lot for anyone to do, so mainly they just drove around to their friend's houses and hung out. That particular night they drove to a gas station where Darrin Carver, a good friend of theirs, worked. While there, they laughed at the old drunks who would come in to buy eighty-cent beers and moon pies. They talked about girls and music, just anything to pass the time.

Just as Gregg and Brian were about to leave, two guys they both knew from school walked in. The two boys walked straight up to them, and with stoic faces, simultaneously asked, "Guys, where is the old murder house?"

"What old murder house," Brian asked in a jovial way before taking a long pull from his freshly cracked Mountain Dew. The two boys looked a bit annoyed.

"We don't know where the house is at, but we were playing with a Ouija Board and we got the ghost." The taller of the two boys said, earnest but with the eagerness of a child on Christmas morning.

Gregg, Brian, and Darrin immediately locked eyes with one another. Gregg a staunch Catholic, Brian a Lutheran, and Darrin a Baptist knew the dangers of messing around with Ojai boards.

"I don't know," Brian said in a disinterested kind of way. Then he looked away.

Not wanting to lie, Gregg tried to be more general. "There are several haunted houses around. I know of one down on the Georgia Road."

After the two classmates were convinced that Gregg, Brian, and Darrin really didn't know about the house, they went on to explain what had happened to them. The two excited young boys told their three classmates that they had been attempting to get in touch with the ghost of the old murder house, and they had done it. They said that the ghost had revealed herself as Frankie, and they said she was asking for help and kept saying over and over again, "Three sixteen in the window."

"I wouldn't mess with that stuff guys," Gregg said, raising his eyebrows the way one does before boarding a roller coaster. "You might get a hold of something stronger than a little dead lady."

The two inquiring friends mumbled around a little then busied themselves in the store. They bought at least ten dollars worth of junk food and sodas, and then drove off into the dripping, wet night.

Immediately after the taillights of the two excited boy's car faded into the foggy night, Gregg and Brian bid Darrin farewell and headed out to the old murder house. The guys had piqued their interest since they knew that the murdered woman's name had been Frances Bullock and that she'd been known as Frankie by those closest to her.

Along the drive to her old, abandoned house Gregg told Brian more about the house and why everyone believed it was haunted. Brian listened carefully as Gregg, like an old-time storyteller, helped him paint the pictures in his mind.

"Frances Bullock, Gregg began, was stabbed to death somewhere in her house in 1963. She was found by worried neighbors who hadn't seen her in a few days. The murder was never solved, and ever since her death, no one has ever been able to live in the house. It's said that her ghost has been seen by anyone who even attempted an over-night stay. It's also said that in the dead of night she can be heard screaming and crying for her murderer to stop. There are like a thousand ghost stories about the old place. You know Jennifer from Biology class, sits behind Bobby, she said she watched Monica get flung right off the steps one night and there's still a blood stain in the wood, won't go away. People have tried to clean it—keeps comin' back."

After the brief description, as Gregg's headlights illuminated the back of the old murder house they were parked directly behind, Gregg decided to tell Brian of his father's horrific encounter with the house. Brian knew Gregg's father was the Assistant Chief of Police of Franklin, North Carolina and had been for years. Brian also knew it was from his father Gregg had first heard about the murder house and the ghost. Brian and Gregg had been to the house several times, but generally just a slow stop in the driveway kind of deal. This time was different. As the two boys sat parked directly behind the house which stood on the outskirts of the city limits, they shuddered with anticipation. Though technically the house was near town, a dense line of pines on three sides of the house concealed it from the sun and the noises of the nearby street.

Gregg turned off the engine. The house was a 1940s model, not some antique Adams Family deal. Its red brick siding glowed from a nearby over-hanging street lamp that stuck up out of the side of the little dirt road to the left of the house. Upstairs, the windows were fully cloaked with curtains, but downstairs they were wide open for viewing.

Gregg's father had been in the house many times during the daylight hours for various reasons, Gregg told his wide-eyed friend, but always accompanied by other officers. Only once did he ever have to venture there alone at night, and the story he had told his son about that night, every detail, filled Gregg's mind like curdled milk. As he and Brian, silent with anticipation, sat staring into the dark windows of the house, Gregg began the story.

"It was a scorching night in mid-August several years back, and my father was working the graveyard shift. Back then there was only one or two town police officers on duty at night, and that night it was just him. Long about midnight, Dad took a call from an old woman that claimed she had been watching strange lights illuminating from within the old murder house. She figured, like so many times before, high school kids had broken in and were ghost hunting. Dad was very reluctant to go, but he told the old lady he'd check it out. The slight drive from the police department to the murder house seemed even slighter that night. He had been telling himself in the car that he was going to pull up in front of the house and watch, and if he didn't see any lights after a few minutes he would go on. He prayed he wouldn't see any lights. As my dad neared the house," Gregg lowered his voice. "He cut off his headlights and let the car crawl slowly up the dirt road that circled around to the house, his path lit solely by the overhanging street lamps. He parked just out of sight. From where he sat he would be able to see into the house, but if there were kids inside, they wouldn't be able to see him. He cut his engine off. After a few moments of

silence, he began to feel uncomfortable about the entire situa-
tion. He began glancing back into his rearview mirror, scared
to death that Frankie's frail and pale face would rise up behind
him. Just as he was turning the switch to leave, he saw a light.
It looked like someone had turned on a bathroom light in one
of the upstairs bedrooms. It didn't fully light the room so he assumed it was a bathroom light. 'Damn it! Damn it!' He said to
himself, reaching for his flashlight. Had the light been a candle
or a flashlight it would have put him more at ease, because he
knew that the house wasn't hooked up to power, and there was
no rational way that a light could have come on. The moon was
hanging high above the red brick home he so dreaded entering.
He stood for a minute on the front porch, cupping his hands
around his eyes and pressing them against the warm glass of
the front door's window so as to be able to see within the dark
house. He saw a grand piano, antique furniture, rocking chairs,
and partway into the kitchen. He then walked quickly off of the
porch and decided to call a county unit to go in with him but
stopped at the last minute, fearing the jokes that could come
of it. After a long string of hushed curse words, Dad cautiously
lifted the garage door which he surprisingly found unlocked.
As he partially closed the door behind him and realized the
darkness within, a solid and unshakable fear swept over him.
He began to feel nauseous and weak. There was, of course, no
electricity in the house so his flashlight was his only source of
guidance. Amid the wintry lawn mowers and stone-solid bags
of half-used fertilizer was a rack of old dresses, making the image of Frankie clearer in his now terrified mind, because now
he could cloth her. His mind could dress her up to chase him.
As he began the slow ascent of the stairs to the first floor, he
was overcome with an extraordinary sense of being watched.
The stairs creaked and popped like a campfire as he felt his way

along the block wall beside him. His flashlight found the door to be closed, and he was hopeful that it had somehow been locked. He took the knob in his hand like it was a red-hot iron that he dreaded touching. Slowly he turned the old brass knob, and with no resistance, almost like someone on the other side had helped him, the door swung open wide. Dad clung to the wall for a second, shining his light around wildly. After he gained his composure, he took the next and final step up to the first floor, up to the very spot where Frances' corpse had been found all those years ago. He turned around and let the light from his flashlight crawl back down into the black basement. Like a sword, he swung the wand of light all over the room, up and down, with an empty feeling in his gut, and deep down praying to God that his beam wouldn't fall across anything unearthly. It's then that it happened."

"What?" Brian asked with mouth gaping. "What happened?"

"He said just as he closed the basement door behind him, he heard what sounded like bare feet running through her kitchen. He froze up and tried to grab at his gun, thinking someone was about to jump him. He couldn't get it fast enough. Whoever or whatever it was jumped on his back. He said it felt real and unreal at the same time. First, he said he felt her arms wrap around his shoulders from behind, and he couldn't move. He felt her knees jab into his ribs. He couldn't even think. It was like a sort of instant paralysis of the senses. He was numb. He could feel her he said. She was cold, and he said the room started to lightly hum like it was filled with electricity or something. He thought he was going to pass out. He leaned against a wall. He steadied himself. Then, he did all he could do."

"What did he do?" Brian whispered.

"He started walking. She was grasping onto him like a child, like someone wanting a ride out of a prison they had for too long been confined to. Strangely, he said that while she was wrapped all around him he was almost too numb to be afraid. He could smell her over his shoulder, and he felt the emotion wrapping the two of them together. She even held onto him as he climbed the stairs to the second floor, the beam of his flashlight still splitting the shadows that lined the walls. At the top of the stairs, he felt her weight increase and was overwhelmed with pain, and for the first time since he had picked her up, she spoke. She whispered, *"HELP ME!"* Dad said it almost sounded electrical, like a fuzzy radio station. He said she clung to him tightly until he reached the basement stairs again. It was there that he felt her fall off. He said he could feel her slide off. He pulled the door open and ran down the stairs. He said he even rolled under her garage door, not bothering to shut it back. He jumped into his car and sped away. His hands shook for days after that. Can you imagine?" Gregg posed the question to his friend who wore an expression that read, I'll never sleep again.

Now, there they were sitting outside of the very same house, in the darkness, after a storm.

"We must be crazy," Brian said while staring at the house that looked so very uninviting.

"Come on," Gregg said in a breathy manner. "Let's go see if Frankie wants to say hello tonight."

Both boys stepped reluctantly out of the car and into the damp night. The street lamp's warm glow was lying across the bushes that lined the old house giving the illusion that behind each one was a black form crouched in wait of two stupid high school kids. The march from the car to the front steps of the house felt so unprotected, like walking down a cold, early-morning road without a coat on.

The steps were steeped in rain, and with every step that the boys conquered, they felt sicker inside. Finally, standing right in front of the back door, they were speechless. The street lamp shown right down into the windows outlining old pieces of furniture and objects they couldn't identify.

"Hey," Brian said, sounding excited. "Look at that!"

There, right before them, seated on the windowsill inside the house was a small Bible; it was turned to the third chapter of John. John 3:16 was lightly underlined and boldly and crudely underlined as if an infant had done it, was the name John at the top of the page. The two boys stared intently at the underlined passage, so intently, that it was a moment before they noticed a rocking chair inside, just beyond the window had begun steadily rocking back and forth.

The two boys screamed as they jumped from the stone steps and raced toward their car. As Gregg fumbled with the ignition, both boys stared vigorously into the windows at the back of the house, fearing Frankie's screaming apparition was in chase, but what they saw wasn't a screaming apparition; what they saw melted their nerves like ice in fire. Gregg and Brian both watched as the curtains from one of the upstairs rooms quickly parted, and a Christmas snow pale woman with short-cropped dark hair peered out at them with the saddest and deepest eyes they had ever seen.

"Drive!" Brian screamed as Gregg worked to start the car. Gregg turned the key, but the engine wouldn't turn over. Brian covered both of his eyes and started praying. Gregg, feigning strength, tried over and over again to start the car, but it just wouldn't start. Then, taking a cue from his friend, Gregg starting reciting The Lord's Prayer. Just as Gregg got to thy kingdom come," the car started, and the two horrified friends sped off into the night.

CHAPTER TWENTY-SEVEN
WE'RE LIVE TWELVE

SEPTEMBER 1, 2013

"OH MY GOD ABOVE!" Dale interjected loudly.

"I know right. It was something else."

"How, how, how do you have sanity man?" Dale quizzed Gregg from Arkansas.

"Who says I have sanity? My wife would beg to differ," Gregg jokingly added.

"Ladies and gentleman, tonight's show may run well into tomorrow or longer," Tony spoke as if reciting an old World War Two pre-movie commercial.

"Did you get all that Dale?" Tony asked his cohort. "Remember Gregg, Dale's filling up a notebook on this one."

"GONNA SOLVE IT!" Dale shouted.

"Solve it, man, solve it!" Gregg enthusiastically followed. "It may as well be you. No one else has been able to pull it off. They'd have had to have some evidence to do that," Gregg flatly finished.

CHAPTER TWENTY-EIGHT
WHITLIN,' TRADEN' AND THROWIN'

You could tell she was so broken-hearted.

From "Brownsville Girl" by Bob Dylan and Sam Shepard

JULY 25, 1964

Sheriff Bryce Ingram sat in his squad car just outside of Angel's Drug Store with his left elbow resting on the base of his open window, his fingers tapping the roof of the car. Though it was barely 10:00 am, the day was already hot, and he could feel the fabric of his shirt covering his lower back already soaked with sweat. His car was idling with the radio turned down to a murmur. He was alone. As the Sheriff sipped coffee from yet another white coffee cup that the Normandy restaurant would never see again, he subconsciously listened to the news of the day, barely audible seeping through the speakers. He heard something about a comic book convention in New York called Comicon set to begin. He heard that the 89-year-old Winston Churchill was to attend a meeting of the House of Commons, and just before sitting his coffee mug on the dashboard, freeing up his right hand so as to turn the radio off, he heard that President Johnson would be sending 5,000 more troops to South Vietnam, bringing the total to 21,000. With the hum of news gone, Sheriff Ingram's attention settled solely on the small mountain town before him.

CHAPTER TWENTY-EIGHT

The little town of Franklin was in full swing of summer. A murder of old crows in filthy fedoras and bib overalls stooped, leaned and hovered gangly and crooked over a game of checkers being played in front of old man Pendergrass's store just up the street from where the Sheriff sat observing the Saturday morning ritual. The men were too far away for Sheriff Ingram to hear their conversations, but their wild sporadic tangles of laughter that erupted every few minutes were audible to anyone on the street.

Early dinner smells were already eking forth from the Dixie Grill and Kelly's Tea Room. The fragrance of hot biscuits, ham and cheeseburgers hung in the sultry July air. Dinner in the mountains was lunch up north, the Sheriff had learned several years back. Across the street from where the Sheriff idled was Peoples Department store and Perry's Drug Store. The owner and operator of Peoples was sweeping the sidewalk. The real action of downtown Franklin though was never the games of checkers or the soapbox preachers. The center ring of the circus had always been town square, and Sheriff Ingram had intentionally positioned his car so as to guarantee the best view of the show as he'd done many times before.

Since it was a Saturday that meant the knives would come out—whittlin' tradin' and throwin'. They would begin gathering on what the Franklin locals referred to as lazy benches or liars benches as early as 6:00 o'clock in the morning, and by nine or ten o'clock it was every man for himself. The old-timers, the last of their breed they'd proudly raise their chins and say, no matter the season were decked out in long sleeve shirts, overalls, boots and fedoras with loud yellow or red feathers as a garnish on their hat bands.

The Sheriff reached for his coffee and pulled his left arm inside the car. An elderly woman holding the hand of a young boy crossed the street to the square. She and the boy had just exited the Macon County Court House which sat cattycornered across the street from the obviously heated or comical Checker game ensuing in front of Pendergrass's Store. As they passed the old men on the lazy benches, one old fellow with tobacco all over his mouth held something out to the boy. The old woman stopped walking.

"Thire ye go young'un. Thire's ye a good knife." The old character said to the boy. In his outstretched hand that looked more like a fat creek rock than an actual hand appeared to be the end of a white pocket knife, maybe Mother of Pearl the Sheriff thought as it had glinted just a touch in the sunlight as he held it out. The boy looked up at the older woman as if mentally asking permission to take the knife.

"Go on." The old woman acquiesced with an impish grin. The little boy, overjoyed at the prospect of being the sole possessor of what appeared to be a true to life, bonified Mother of Pearl handled Barlow pocket knife slowly took the knife from the old man's thick dirty fingers only to have his short-lived happiness crushed like eggshells at his feet, for the knife was single-sided. There was no blade. The old men, upon seeing the young boy's smile turn into a look of confusion then utter sadness, whipped themselves into a frenzy of knee-slapping, head held back coughing and wheezing laughter at the little boy's expense. The boy had been tricked. The old man had thrown the knife. The Sheriff couldn't help but smile, as he remembered the same thing had happened to him on a similar Saturday morning in and around 1929.

The old-timers throughout the day would rotate positions. They would take turns looming over games of checkers. They'd go from bench to bench telling and retelling new and old dirty tales and jokes, leering and catcalling women from fourteen to forty, but all of this was icing on the cake of the knife business really, for if any one of the old buzzards roosted on the benches had been quizzed about his reason for being there, he'd say snake-bite quick, "Come to town to trade a knife."

The Sheriff watched as the old woman led the child away from the guffawing mob, and before long it was business as usual back on the lazy benches. Beech-Nut chewing tobacco was pulled from and stuffed back into overall pockets, as the rickety old men settled themselves back into the groove that had been interrupted by the cruel joke upon the little boy. Some old timers, still wheezing or catching their breath from the joke that had been played at the little fellow's expense, cut their tobacco with their pocket knives and placed the freshly cut slices into their waiting mouths upon their blades. After the old men were settled, still, and sucking on tobacco, the knives came out. Some pulled small chunks of wood from deep pockets and commenced to whittle. Others eyed the knives doing the whittling, while others passed knives around they'd brought to town specifically for trading. The Sheriff knew the trading could go on for several hours. It wasn't the trading the old men loved so much. It was the boot. One old fellow would say.

"I'll trade you this here Old Timer knife for that yeller Barlow." If the crooked old crow who owned the Barlow didn't respond in time or in-kind the other old crow aiming to go home with that Barlow might say, "Old Timer and a dollar bill." The dollar bill was the boot. And that was trading knives. Sometimes the old men would go home with a better knife than they'd arrived with. Sometimes they'd leave with a lesser knife and a handful of money. The smartest old birds often went back home with the very knife they'd brought with them that morning and a handful of money. Throwing knives was altogether different. Throwing knives was gambling. A man would let another man see just a little bit of the knife he'd brought. The other man seeing this little visible part, if he liked what he saw, might trade the knife he'd brought to town to trade. The gamble was, he might get a good knife or he might end up like the little boy with nothing but a piece of what might have been a good knife at one time or another, and Oh the laughter and merriment that ensued when that happened, not to mention the cursing and oaths from the deceived.

Sheriff Ingram knew every man on the square. There were about twelve in all. Most of the men were in their late seventies or early eighties. One old man, he knew to be ninety-one years old. The youngest among them consisted of Asa Morgan, Beulan McCall, Furman Welch, Arthur Holden and the baby of the bunch was Joe Burnett, hardly thirty years old, and with the exception of Burnett, who would be sleeping off a hard drunk on the bank of the Little Tennessee River the next morning, Sheriff Ingram knew that each and every man on the square, lying, cheating, gambling, catcalling, belly laughing to the dirtiest of stories and jokes, would be filling their respective pews and roles as deacons, superintendents, Sunday School teachers and in the case of Asa Morgan, preachers, the next morning in little Baptist Churches all over Macon County. "Saturday sinners and Sunday saints," the Sheriff mumbled to himself.

"Sheriff." A timid female voice spoke, startling Sheriff Ingram in the process. The Sheriff turned toward his open window. Standing a respectful distance from Sheriff Ingram's car was the last person the lawman wanted to see, Odessa Stanfield, the mother of Frances Bullock.

"Yes ma'am," Sheriff Ingram replied. "And how are you this morning?"

"I'm fine." The older woman weakly responded, weak as it was half-hearted and a lie at best. She wore a plain cream-colored dress, a simple string of small beads around her neck and clutched, with both hands in front of her, a brown purse. The Sheriff noticed a tremor in her hands right away as the sidewalk put her hands at eye level.

"Are there any new clues?" Frankie's mother asked the Sheriff, lowering her eyes to the cracked sidewalk in the process. "Has anyone heard anything? Are any new suspects being questioned?" The Sheriff wanted to step from the car and take the old woman's hands, but though she wasn't right upon his car, she was still close enough that he'd have to ask her to back up in order for him to get out, so he chose to stay seated.

"No ma'am, but CD and I, we've not given up on it. In fact." The cold squeeze Sheriff Ingram's heart had been experiencing loosened as Chief of Police CD Baine's motorcycle pulled up and parked behind his squad car. Ms. Stanfield watched as the wiry, little lawman dismounted and walked her way.

"Thank God!" The Sheriff mentally shouted.

"Ms. Stanfield, you look pretty this morning. How are you getting along?" Chief Baines asked the visibly frail woman standing at the Sheriff's car window. Sheriff Ingram couldn't believe his luck, but he *thanked God* for the Chief's perfect timing.

Each day since the slaying of Frances Bullock, both lawmen in some form or fashion had had to allay the fears of family and friends by letting them know that both departments and the State Bureau of Investigation were doing all they could to find the killer, but both men believed the case had been closed before it had ever been opened. Both men in their heart of hearts believed the case would never be solved.

After thanking both lawmen in hardly more than a whisper, Ms. Bullock crossed the street behind the Chief's motorcycle and entered People's Department Store.

"Expecting a blizzard?" The Sheriff teasingly asked Chief Baines who was, as usual wearing a black coat.

"Never know." Chief Baines fired back. For a moment both men were silent and the Chief, as the Sheriff had done all morning, assessed town square with roving eyes. Sheriff Ingram took the last sip of cool coffee from the mug he'd sat upon his dashboard.

"You'll lose Ed's vote next time Bryce if you keep runnin' off with his mugs." Chief Baines teased.

"I got about four of em' in the office. I do need to get em' back to him though. Don't want to end up like old Mr. Rankin. He'll slip something in my grits won't he?"

After several more silent seconds, it was Chief Baines that took the wheel.

"Come on Bryce! Let's go call Cole, see if they have anything new." Sheriff Ingram reached to turn the key of his squad car. Chief Baines, who'd earlier placed the palm of his right hand upon the roof of the Sheriff's car, slapped it hard three times.

"Ride with me." The Chief demanded with a grin.

"Hell, it ain't eighty feet!" Sheriff Ingram crowed.

"I know. There ain't no reason to move your car though. You need to keep it sittin' right where it's at between Angel's and Perry's drug stores. I'm just waitin' on the day they take it to the street out here like the OK Corral," Chief Baines said with a slick grin. Sheriff Ingram smiled. It was a running joke about the two competing drug stores that sat directly across the street from one another.

"Sheriff Ingram opened his door and got out. He followed the much smaller man to the motorcycle parked behind his squad car and saddled up behind him. When the Chief kick-started the motorcycle, the early morning town clowns all craned their heads in unison. Chief Baines with Sheriff Ingram holding to his waist, pulled into the street, passed the square and turned left toward the 1850 Macon County Jail that still served as the Franklin Police Department and jail.

"There go are two fearless leaders!" The tobacco stained relics bellowed from their benches with gaping dirty mouths and slapping hands. "They went thataway boys!" One old man called out, crossing his arms before him with both index fingers pointed in different directions.

Chief Baines came to a stop in front of the police station and both men dismounted. They greeted the mayor who was just exiting the station with a file in his hand. They then walked inside. Inside the Chief's office, scattered with papers, busted motorcycle helmets, wanted posters and ashtrays the two men sat down, the Chief at his desk and the Sheriff right across from him.

Chief Baines thumbed through an old Rolodex, licked his thumb and tried again. After a moment, holding open the Rolodex with his thumb, the Chief picked up the phone and began dialing. He then leaned back in his chair and closed his eyes while the Sheriff waited.

"Yes, this is Chief CD Baines in Franklin, North Carolina. I just wanted to check up on the Frances Bullock case, see if there's anything new I might tell her momma." Just then the Chief sat up straight. Sheriff Ingram, recognizing the seriousness in the Chief's eyes, asked,

"What is it?"

The Chief responded, not to the Sheriff, but to whoever was on the other end of the line.

"Lost! Hell you mean it's lost?"

The Sheriff stood up and started pacing the cluttered floor. Within seconds the Chief hung up the phone. Not only was there nothing new with the case, but what little evidence there had been, Ms. Bullock's bloody dress, a kitchen knife, her sandals, all were missing. The State Bureau of Investigation agent Nathan Cole had told the Chief curtly and without frills or apology that somehow all of the evidence in the Frances Bullock case had gone missing. Outside the old men laughed and catcalled as the Cicadas sang in the trees.

CHAPTER TWENTY-NINE
WE'RE LIVE THIRTEEN

SEPTEMBER 1, 2013

"Dale threw his pencil, Gregg!" Tony informed his radio guest from North Carolina. "I don't think he can take anymore."

"I get it. It's unbelievable, but it's all true. Everything was gone. So there were no pictures or any evidence to speak of to analyze. Somebody had worked hard, and somebody had some real pull high up somewhere. It's not so hard to see how a small town newspaper photographer could be strong-armed or coerced into losing all of his pictures, but it's something else altogether for the State Bureau of Investigation to come up short."

"Gregg," Dale said, though hardly intelligible.

"Get your hands off your mouth?" Tony jokingly commanded his partner.

"Gregg, I've got pages of notes here. I've circled the names of the suspects that I think sound the guiltiest, but they wouldn't seem to have much pull from anybody. Meaning, I can't imagine if they'd killed Ms. Bullock there would be anyone high up who'd care enough to help them. Does that make sense? For example the boy at the hospital. He had a bloody knife, ranting and raving about Ms. Bullock, but he seemed too sloppy, too young to have elicited a cover-up of any sort."

"I agree, but like the coroner, his death painted him as guilty of something."

"OH HELL!" Dale said with a wheeze as if he too were losing hope.

CHAPTER THIRTY
A BROTHER COMES HOME

Well, you saw my picture in the Corpus Christi Tribune
Underneath it, it said, a man with no alibi.
You went out on a limb to testify for me. You said I was with you

From "Brownsville Girl "by Bob Dylan and Sam Shepard

FEBRUARY 21, 1984

The seasons continued to change, and the calendars, one by one, came down and were replaced. Chief C.D. Baines went home and grew old, the same with the Sheriff. The Franklin High School graduating class of 1963, fresh and full of promise, quickly became the class of 1973, then 1983. The young officer Ernie Caswell, who'd been one of the first officers on the scene of Frankie Bullock's murder had become Chief of Police and was himself becoming an old man before his time. For officers Gene Southards and Sonny Welch, it was a Tuesday.

"Footloose." Officer Sonny Welch read the marque at the Macon Drive-in Theatre as he and his partner Gene Southards passed it on their left. "What ya' reckon that one's about?"

"Don't give a rat's ass," Gene responded quickly and without looking toward his partner.

"Saw on TV that ole Dan Aykroyd and Bill Murray's gonna be in one about ghosts. That'll be good. I'll see them and Chevy Chase in anything. They tickle me to death." Sonny continued on the topic of movies regardless of his partner's seeming lack of enthusiasm.

Gene caught the red light at the top of Frog Town. Frog Town had once been a swamp, just a big, wet nasty valley with woods on both sides. At present, and for as many years as either man could recall, it had been a thin roller coaster of a road that connected Franklin's business district to the Franklin High School and the Drive-In Movie Theatre, a natural fit due to the big geographical dip Frogtown provided.

"I need to swing in here and ask Shorty somethin'," Gene mumbled after the light had turned green. Shorty Mason's grocery store sat just to the right of the red light, directly across the street from the Macon Barber Shop. Gene cut his wheel to the right and parked the squad car in front of the door. He killed the engine. Sonny waved to the barber, Frankie Bowers, across the street, whom he could see clearly through her window as her blinds were pulled up. Gene had already darted inside the market. Inside Mason's Food Mart, Sonny found Gene showing Shorty something on a little slip of yellow paper. He couldn't make out their conversation. Meanwhile, Sonny picked up a TV Guide and started thumbing through it. After a minute or two, Gene passed him and stepped up to the counter. Sonny had taken the TV Guide from the rack near the register. He eased it back into the slot from which he had plucked it up.

"I think Norm's my favorite. I like Cliff awful well though. I watch it for Norm though," Sonny said while tapping with his right middle-finger the cover of the TV guide he'd just replaced above a box of Wrigley's Spearmint Gum. He then picked up a pack of multi-colored gum with a cartoon horse on it and rolled it between his fingers. "Ever chew any of this? It's good but the flavor dies in five minutes." Sonny said to his partner, who had yet to respond to his first inquiry. Gene nodded no to the gum, then after squinting his eyes at a tabloid headline, slowly responded.

"He's good. That's a fact. And that Cliff's a mess ain't he?"

The two officers, twenty-some-odd years behind them, had moved on. They rarely mentioned the Frances Bullock case due to pure disgust and disdain, but on that day, in Shorty Mason's grocery store, all of the old demons would come back to the door knocking with both fists clenched tight and cold.

"Gene!" The clerk at Shorty's called out for the lawman's attention. "Didn't you always think them Mashburn brothers had something to do with the Frankie Bullock murder?" Gene looked up at the clerk without a response, so the clerk continued. "He was in here yesterday, the reason I was askin', the youngest brother that is, the one that had that knife up at the hospital that time—hadn't seen him in years. Said he'd been livin' down in Corpus Christi, Texas—said his momma was sick or something."

"Yeah, well," Gene responded without looking at the clerk. He was unfolding a dollar bill from his front left pants pocket. "He left town right after the murder—figured he'd stay gone." Gene quietly replied. Sonny lifted his eyes but didn't speak.

"Have a good one," Gene proffered. The clerk nodded and lifted a grimy looking bottle filled with sloshing green liquid from somewhere below the counter. He began straying the counter before the two officers were fully out of range. Gene cut his eyes sharply at the clerk as his exposed forearm was peppered with cleaner.

"Well Hell!" Sonny spoke out loud as the store's door swung shut behind the two men with a suction sound. "What do you make of that?"

214

Gene just shrugged his shoulders. The two officers got back into their squad car just in time to hear their CB radio call for them.

"Southards!" Gene spoke into the cool grid of the CB radio. What the dispatcher had to say, ran like icy fingertips up both men's spines. There had been a suicide. The last name was Mashburn.

Several officers worked through the afternoon to put the suicide to bed. There was no suicide letter, no recognizable reason for the deceased to have shot himself; however, as Gene and Sonny knelt down beside the dead man whose lower jaw was lying beside his face, connected by a thick bloody cord of flesh, all they saw was a scared teenage boy in the rain.

CHAPTER THIRTY-ONE
WE'RE LIVE FOURTEEN

SEPTEMBER 1, 2013

Little Rock was silent.

"So, he was gone," Gregg said.

"I don't know what to say," Tony spoke. "I'm at a loss."

"So, it was the same boy from all those years ago," Dale asked, this time with an absolutely stone-cold, earnest and morose tone.

"Same one."

"So he came home to die?" Tony asked.

"Seemed that way."

"Whhheeeeww." One of the men blew into the phone.

"What about the Bible Gregg?" Dale asked.

"What's that?" Gregg asked for clarification.

"The Bible. I'm writing all of this down, and it's the one piece that doesn't fit anywhere. You said the boys in the gas station, boys you went to school with in 1993 were playing with a Ouija Board. You said the board was telling them three sixteen in the window. Then you said when you and your friend drove out there, there was a Bible on the window sill inside the house turned to John 3:16. Now that's strange as Hell. What do you make of that?" Dale asked.

"I can't say for sure, but I came so close to getting that Bible." Both Tony and Dale broke out into laughter.

"You were going to break in and get it weren't you?" Tony asked, mid-laugh.

"No, actually the Bible was coming to me." Gregg soberly replied.

CHAPTER THIRTY-TWO
WHAT ARE THE CHANCES

You always said people don't do what they believe in they just do what's most convenient, then they repent.

From "Brownsville Girl "by Bob Dylan and Sam Shepard

JULY 27, 2013—MID-MORNING

"Thank you so much for meeting me, Gregg. I wish we could have talked last night, but my wife was with me, and it was late." A heavily bearded man said while enveloping Gregg's hand is his much larger grasp.

"Any time Barry—You know that." Gregg replied to the man who of late had become a dear friend. Barry Houston, the young man of years before who, with a friend, had claimed to have contacted the ghost of the Murder House on a Ouija Board, had attended his presentation of the life, death, murder, and mystery of Frances Bullock the night before. Prior to leaving the venue, Barry had asked Gregg if he might be able to meet him for a few moments the next day at the Rathskeller Pub, as he had something he'd like to share that wouldn't take long but required some privacy.

"You're my early appointment," Gregg said with a smile, as he lifted the beer he'd purchased prior to his friend's arrival to his lips. "I've got to meet an older lady this afternoon at the Museum.

"Is that right?" Barry asked a second before telling Adam, the owner, operator and bartender of the Rathskeller Pub that he'd like a coffee to go. As Adam turned to tend to Barry's order, Barry turned back to Gregg who was seated to his right on a bar stool.

"So, what's up buddy? Did the guilt get to you? Did you kill her?" Gregg teased. The two had graduated high school together, and both men had been born thirteen years after Ms. Bullock's untimely death, so the joke had shallow roots.

"No, can't say that I did, but I do want to get something off my chest," Barry said in a hushed tone.

"What's that?" Gregg took another drink. Barry lowered his voice to a whisper.

"I took the Bible. I took it that very night. In your presentation last night, you told of going to Frankie's house with Brian, seeing the Bible in her window after me and Eddie had said what we said about the Ouija Board. We found somebody later that night who knew where she had lived. We all drove out there around three in the morning, and we didn't just look through the windows." Barry leaned into Gregg's ear for the last part. Gregg was stunned. He didn't speak for a moment. Adam handed Barry his coffee, and Barry paid.

"Well, you shocked me boy!" Gregg said, sitting his beer upon the bar. Barry flashed a chicken-thief smirk.

"That's not all." Barry continued in the same whispered tone. *"I saw her that night. Just as I leaned over to pick up the Bible from the window sill—I saw Frankie's reflection directly behind my own in the window. The guys had a light of some sort on behind me, lantern or flashlight. Tell the truth, I don't remember, but it made it to where I couldn't see outside but could see the rest of the guys*

back behind me about six feet or so. She was much closer. I spun around like nobody's business, mouth agape. She wasn't there, but she had been Gregg. She was standing right behind me that night."

"Where's the Bible now?" Gregg asked, mimicking Barry's tone for reasons he couldn't comprehend.

"Shandra's got it—my ex-wife. I have no idea what she's done with it. You can ask her." Barry said while slipping off the bar stool he'd been perched upon. "I've got to go. I just wanted to tell you. That's bothered me for years. Oh, and I remember the underlined parts that you talked about last night—looked like some kid had done it."

Barry walked away. He climbed the ramp toward the only door in or out of the bar and disappeared around the corner of the building. He never looked back. With Barry gone, since it was early in the day, Gregg was all alone in the place, with the exception of Adam of course, but he was nowhere in sight at the moment. Gregg stood up, chugged the last half of his beer, and as always, looked at the big wooden urn on the shelf across from the bar. *Who were you?* Gregg wondered as he slowly strode toward the door, whose window, like a prism, was casting pillars of light across the barroom floor.

CHAPTER THIRTY-THREE
WE'RE LIVE FIFTEEN

SEPTEMBER 1, 2013

"What are the chances?" Tony roared.

"I know. I was astounded."

"Did you get it? Did you get the Bible?" Dale asked in the same child-like manner he'd adopted most of the night.

"No, I got ahold of his ex-wife, *wonderful lady,* I'd known her forever but hadn't spoken to her in years. She says she remembered the Bible but had no idea where to even begin in locating it. She said she thought it might be in a storage unit somewhere."

"AHHHH MAN!" How cool would that have been, and how cool that Barry was there the night before and heard you talking about him." Tony interjected.

"It was crazy. The whole thing is crazy." Gregg insisted.

"What about an urn? You said you looked at an urn in the bar," Dale said, almost immediately. "I'm not even surprised now. Of course, the bars in Franklin, North Carolina have human remains in them. Why would they not?" Tony joked.

"Right, before the recent owners bought the place it had been owned by a husband and wife. When they were gutting and restoring it in the year 2000, they found multiple small urns filled with human remains in a back closet. Having no idea who they'd belonged to and knowing the history of the building, they went and bought a large wooden urn to house the remains.

They just poured them in and set them on the shelf, decided to let them be a part of the party I guess."

"You said the history of the place. What is the history of the place?" Tony asked, sounding not unlike a college student with a raised hand.

"It's where Franklin was formed. In 1818 directly where the Rathskeller Pub sits today a Cherokee cabin sat. That's where the founding fathers hashed out the town. All the minutes to those original meetings are in bound volumes at our library. We keep meticulous records."

"Tony!" Dale exuberantly called out. "I can't wait to get to this little town. I want to get drunk with a bunch of ashes sitting over my head." Both men laughed heartily.

"Ok, Ok," Tony tried to reel the line back in. "Was there ever anything, any evidence, any slip-ups? I know the coroner was trying to tell his friend something that day, but we know how that ended.

"Oh, there was a full confession of sorts." Gregg teased the two DJs.

"Dale's licking the tip of the pencil Gregg. His eyes are wild."

CHAPTER THIRTY-FOUR
I KNOW THINGS

*Then when I saw you break down in front of the judge and cry real tears
it was the best acting I saw anybody do.*

From Brownsville Girl by Bob Dylan and Sam Shepard

JULY 17, 1993

The Bryant Funeral Home calendar that hung behind the Chief of Police's desk read July 1993.

"How long has Bryant been putting out them calendars Chief?" Tracy Chastain, one of Chief Ernie Caswell's newest hires, asked as he was attempting to white out a mistake he'd made on an arrest report. Chief Caswell looked up from a form of his own he was scrutinizing and then over his shoulder at the calendar.

"Long as I can remember. Old-timers still live by that thing. They plant by the signs and all." Chief Caswell mused.

The Chief then tossed the form that he'd been previously engrossed in across the desk to the neatly-dressed young officer and told him to file it away.

"I'm going home. FP2 just hit the city limits. He'll be here in about five minutes." Chief Caswell said to the much younger officer as he wove his way through his cluttered office, grabbing his hat and jacket.

"Tell him when he gets here that Charlie McFalls was seen out on White Oak Circle drunk again. Tell him I went looking for him, but I couldn't find him. He lays down in the grass, old bastard, and tell him that we had to take ole Flora Spindale back to the second floor. He might want to run up there and check on her."

As Chief Caswell, with haste, while gathering his things, laid out to Chastain the list of things to mention to the Assistant Chief upon his arrival, the new officer recalled the events of two-hours prior. He and the Chief, while driving past the hospital had to forcibly place an old lady in the back of the squad car. She'd been running up and down the sidewalk in an old nightgown, barefoot and hair wild as it was white. The whole ride back to the hospital, with her gripping the metal grid behind their heads had been very uncomfortable. He'd never been on the second floor of the hospital; however, all his life he'd heard references to it. Everyone knew it was the psych ward. When anyone would do anything a bit off, people would grin and tell them, "You'd better be careful. You'll end up on the second floor." Adding, at the hospital, was totally unnecessary.

The young police officer grabbed a scrap of paper from the Chief's desk, as he had already heard him exit through the front, and jotted down:

Flora Spindale, second floor, Charlie McFalls, White Oak Circle, drunk.

Charlie McFalls, thirty years prior had been seen banging on Frances Bullock's door asking for payment for some yard work he'd done. He was also thought to have been in possession of the broach watch Ms. Bullock carried in her purse. It was his name given to authorities as to the seller of the watch, and it was Charlie McFalls, while Frances Bullock's body still lay in her home, amid the circus investigation, who walked right into her living room as calm as a sinking September sun.

Not unlike other suspects in the murder, Charlie had changed. Well respected ladies who'd been whispered suspects left within days of Ms. Bullock's murder on extended trips to London or to visit family in distant states. Upon their arriving home, some became reclusive, resigning from clubs, groups, and organizations, pulling curtains and shutting doors. Some of Ms. Bullock's male friends had moved out of town entirely. Frances' brother, Willie, finding it hard to dispel the gossip, settled into a quiet life as a small, out of the way gas station owner, but of all the suspects, it was Charlie McFalls who decided to drink away the past, to drown the accusations in the bottle, to numb the rumors. McFalls had moved into a falling-down shack on the edge of the Woodlawn Cemetery. Weaving past Frances Bullock's tombstone each night, he became the town drunk and more of a ghost than a man.

Jimmy Clark, FP2, the Assistant Chief of Police, was like a mirror image of Chief CD Baines of years ago. He too rode a motorcycle. He too was a small man in stature but was feared upon the streets. He strode into the police station, picked up a walkie-talkie and tested it. He then, without speaking to the younger officer, sat down at his desk which was situated across the room from the Chiefs and picked up the phone. He talked for several minutes to someone at the Sheriff's department then hung up the phone, smiled at the rookie and said, "Let's ride Chastain."

For hours Officer Chastain, though he was deep into his third year on the force, listened to the Assistant Chief explain protocol, numbers, codes, actions, personalities of potential future and past offenders and how best to relate to them with force or words. Clark loved his job. He loved the power and the position. He loved moving, always being on the go, always something new.

As the hour grew late, after the two men had stopped for dinner, Clark drove out to the west end of town.

"Where are we going?" Chastain asked.

"Woodlawn," Clark replied.

The new lawman had been born and raised in Franklin. He knew Woodlawn was a sprawling cemetery on the outskirts of town.

"What for?" Chastain inquired.

"Damn Chastain, you know what for. The kids go out there at night. There's a rise in the middle of the cemetery where they jump their cars."

"Thrill Hill!" Chastain said with a big American boy smile. "I bet I've done that a thousand times."

The Assistant Chief didn't smile. "Don't do it again." He drawled as if he'd been the young man's father. Just as the two lawmen were nearing the entrance to the boneyard, Assistant Chief Clark slammed on his breaks. His tires squealed, and both men's heads were jerked like a rag- dolls.

"What the Hell?" the Assistant Chief called out while jerking the car into park.

Sitting in the dead center of the road, mere inches from the Assistant Chief's bumper, was Charlie McFalls, eyes closed, drunk as a skunk.

"Is that Charlie?" Chastain spoke hurriedly, praying the elder lawman hadn't noticed a slight tremor in his voice due to the fact that until that very second he'd completely forgotten the folded paper he'd tucked inside his pocket listing the two meager things he'd been instructed to tell the Assistant Chief.

"Hell yes, its Charlie. Who else would be sitting outside the damn graveyard, in the middle of the damn road, in the middle of the damn night?"

"Chief said he'd been seen today." The young officer spoke as the two men exited their car to place the slobbering drunk in the back seat.

Clark, very used to McFalls, thought nothing of grabbing him up by the back of his filthy pants and hoisting him horizontally into the backseat of the squad car, but McFall's smell, a thick hot blend of sweat, Rot-Gut Whiskey and weeks without a bath was something altogether new for Clark's young partner. He'd met the man, but had yet to manhandle him. Chastain gagged twice before getting back into the car. The Assistant Chief pulled into the Macon County School Board parking lot and turned around. With the nose of their squad car headed back toward Franklin, Chastain started talking.

"Chief said you might want to go up to the hospital tonight."

"What for?" Clark asked, almost before Chastain got the words out of his mouth.

"Said,...hold on." Chastain paused and dug his hand into his right pants pocket. He pulled out and unfolded the paper he'd placed in his pocket earlier. "Said Flora Spindale was up there on the second floor. I couldn't remember her name right off. We picked her up this afternoon—crazy as Hell."

"That's a fact," Clark replied. "Guilty as Hell too."

"Guilty of what?" Chastain asked.

"I don't know," Clark said with a smile. "She's the one found Frances Bullock thirty years ago. She was the last one to see her alive, and she's the one that found her body. All kinds of people for three days stared into her windows, watched her house. Nobody saw hide nor hair of her, then Flora Spindale shows up on that Monday mornin' and looks through the window and finds her pretty as you please. Ask the Chief. He's got all kinds of theories."

"You think she killed her?" Chastain asked, betraying his earnestness with youthful zest.

"Oh, I have no idea who killed her. I just think every-damn-body is guilty. Have you not met me?" Clark grinned and sped up. The Assistant Chief, without averting his eyes from the road before him, simply by instinct and familiarity, flicked on the radio. "Pick somethin'," Clark said to Chastain. For the previous two and a half years, Clark had always allowed the younger officer to choose the radio station, and it hadn't been lost on the rookie. The young officer leaned slightly forward and within seconds located a decently clear station playing a song by the Damn Yankees before settling himself back into his seat.

"There's your boy," The young officer spoke out as he pointed to a car stopped at the red light in front of the Old Ingles grocery store. The young man in his son's passenger seat lifted his hand in a wave. Music was blasting from the open windows of his son's car.

"What the Hell's he listening to?" Clark rhetorically asked the air around him.

"Guns and Roses," Chastain answered back. Clark cut his eyes in the direction of his young sidekick.

"You'd know," the Assistant Chief mumbled while motioning with his right thumb toward the car's radio. Chastain smiled.

"They've been around a while." He informed the Assistant Chief, whose sole response was an almost imperceptible eye roll. Far too quickly, Clark swung his squad car into the parking lot of the Ingles grocery store and pulled up near the door.

"I'll be right back. You watch sleeping beauty back there. I've got to get some chapstick. Lips are about to by God kill me," Assistant Chief Clark said through the open window of his already slammed car door.

A big archaic pickup truck rattled in beside the squad car as the young officer stood guard over the town drunk who looked as dead as any actual corpse the young officer had ever seen. Inside the store, Chastain watched as the Assistant Chief belly-laughed with Dale Duvall and Mark Pruitt, the store managers, every now and again casting glances his way. He assumed the laughter had to do with his being left alone in a hot car with Charlie McFalls, but he wasn't certain. Beyond their conversation, that to him was mute behind the glass, Chastain saw that Debbie Doster and Laura Cabe were working the cash registers. Laura's brother Johnathan was collecting carts to his far left, and Ulla and Dorothy were standing at Debbie's register. The young officer smiled. Ulla and Dorothy were elderly sisters. Ulla wore enormous crooked sunglasses whether it was day or night, and Dorothy always sported a platinum blonde Dolly Parton style wig. Both women chain-smoked and laughed as if God or the Devil one were incessantly whispering barbed off-color jokes into their ears. The Assistant Chief exited the store applying the chapstick he'd stopped for. He slipped it into his pocket before opening the door.

Back at the station, after managing to get the local drunk into a chair in front of Clark's desk, Chastain's time was up for the day; so was Clark's, but the Assistant Chief had to run the normal paperwork on McFalls before hauling him up to the Sheriff's department for his accustomed night in the drunk tank.

"You go on home. I'll get him up there." Clark told the tired-eyed young lawman.

"Are you sure?" I can stay." Chastain pleaded.

"No, go on. I'll see you..." The Assistant Chief paused as he peered across the room at the Chief's calendar. "Next week. Go on home to April. Go home and wash Charlie McFalls off of you," the Assistant Chief said with a childish smile.

"All right," the young officer said quietly while turning to go. After Charlie and Clark were alone, while the Assistant Chief was signing all the boxes and dotting all of the Is, the drooling, sleeping drunk revived somewhat.

"You think you're better than me don't you? Well, you ain't no damn better than me Jimmy, and Ernie ain't no damn better than me, and..." He lost his thread, and his words rolled off down the gutter.

"Calm the Hell down Charlie," Clark said, without even looking up. I'll get you to bed in a few minutes."

Charlie started up again. This time Clark looked up and gave him the eyes that meant—end it here son. The town drunk mumbled then sat up reasonably straight.

"You don't know do you?" McFalls asked Clark.

"What don't I know Charlie?" Clark asked, again without looking up.

"I know," McFalls said with a toothless grin so slick with sweat and snot it appeared he'd been eating mustard and fried chicken.

"That's nice Charlie. I'm glad you know something." The Assistant Chief responded facetiously, humoring the old drunk. Charlie just laughed knowingly and leaned back in his seat. He cleared his throat. He then leaned forward and spoke with perfect clarity, and the room filled with bristling electricity.

"I know who killed Frankie Bullock. I know where the murder weapon is right damn now! I KNOW THINGS DAMN IT!" The old drunk screamed.

Never to Clark had the police station felt so closed in, so tight like the walls were being sucked inward.

Barely alive on the outskirts of town, the old Chief CD Baines sat bolt upright in bed, his lower lip quivered. Chief Caswell stirred and called out in his sleep, and Gene Southards and Sonny Welch, both lost in peaceful dreams, opened wide their eyes, and in the stillness of Frankie Bullock's dark and empty house, something exhaled.

Breaking the silence that had fallen over the police station like a death pall, Assistant Chief Clark spoke.

"You don't know nothin', Charlie! You're just talking. Shut your mouth!" Clark did this on purpose. For whatever reason, he believed the drunk. There was something new in his voice, a certainty, an alertness that he'd done his damnedest to douse for the past thirty years.

Purposely feigning indifference, the Assistant Chief actually turned away from the town drunk to prove his disbelief.

"I said I know who did it and where the murder weapon is," McFalls said this time with real anger behind the words.

"I heard you the first time Charlie." Clark grinned and went about his business. The Assistant Chief was trembling inside. He felt in his gut the man was speaking the truth, but he knew if he showed even a sliver of interest the drunk would shut down, so Clark, against every fiber of his being, pretended not to even care.

"I didn't kill her, but I saw her body, and I hid the knife." McFalls leaned in close for the word knife, filling the Assistant Chief's personal space with his stench.

"Well," Clark spoke, still without looking up, "Where'd you put it?" The old town drunk laughed.

"I took it out to the fairgrounds. I found me a dead dog on the edge of the Georgia Road. I buried that knife under that damned ole dead dog. I knowed if anybody saw that the ground had been dug up they might get suspicious, and I knowed if they come upon a rotten ole dead dog they'd quit digging, figure somebody just buried a dog." Charlie McFalls, reeking of week-old filth, shirt untucked, shoelaces untied as always, boots just barely on his feet, sat tapping with his left index finger, his left temple, the universal sign for not too dumb huh?

After the town drunk was locked away for the night, curled into a tight fetal position on a cot he knew all too well at the Sheriff's Department, Assistant Chief Clark drove out to the fairgrounds. He parked his car on the edge of the highway and stood gazing off into the night. From where he stood at the highway's edge, the Assistant Chief could see the promise in the east of a sunrise. Car after car passed by lives being lived, headlights burning up the last wisps of darkness, people moving, people waiting for them somewhere. The highway, Clark thought, seemed like a line of life, a vein of movement, an artery of intentions, of smiles, dreams and tomorrows, yet just on the edge of this vein, literally on the grassy edge, he imagined the rusted old knife, hidden away, most likely forever. Just as the first purple and orange hues made the tall pines into lanky inky outlines, the Assistant Chief got back into his car and joined the vein of life. His headlights burned with the rest, and the morning broke. His family was waiting for him, but first, he'd look in on an old woman with ghosts in her eyes on the second floor of the hospital, who, like the coroner, the boy in the rain and the town drunk, was guilty of something......something.

CHAPTER THIRTY-FIVE
WE'RE LIVE SIXTEEN

SEPTEMBER 1, 2013

"Finally, we've got something!" Dale shouted.

"You hear that Gregg, *we*." Tony broke in. "Old Dale here's part of the investigation now. So there was someone to talk to, to interrogate at least. I hope he didn't get all tight-lipped when he sobered up the next day."

"No telling what he would have said," Gregg replied.

"Would have?" Dale's voice crept in from somewhere in the background.

"Yeah, would have. Charlie McFalls was killed in the street the next day. Run over." Little Rock grew as static and quiet as Gregg had heard yet. After several seconds Tony spoke. "We're not even surprised."

"You know out of the entire story, from my learning about the case as a boy in the barbershop to this very minute, what happened after that confession has always bothered me the most and definitely scared me the most," Gregg said.

"What happened," both DJs spoke in unison.

"A few days after Charlie said what he said in the police department, dad purchased a metal detector. He went on his own time out to the fairgrounds hoping against hope to find something, anything, but someone was watching him."

"Who?" Again in unison, both men asked.

"We have no idea, but the night after he'd taken the detector out to the fairgrounds for the first time, we started getting phone calls. The calls came in the wee hours of the morning. It was generally dad who answered the phone, and I could hear him cussing out whoever it was on the other end from my bedroom. Then I'd hear him slam the phone down, and if that's not spooky enough, here's the kicker; it wasn't a person on the other end of the line."

"What?" Tony interrupted. "What do you mean it wasn't a person? You mean they weren't speaking?"

"No," Gregg assured them. "It was most definitely speaking."

"You've lost us, Gregg."

"It was a doll," Gregg said. "It was a pull-string doll. You could hear the string being pulled right before a high-pitched little voice said, "BEWARE! BEWARE! BEWARE!"

"You're shittin' me!" Tony slurred. Dale busted out laughing at his partner's slip up.

"Sorry about that language Gregg. That just slipped out."

"Oh, it's fine. I wouldn't have known what the voice on the other end was saying because mom and dad just whispered about it, but one morning that week, mom was gone and dad was in the shower, and the phone rang. I picked it up and said, 'Hello.' That's when I heard it for the first time, and it's still, to this day, one of the scariest things I've ever heard in my life."

"Again, Gregg, I'm sorry about the profanity. That one snuck up on me man. I wasn't expecting that."

"Yeah, we weren't either. The phone calls stopped when Dad stopped going out to the fairgrounds."

"Was the town drunk the only one to ever confess to any part of it?" Tony asked.

"No, actually there was someone else. A few months ago I was contacted by a lady who said she thought she might have some information I'd be interested in. She told me a dear friend of hers had told her of a phone call her friend had gotten the previous night. Her friend was well into her seventies and claimed to have been childhood friends with the daughter of a lady who'd been a whispered suspect in the Frances Bullock murder. The woman told me her friend's friend had cried so pitifully on the phone, afraid that her mother had secrets she'd never revealed."

"What made her think so?" Tony asked.

"A Protestant confession."

CHAPTER THIRTY-SIX
SHE NEEDED TO TALK

The memory of you keeps callin' after me like a rollin' train

From Brownsville Girl by Bob Dylan and Sam Shepard

AUGUST 21, 2013

"Momma, do want some water?" The dying old woman's daughter asked with a bit of a slur in her voice, having just woken from a nap. She tried to sleep between feedings and cleanings.

"Do you?" She asked again, as soft as morning rain. Her mother, staring off into oblivion, seemed not to even notice that her daughter was there.

"Momma." She spoke again. "Would you like something to drink?"

"Odie Westerner. I need Reverend Westerner." Her mother spoke without linking eyes with her daughter at all.

Reverend Odie Westerner was ninety-three years of age and living in another state. Reverend Westerner had been their family's minister for well over fifty years in their hometown of Franklin, North Carolina.

"Momma, you're with me now in Florida remember? Reverend Westerner lives in Franklin, way up in North Carolina, remember? Remember you came to live with me? Reverend

Westerner can't come all the way down here momma." The weak-eyed old woman, with brimstone in her voice, turned her eyes toward her daughter this time and demanded with clenched fists that her daughter contact their old preacher.

"I've got to talk to him!" The dying old woman demanded.

"Ok, momma. I'll see what I can do. Maybe we can at least get him on the phone, alright."

After a single phone call, three days later the old preacher was easing his way through the two women's home in Ustice, Florida. For reasons foreign to the dying woman's daughter, the old preacher seemed to jump at the chance to speak with her mother. Getting him to the Sunshine State had been as simple as a single request. He had his son drive him down.

The old minister, per his dying friend's request, shut her bedroom door for their clandestine meeting. When the old man of God came forth two hours later his shirt was wet with tears, and his eyes were bloodshot.

CHAPTER THIRTY-SEVEN
WE'RE LIVE SEVENTEEN

SEPTEMBER 1, 2013

66 So nobody knows what she said to the old preacher do they?" Dale asked, sounding far more crestfallen than earlier.

"Just him and her and they're...."

"Dead! We know. We know." Dale finished Gregg's sentence for him. "Let's see here," Dale perked up, but with a facetious tone. "Teen boy brandishing a bloody knife kills himself years later. Town drunk gets crushed by a car a few hours after a semi-confession, coroner dies mysteriously after attempting to confess something. Who in the Hell could be pulling strings thirty, forty, fifty years later? Who's got that kind of clout Gregg?"

"Well, I know it sounds crazy, but the old Chief of Police, C.D. Baines had theories stretching far beyond the confines of Franklin, North Carolina or even the American South."

"What did he think?" Tony asked.

CHAPTER THIRTY-EIGHT
GHOST INDIANS AND THE MOB

Oh if there's an original thought out there, I could use it right now

From Brownsville Girl by Bob Dylan and Sam Shepard

SEPTEMBER 16, 2012

❝They may come out of there tonight, seein' as it's a new moon." Someone spoke behind Gregg's back, startling him in the process.

"What's that?" Gregg replied in the midst of a whipped turn around.

"Noonei, they may come out tonight." The voice reiterated, making for a bizarre refrain. The strange interruption that had woken Gregg from the reverie he'd walked into like one lethargically advancing into a bog of thick sucking mud had come from Joe Baines, the son of the late Chief C.D. Baines. Gregg knew Joe well. Baines, a wild, intensely-intelligent though thoroughly eccentric bit of Franklin local color, had unintentionally snuck up on Gregg.

"Hey man, how are you?" Gregg asked the lank bearded man who had sidled up right beside him.

"Oh, fair to middlin' I'd say. How are you?"

"I'm fine, just doin' a little studying'."

"I see that. What angle you got? You already know all about the Noonei, so what are you studyin' on?"

"Oh, nothin' in particular. I just hadn't read this marker in a while." Gregg said. "We may stop here on a tour next year." Joe didn't say any more. He lifted the gargantuan handled coffee mug that Gregg believed was somehow soldered to his fingers, as he'd never known him to be without it, to his lips. He assumed it was coffee anyway. In Joe's other hand he clutched a small green notebook with a pen jabbed down inside the white spiral binding ring.

"So what's up with you today?" Gregg quizzed Joe.

"Oh, just waitin' for original thoughts to hit brother; writing songs you know," Joe answered. Gregg knew how brilliant Joe was. There were times when Gregg had stood directly beside Joe in a café while Joe was waist deep in thought, and he hadn't been aware of Gregg's presence in the least.

"Songs about what?" Gregg dug in deeper.

"Life man," the steely-eyed artist answered.

"You should write one about the Frances Bullock murder, a folk song. You know how the old mountain balladeers used to write songs about brutal murders, famine, disease, hangings and such. That would make a killer song, no pun intended."

"Maybe I should write one about the Noonei!" Joe proclaimed with no discernable expression.

"Yeah, that would definitely be a colorful tune," Gregg replied, turning away from the historical marker he'd been so engrossed in, to begin with. The Noonei, both Gregg and Joe, and for that matter anyone who might find the time to stop and read the historical marker Gregg had been scrutinizing, knew all too well were the legendary ghost Indians the ancient Cherokee believed lived deep within the gut of the Nikwasi Mound. The Nikwasi Mound, on the edge of which both men were standing, had been and was still considered by the Cherokee to be the spiritual epicenter of the entire Cherokee Nation, and it sat smack dab in the center of Franklin, North Carolina. Abruptly, and hot on the heels of Joe's last sip from his mug, the skinny songsmith began singing.

"Bryce Ingram's mind was stolen. Chief Baines, he lost his too, a single year beyond 1962. Ms. Bullock, she would lose her life to a wicked heart and long lost knife, and the town of Franklin never would be free, of three bloody days in 1963."

"Damn man! Did you just come up with that on the spot?"

"Come up with what?" Joe quickly spoke back, his face still boasting no recognizable expression. Then he possum grinned and slapped Gregg on the back. "Yeah, wasn't bad was it?"

"No, it wasn't bad. You should finish it. Make your daddy proud." Joe took another long drink from his mug.

"Hey, while I've got you here," Gregg said. "You know I've told you I'll be doing the presentations about the Frances Bullock murders next July. You and I have already talked about your dad and the time period, but I've been meaning to ask you what your dad thought. Did he have a favorite suspect?" Joe's eyes changed.

"You really want to know?" Joe teased Gregg between pulls from his mug.

"Yeah, who did he think killed Ms. Bullock?" The corners of Joe Baine's mouth turned up for the first time since he'd startled Gregg from his contemplation earlier. Both corners getting lost beneath his long and wiry salt and pepper mustache.

"The Mob!" Joe whispered, though there was not another soul in sight." Like a screaming football team tearing through a homecoming game banner, a rush of Turkey Buzzards erupted in song from somewhere behind the two men, tearing to shreds

CHAPTER THIRTY-EIGHT

the awkward stillness that had ensued after Joe's words had crawled into Gregg's head and taken root.

CHAPTER THIRTY-NINE
WE'RE LIVE EIGHTEEN

SEPTEMBER 1, 2013

❝ What? Mob? You mean like Mob Mob, like the Mob, like Al Capone Mob, like John Dillinger Mob?" Dale and Tony traded lines.

"One in the same," Gregg assured the radio hosts. "And so much more."

"Alright, Dale actually just put his feet up and licked the end of his pencil Gregg. We're ready, GO MAN!"

"So Joe said his father's last two years of life were spent more in his past than his present, and the Frances Bullock murder of decades before consumed him—engulfed him. Joe said that's all he wanted to talk about. Now what I'm going to say will sound absurd, insane, and unbelievable. I felt the same way. To tell you the truth I just humored him at first. I just listened out of kindness, because I thought the mention of the Mob was too far-fetched, to begin with, not at all possible, but then, I dug a little, and damn if my eyebrows didn't raise. Joe said his father was convinced that Ms. Bullock was somehow involved in a drug ring, and, I know what you're thinking. Drugs weren't a real issue in America till later in the decade, but I listened. He said his father had notebooks filled with sketches and notes, scraps and hints, numbers. Chief Baines believed the multiple flights to various cities Ms. Bullock was taking were inconsistent with the funding she'd have available for such things, and he believed the mystery man she was always talking about to close friends and family, always altering the location of when and how she'd met him depending on her audience, was further proof of something larger than Franklin, North Carolina. Now hold on to your hats if you're wearing them."

"Dale's wearing a powder blue bonnet Gregg," Tony remarked so slick and quick that Gregg laughed out loud.

"Ok, well keep your bonnet on Dale. The old Chief believed there were links to Hollywood California and the White House." Both DJs laughed.

"Alright, now we're havin' fun!" Dale chuckled, more like a child than a man.

"Stay with me guys. I swear this plane will land on solid ground. Somehow or other word had gotten to the old Chief sometime after her death that Ms. Bullock had been somehow affiliated with a man who was himself affiliated with some of John F. Kennedy's secret service agents, and that they were in turn tangled up with the Mob. Furthermore, word had gotten to the old Chief that Ms. Bullock had somehow, on one of her many trips, crossed paths with a movie star with links to her region."

"Sounds like the old Chief had slipped a little Gregg. The cheese had fallen off his cracker maybe?" Tony said with an undertone of laughter.

"I thought the exact same thing until I went to Green Hill Cemetery. Turns out in 1966, William Greer, the Secret Service Agent who was Kennedy's driver in Dallas the day he was assassinated, escaped to the mountains of North Carolina. I say escaped because he never could manage to get out from under a cloud of suspicion. Due to so many people thinking that he had some involvement in JFK's assassination, Greer retreated to the mountains. From 1966 to 1985 when he died, he lived as a recluse in Waynesville, North Carolina, about a forty-minute drive from Franklin. He's buried in the Green Hill Cemetery over there.

"No way! No way!"

"He's there, and he's not alone. In 1978 the Hollywood actor, Gig Young, who won an Academy Award for a film he did called, They Shoot Horses Don't They, shot his girlfriend in the head before turning the gun on himself in their New York City apartment. After a big Hollywood funeral, his body was placed in a hearse in California and driven all the way across the country to Green Hill Cemetery in Waynesville, North Carolina, and his story is awesome. He worked with the likes of Elvis Presley, John Wayne, Bogart, Hepburn, Gable you name it, and he played with em'. He starred in multiple Twilight Zone episodes and classic horror films, but creepiest of all, years after Bruce Lee's death, they cast Young to act in Lee's unfinished movie, the one he'd died filming. So right before he wrapped his lips around a pistol barrel, he 'd helped finish a movie for a ghost. Crazy huh?"

"Gregg, I have to tell you, at this point, Dale is Googling this, and I'd like to announce to everyone out there listening tonight that, GREGG'S TELLING THE TRUTH!! THEY ARE THERE AT GREEN HILL! My God above, we thought we had a great mystery with two boys in the rain, dead coroners and such. We never thought when we signed on tonight we'd be dealing with the Mob, Hollywood, and JFK. You've got us scared now Gregg. Damn, we'll be lookin' everywhere for long black cars and jet black helicopters!"

"Sorry guys, but that's part of the story. The old Chief died certain of some connection. We'll most likely never know what, but I don't disregard his theories, though wild they may be."

"Oh, we completely agree Gregg. Let's hear em' all. After that though, to top it, you'd honestly have to tell us that Yogi Bear and Fred Flintstone had somehow been whispered conspirators as well," Tony joined with the wheeze of laughter dying on his breath.

Both DJs again traded comebacks of amazement and awe before Tony audibly sighed and said, "We're runnin' out of time Gregg. We have about twenty more minutes. Man the time has flown by tonight. I know I speak for Dale when I say that this has been our best show ever. When we hang up tonight, I don't even know where to begin in thinking about this story. Dale's got enough written down for a book. This story would make the most incredible book, but I can't imagine anyone would believe it. This is a perfect example of truth being stranger than fiction."

"You're right. It would make an awesome book. I'll think about that."

"Well in about nineteen minutes what do we have time for?" Tony asked.

"I have a question?" Dale rattled in. "Maybe it's more of a statement slash question, and I mean absolutely no disrespect to women in saying this, just the opposite actually. Women are the keepers of secrets. Women are the ones who retain details. Women, as the great Texas singer-songwriter, Billy Joe Shaver said best, are the wonder of the world. Have you ever asked women in and around Ms. Bullock's age range about the murder? She'd have been what," Dale paused, "Ninety years old today, had she lived. Have you ever asked women say eighty to ninety years old about the murder? I'll guarantee you, they've got stories to tell."

"Funny you'd ask that. Just a week ago...."

CHAPTER FORTY
D.A.R.

Way down in Mexico you went out to find a doctor
and you never came back.
I would have gone on after you
but I didn't feel like letting my head get blown off

From Brownsville Girl by Bob Dylan and Sam Shepard

AUGUST 25, 2013

❝Did you see the sky out there?" The youngest looking woman in the room asked while placing her purse down beside the chair she was simultaneously pulling out from the table.

"Oh, yes!" Another woman replied while shifting her water glass to the left with her left hand and lifting her cell phone with her right. "I stopped and took a picture of it."

"You did?" Another woman, seated to Gregg's right, obviously twenty years their senior, asked in a facetious tone. "I thought you hated those phones, Mary Lou."

"I do, but my grandkids insist that I have one, and I've got pretty handy with it."

"Well, well." The sarcastic old woman said before lifting her own water glass to her heavily painted lips.

"It was beautiful." A fourth woman joined in, poking a cell phone of her own in the process.

"I haven't seen colors like that in forty years." The woman who'd raised the question in the first place elaborated. "Me and Guy were down in Mexico. We were staying in this awful little motel. He started having pains in his side. I told him I'd get my head shot off if I was to go out by myself and try to find a doctor. We just barely made it back into Texas when he had to be admitted to the hospital. His appendix just about burst." The woman finished with four rhythmic taps of her fingers on the wooden table before her.

"Aaaand?" The sarcastic old woman who'd feigned being impressed at her peer's technological advancement earlier, asked, offering further evidence that her hateful tone to Mary Lou hadn't been pointed but was one she most likely wore like a cool shawl about her shoulders all the time.

"Oh, I just remember how pretty the sunrise was down there in Mexico. That's all I was saying." The old woman with the cherry red lips rolled her eyes then plunged her hand down into her purse which she had sitting directly in front of her on the table. Momentarily, she pulled out what appeared to be a plush green case and slid the glasses she'd been wearing into it.

One by one they arrived. Franklin, North Carolina's chapter of the Daughters of the American Revolution One by one Gregg watched them and listened. One of Gregg's favorite things to do, and had been since he was a young boy, was to watch and listen to people, especially elderly people, as their expressions and often their words were no longer veiled in the pleasantries and learned niceties of youth. Their authenticity intrigued him. It was almost eight o'clock on a Saturday morning at the Sunset Restaurant. Gregg had been asked to be the guest speaker at the D.A.R meeting, and he was actually very excited. It didn't bother him in the least to meet with the large group of elderly ladies so early in the morning. In fact, it wasn't his first time doing so. He'd spoken to their group once before, wherein he'd garnered several tidbits of history he'd since been using on his tours. He hoped the current meeting would offer up similar if not better fodder.

"Well, let's get started," a heavy-set elderly woman wearing a light yellow blouse said as she slowly stood to her feet. "Betty, if you'll lead us off with the pledge and Dee, if you'll offer grace after that, we'll go ahead and eat so we can get to Gregg. We'll have the business meeting after he's finished in case he needs to go."

After everyone rose to their feet, Gregg included, the Pledge of Allegiance and a tight little prayer was said. Then, an hour passed, an hour filled with laughter, eye-rolls, whispers, jokes, spilled coffee and the shuffling and clinking of plates, glasses, and silverware. When all of the plates, bread baskets and glasses were cleared away, when the steam from freshly poured coffee was rising all over the room and when the door was closed between the rather small private room the D.A.R. had reserved and the rest of the noisy restaurant, Gregg was introduced to kind and generous applause. After introducing himself to some and reintroducing himself to most, Gregg began what would prove to be an hour discussion of new, yet historical information that he'd been presenting in various forms throughout the year on his tours. To the crowd of women before him that ranged in age from their sixties to their early nineties, the information was either old hat or brand new depending upon whether they were Franklin natives or not, and after multiple handshakes, some gentle hugs and several quick conversations just after Gregg had arrived earlier, he'd learned that many were not. Gregg's topics ranged from Grand Ole Opry stars to witches, Walt Disney and Frank James to local legends and American Presidents. The women, whether they knew the material or not, sat with warm smiles and often excited eyes. They'd offer up simple phrases of awe in the breaks between tales like, "They!" or "Well I'll be!" or "If I had to never!"

Gregg told of how in the 1940s and 50s the Grand Ole Opry stars used to perform at Franklin's second courthouse which had been built in the 1870s and had been torn down in the 1970s. He painted for his audience Franklin's Main Street in the late 1800s when the entire street would be cordoned off so as to host boxing matches. He told the ghost story of the postmaster that still haunts the old post office on Franklin's Main Street. He got a myriad of responses when he told the ladies of Lawyer and Mrs. McCoy and their son Crawf', of how they ran from their home in the dead of night in the 1920s never to return, due to a supernatural creature they all three claimed crawled through the center of their front room snarling and growling. Gregg received proud knowing head nods from the women when he talked of Franklin's own Lassie Kelly and how she'd been one of North Carolina's first female lawyers, the yeoman to the Secretary of the Navy during World War One and much more. He talked of old Sheriffs and outlaws, particularly of Sheriff William Huffman Hidgon and the Willie McMahan hanging of 1884. Gregg taught many of the ladies that President Grover Cleveland and Franklin's own Kope Elias, a very famous southern lawyer, had been fast friends in the closing years of the nineteenth century. He told of how the Governor of North Carolina, James Lowry Robinson, had lived in a fine mansion of Franklin's Main Street in the late 1800s. The ladies squalled when they learned that Walt Disney had made a movie in Franklin in 1955 but mostly because Disney had tried and failed to buy portions of the town.

"Lord, we could be sittin' by Space Mountain right now!" One particularly short woman called out. All the ladies laughed.

Gregg told of when Frank James and Cole Younger of the famous James Younger gang came to the area in 1904 with the Wild West Company. The talked of famous Franklin witches, Vice Borden, Anne Cameron, Aunt Mahalia, Granny Beck and more. He told the ladies the story of the Spanish Fort Flag, a Confederate battle flag that had been hidden away in Alabama after a Union victory, preventing the Union soldiers from taking it as a spoil, and they giggled and wiggled in their seats when he told of how the flag was later raised up on a Franklin flag pole at a 1911 Confederate veteran reunion to a full salute. He talked of the great Franklin scientist Silas McDowell and the apples he learned to grow out of season, creating, in turn, quite a name for himself in the science community in the early 1800s. Gregg talked of Confederate Major Nathan P. Rankin and how he'd started so many schools in Franklin, but when Gregg mentioned another Franklin legend, Tom Rickman, a locally renowned store keep who'd been dead for years, one exceedingly thin woman asked Gregg if he knew the story of Mr. Rickman and Elana Carlson. When Gregg smiled and said that he didn't, the waif-like lady took the wheel, and Gregg was glad she did. The story was wonderful. In summary, a very young woman from Peru had moved to Franklin many years before. She spoke no English. She knew no one. She learned the English language by sitting around a potbellied stove in Rickman's old country store. She'd gone on to be an educator in Franklin. Gregg knew her well but had no idea of how she'd learned to speak the language. After the lank elderly lady's addition, time was getting slim, and Gregg could see some of the ladies checking their watches and phones. Gregg, fully intending on wrapping up and easing on out, was caught off guard when a lovely older woman with snow-white hair sitting near the door that separated the private room from the main floor asked:

"Do we not get anything about Ms. Bullock, Gregg?" The room grew absolutely silent upon her words. No one spoke. All eyes, if they'd been looking at watches, phones, coffee mugs or each other, beat a path to Gregg's eyes.

"Well, we can talk about whatever you want, but I assumed you'd like to get to your business meeting. I figured you'd had enough of me already," Gregg said with a genial smile.

"Oh, business Hell!" One of the ladies replied. Multiple women began speaking at once. Gregg listened as the woman who'd invited him in the first place hushed everyone then looked his way.

"We have the room. Nobody's booked after us. If you need to go, that's perfectly fine, but we wouldn't mind hearing a little about it, would we ladies?" A unanimous "NO!" filled the room, and once again the ladies grew quiet.

"I know some of you were at the presentations we did last month," Gregg said, "I don't want to beat a dead horse, so..."

"I wasn't there. I couldn't make it." Mary Lou piped up. Gregg knew Mary Lou from their joint affiliation with the Macon County Historical Museum. They were both on the board.

"I want to hear it all!" She further exclaimed.

"Lord, that would take all day Mary Lou," Gregg said before taking a sip of cold coffee.

"Well, we don't have all day," one woman remarked, "But tell us something." Gregg was just about to begin a summary of the case when Mary Lou piped up again.

"My dogs went crazy that night!"

"What's that?" Gregg replied.

"I said my dogs went crazy that night. I lived right across the street from Frankie. I remember that night like it was yesterday." Instantly, Gregg became an audience member, a voyeur, and not unlike Gregg, all of the others turned toward Mary Lou as well, giving her one hundred percent of their attention. With bold words and animated gestures, Mary Lou relived the night. She told of how all of her windows had been open because she'd been painting, and how her husband wasn't home. She told of how she sat bolt upright in bed that night of the 26th when her dogs outside started barking, as she put it, "To beat the band." Barely had the new tale-teller finished entertaining the room when another woman spoke out.

"I was with Wayne and Helen when the police came to talk with them after the murder. I remember Helen was so scared. She locked up everything, and none of us had ever locked up anything! We everyone changed after that didn't we?" Whether the woman's question had been meant as rhetorical or not, it was answered over and over across the room with resounding acquiesce.

"What I remember was how shook up little Eddie Stanfield was." Another woman added. "Old Bryce questioned him because he used to walk past Frankie's house on his way to work. Sweet little thing. It killed him just being questioned."

"I was working at the hospital." Yet another woman leaped on board the train of stories. "I was working with Dr. Ed Angel's nurse. We got to talkin' about Ms. Bullock. She said she'd never forget the autopsy and what Dr. Angel had said to her. Said he leaned over to her and whispered, *"This is the work of a woman."*

The spotlight had shifted, and for the next forty minutes, Gregg never felt its glow, but he was overjoyed, for what unfolded before him was better than anything he could have dreamed up for the day. One by one, and story by story, the ladies told of their suppositions, their theories, where they'd been that night or where they'd been when they heard of the murder. Between them, they knew the actions and often the exact words of almost every neighbor that had been questioned in the days after the murder, and not one of them hesitated in sharing....

"I know in my gut it was him!"

"I know many a lawman said to many people that they could go lay their hands on the killer's shoulder anytime they wanted, but they'd never work again if they did, and like as not they'd be killed too."

"It was in her eyes! Till she died, I could see it in her eyes what she'd done."

"It was that IRS agent, sure as the world." The ladies went on and on.

"I heard from...."

"Down at Conley's Barber Shop, they said that...."

"Momma told me to my face that...."

"Weren't hardly anybody at her funeral poor thing."

"I'm afraid she knew somethin' or she wouldn't have done it there." A woman to Gregg's left mumbled.

"Who wouldn't have done what where?" Mary Lou inquired.

"Ole Ella Dean, out at Woodlawn." The lady whispered.

"Oh yeah, I've heard that." Mary Lou said while popping the cap off a tube of chapstick.

"What about Woodlawn?" Gregg asked the lady to his left. The lady, acting for all the world like the consummate southern bell, whispered.

"The suicide."

CHAPTER FORTY-ONE
WE'RE LIVE NINETEEN

SEPTEMBER 1, 2013

"I knew it!" I knew they'd be the ones with the stories to tell."

Dale boasted from Little Rock.

"You're right. I got more from those ladies than I'd gotten from a lot of people, and I hadn't even entertained the notion of gathering information about Ms. Bullock from them. I'd simply been asked to tell some stories and introduce what Pauletta and I had created with Where Shadows Walk. Like so many times before, that's just the direction the needle on the compass went. It's what they wanted to talk about."

"What about Woodlawn and a suicide Gregg? Nobody elaborated." Tony requested.

"Crazy stuff man, I tell you. There were two sisters that lived beside Ms. Bullock. After the murder, their brother told the police that they should interview them, his sisters, due to how close they lived. He thought they may have heard or seen something. Well, they hadn't heard or seen anything. Twenty-four years later, in 1987, the brother to the ladies who lived so near Ms. Bullock received a visit from the Franklin Police Department. Seems his wife had driven her car out to the Woodlawn Cemetery, wrapped the inside of the car with plastic wrap and shot herself in the heart.

"My God! Is there no end to the death in this story? Why did she do it?" Tony asked.

"Nobody knows. She nor her husband or his sisters had ever been considered suspects in any way, and I had never heard about it till last week. I've of course looked it up since, but it just seems to be another tragedy, just another awful tragedy."

"Well, let's lighten the mood. Let's discuss the elephant in the room, Dumbo more specifically," Tony said. "If not but for a simple twist of fate you'd be living in Disney World!" Both men laughed.

"That's right," Gregg answered back. "It was close."

"If Dale wasn't Googling as fast as you're talking, I swear to you Gregg, I wouldn't have believed half of what you've told us tonight, but damn if it don't all check out: Walt Disney, Glover Cleveland, Grand Olé' Opry. Franklin, North Carolina must be the coolest small town in America, not to mention the final surrender of the Civil War, all the witches, and ghosts."

"We like to think so," Gregg replied.

"And, AND," Dale broke back in. "I just found that Gregg's little haunted hideaway town in Appalachia is home to the only Scottish Tartan Museum outside of Scotland."

"We've got about four museums in Franklin," Gregg replied, taking the baton at a full sprint with the freshly introduced topic. Better late than never, he thought. "We've got the Scottish Tartan Museum, the Gem and Mineral Museum. That one's housed in an 1850 jail. We've got a classic toy museum and the Macon County Historical Museum sits right off of town square. That's where I do lots of my presentations, and we go inside there on the tour some nights."

"That's where you did the Frances Bullock presentations right?" Tony asked.

"It is."

"And that's where you met with the lady with all the information about the coroner right?"

"That's right."

"Other than the lady wanting to talk with you privately, did anything ghostly happen when you were telling Ms. Bullock's story this last July, anything spooky?" Dale asked like a little boy.

"Going by the images on Dale's tablet seems like that place should be filled with ghosts."

"Oh, it's a very haunted location. We've got incredible stories we tell there, but I can't think of anything otherworldly that happened during or after the presentation; however, last Christmas, we most certainly had some spooky stuff go down. Pauletta and I had decided to do a Ghosts of Christmas Past presentation which consisted of hot drinks, cookies, stories, and I ended it with a recitation."

"A recitation?"

"You know like Porter Wagoner or Red Sovine used to do. Teddy Bear, Phantom 309, you know spoken word songs."

"Oh, yeah, so you wrote it about ghosts?"

"Yes and no. It's kind of hard to explain. I created a character, a fictional old hobo. I used his third-person perspective to tell a Christmas story meant to be nostalgic and festive while still keeping with the theme of hauntings. We have a man here in Franklin that goes by the nickname of Rocky; he's a painter, but he's also pretty much homeless. He spends as many nights in jail as he spends out. The thought hit me when I was mentally constructing this old hobo that Rocky would be a fitting gatekeeper to the other side, kind of like Charon the ferryman to Hades who carries the souls of the recently deceased across the rivers Styx and Acheron. So, yes it is about ghosts but not in the traditional ghost story sense. It's more about the metaphori-

257

cal spirit of an American small town told by a lost soul coming home. Anyway, back to the spooky, that night Pauletta decided to leave a lot of the glassware at the museum because the presentation had run so late. We were going to run by the next day and pick it all up. Mind you, we were the last to leave and lock up and seeing as it was a weekend, we were the first to open the museum back up the next day. When we opened the museum the next day we found that our punch bowl had shattered and in the strangest way. A large framed picture that had hung on the wall for years had somehow fallen and destroyed it. Man, glass was everywhere. The picture that fell was a black and white image of the Museum's first curator—a stern looking old lady. The best part was that the picture had been hanging by a wire on its back. The wire wasn't broken, nor was the nail out of the wall. Someone or something would have had to lift the framed picture off of its nail in order for it to have fallen as it did."

"Old gal didn't want all that Christmas frivolity about the place did she?" Dale joked.

"Maybe not."

"I've never even been to anything like that, but I can imagine that Christmas presentation would have been great." Tony joined in.

"Did sound warm and cozy didn't it?" Dale said, sounding for all the world like he was wrapping his arms around himself and shaking as he said it, due to a noticeable quiver in his voice.

"I'd have loved to have heard that recitation." Tony broke in again.

"It was fun to write. Took some time though."

"Gregg, we're almost out of time, and you're killing the both of us here. Now we've got to have you back on to talk about, Wal Purgus Night, death signs, Banshees, and I don't know what else. Stop it, man! Stop it! We'd stay up all night talking about this if we could. Like as not the two of us will stay up the rest of the night talking about it anyway. Ok, Gregg, Dale believes he's got it solved, but we'll save that for the very end. Dale wouldn't have it any other way would you Dale?"

"No, sir. I got this thing wrapped up." Dale proudly announced.

"Well before we let Dale close this cold case, we have a very few minutes left. Gregg, do you have anything else you'd like to say, anything else you can recall that might help Dale out."

"I don't need help!" Dale shouted. "As I said, I've got this thing wrapped up!"

"Guys, I've actually been jotting down a few things as we've been talking tonight, things that I didn't know if we'd get to or not, things that I've remembered as we were talking, but since we're almost out of time...." Tony abruptly interrupted.

"No, no, tell us!"

"Ok, I'll try to make it quick. Remember Janice, that met me at the library, the wealth of information? Well, an old woman contacted her recently. She said her husband had been a doctor during the time of the murder. They'd lived near Frankie. Anyway, she called Janice and asked her to meet her at the Franklin Golf Course. Janice agreed and met her there. The old woman told Janice that her husband had begun acting strangely shortly after Ms. Bullock's murder. She said one day she followed him because he'd taken a bag from their garage and had walked up into the woods with it. She said she watched, concealed by trees, her husband bury whatever was in the bag. However, when she attempted to show Janice where her husband had buried the bag so many years before, it turns out the highway had been built over it." Gregg was cut short.

"Unbelievable. Actually, why did I say that? That fits perfectly with this case." Dale remarked. "It's absolutely believable. Go on! I won't interrupt again."

"Hush it boy, or you'll never get your chance to solve it. Let the man speak." Tony overlapped Dale's closing words apologetically.

"Don't worry about it," Gregg reassured the DJs. "Another thing I'd penned down concerned the old Chief of Police, Ernie Caswell. It was told to me by some of his family members that right before Chief Caswell died about fifteen years ago, he instructed his wife to burn anything in their home that had the name Frances Bullock on it. He didn't want his family involved in that Hell in any way after he was gone. The case had haunted him his entire career. Like my dad, Officer Southards and Chief Baines, Chief Caswell was a fine man, but that case almost killed him, maybe it did.

Next, I was recently asked to speak at a historic store in Franklin called the Rickman Store. It's an 1895 store that ran full steam till the 1990s and has since been bought and preserved by a preservation group. Anyway, you don't need to hear about all that. Since its purchase and preservation, the old store hosts musicians, storytellers, speakers and such. I was asked back in June to come and read an excerpt from the written portion of the presentation I was going to deliver the following month on Frances Bullock at Franklin's Historical Museum. I was excited and honored to have been asked. Anyway, there was a packed house. That excited me further. I had barely introduced myself and my topic when an elderly man jumped to his feet in the back row of folding chairs and shouted, "She was a drug dealer!"

"What!" Dale blurted out.

"Settle down boy!" Tony reprimanded. "Let the man speak."

"I was in shock. I'd expected to read from the excerpt and maybe, maybe field some questions at the end. So, since the gentleman remained silent and standing after his unexpected outburst, I had to address his wild exclamation while all eyes in the house remained fixed on him. It was tense. My first emotion after the shock wore off was anger at having been interrupted, but I knew that would seem unprofessional, so I chose to smile. I told the older gentleman about the old Chief of Police CD Baines having had similar concerns. This seemed to only anger him further. That's when he spoke again.

"She'd bring em' back from cities she'd go to. Sold em' from her house at night. She sold em' to my cousin. I know for a fact." My smile faded because, at that point, he was messing up my presentation. He nearly tipped his chair over when he spun around and walked out the door."

"He didn't stay for the reading?" Tony queried.

"I think that was the most shocking part to everyone. He'd obviously come with the sole intention of relaying his message, and when he'd said what he'd come to say, he was gone, and no one had ever laid eyes on him before. The room was filled with locals, some elderly, who'd lived in Franklin their entire lives, and he was a stranger to them all. What else, what else? Guys, I swear I'm hurrying here."

"No, please don't stop!" Tony reassured his guest.

"If you recall, all of the evidence was lost early on. Well, it came back. Someone anonymously returned the evidence in and around 1995 wrapped in plain brown wrapping paper. Shoot guys, I've got way too much to tell here. I can't talk about it all, and I'd be skipping around all over the place, decade to decade, so I'll end my part with what we do best, a little ghost story. How about that?"

CHAPTER FORTY-ONE

"Yeah, let's do that. We've got about five minutes," Tony instructed.

"A lady came to us, not unlike so many others have recently. She wanted to tell us about her experience at Frankie's house. She said she and her cleaning crew had been hired to clean Frankie's house in 1978. She remembered that the family member who'd hired her said the family was going to have a reunion of some kind in the house. Anyway, she said her crew knew absolutely nothing about the house, but they hadn't been there twenty minutes when each one of them started complaining about how the house felt.

They told her the house didn't want them in it. She said she felt the exact same way but told them it had to be cleaned because they'd been paid already.

After a few more minutes she told me she had to let the others go outside. Some were even getting sick to their stomachs. She said she tried to hurry and finish on her own. She told me she'd just finished the kitchen and was just about the clean the living room when every picture hanging on every wall downstairs turned right or left a few inches. She said she just stood there with her mouth agape. She then told me that there was a large framed map of Macon County, our county, hanging over a couch and that it went sailing off the wall and shattered into a million little pieces. She said glass went absolutely everywhere."

"Maybe that's what happened to your punch bowl at the museum," Dale said.

"Maybe." Gregg laughed. "Maybe so."

"Alright Gregg, Dale's going to solve this case in the two and half minutes we've got left. Can you do it, old boy?" Tony asked enthusiastically.

"Can I do it? I've been sleuthing this one since Gregg signed on tonight," Dale replied.

"Well go!" Tony commanded.

"Ok, just like the ladies believed at the DAR meeting, I believe it was a woman that killed Ms. Bullock. The stab wounds were too low, too personal, but I think several of the suspects had a hand in it. The two boys in the rain. I believe they were watching Frankie's house because they were going to break in that night. They knew she had valuables inside. I believe when Gene and Sonny drove away, leaving them walking in the rain that they doubled back and did break in. I believe it was their footprints Gene saw in the mud outside of Frankie's window, and I believe they were the ones that took the screen out of the window.

Did they kill her?— No! I believe they were hiding in her house when she came home that night. I believe they watched the murder take place and couldn't say or do anything because of how they'd gotten into the house. That's why the one was raising Hell at the hospital a few nights later, and that's why he eventually came home to commit suicide.

Next, I believe the coroner cleaned up the mess. Like the lady that came to Gregg with all the details believed, he was the one with the tools and the know-how. Why?—Because whoever killed her had sway and power enough or their family and friends had power enough to make sure their tracks were covered.

Next, the town drunk. I believe he aided in moving her body downstairs to the garage for those three days, hence the blood droplets along the wall leading down to the garage, and I believe he helped move her body back. I believe he did bury the knife, but he didn't kill her.

As far as the actual crime scene investigation, I believe it was botched simply because of untrained early 1960s police work and nothing more.

Next, I believe, like I've already stated, that someone with some serious connections saw to it that all of the photographs and evidence went missing right away. Was it someone associated with JFK, Hollywood, Secret Service, the Mob, drug running?—I don't think so. I think all of that is interesting but most likely purely coincidental.

Next, I believe that the coroner was a decent person. I believe guilt was eating him up, and he was just about to talk, going by what he did at the Woodlawn Cemetery. I believe he was silenced that night because the whole house of cards would have fallen with his confession.

I believe Frankie knew her killer but felt uncomfortable enough not to go about her normal routine that night. Normally she would have pulled her car into the garage, but she didn't, and normally she would have never let onions permeate the inside of her nice new car, but she did. That tells me she pulled up to her house. The killer was either on her porch or in her yard. She deviated from her normal routine and asked them to come inside. Two chairs were pulled out, and two empty wine glasses were sitting there. That tells me there was a discussion of some sort.

Finally, and probably the spookiest part, whoever had enough care, concern, clout, sway, say, connection or influence to ensure such a brutal murder remained unsolved for decades is most likely still around else there never would have been the threatening phone calls in the 1980s, the pull-string dolls of the 1990s or the suspicious deaths that seem to still be occurring. And, DONE!" Dale panted, acting out of breath.

"My turn," Tony said, not boisterous but sure of himself.

"Whoa, whoa, whoooaaa!!!!!— What? You haven't written one thing down all night," Dale shouted.

"It's all up here Bucko," Tony said. His response slathered in laughter. Gregg assumed Tony had tapped his temple with his index finger as he'd said it.

"Well, this I gotta hear," Dale said, in a self-satisfied voice that Gregg imagined came accompanied by crossed arms and a leaned-back chair on Dale's part.

"It was not a woman at all. The lawn man had nothing to do with it, hence his banging on her door demanding back pay for work that Saturday she lay dead in her home. The Coroner did die of a heart attack like his cause of death proclaimed. The timing of his death was nothing but pure coincidence. Ms. Bullock's brother's fury with her was just that, sibling fury. In fact, none of the classic suspects had anything to do with the killing, no lawn man, no coroner, no boys in the rain, no angry females, no sitting Presidents, no Mob, no Hollywood celebrities. If you'd been listening closely, you would have heard the killer's name spoken loud and clear, and from none other than the slain woman herself."

"Go on Mr. Holms," Dale said when Tony paused in his narrative.

"Earlier in Gregg's narrative," Tony continued, "we learned that two teenage boys had garnered a very unusual Oijua Board message—3:16 in the window to be precise. We learned that Gregg himself saw the Bible in the window that very night turned to the book of John. We learned also that the name John in the upper corner of the page had been crudely underlined like a child might have done it. Instead of a child, I see an unsteady hand, a dead hand, the hand of a ghost doing its best.

Later on in the story, we learned that the boy who'd captured the message on the board went and took the Bible but not before actually seeing Ms. Bullock's apparition inside her home, a home she'd died in thirty years earlier.

Don't you see? Frankie was telling the boys, showing the boys the name of her killer, John Peterson. In Gregg's story we find that Frankie's friends and family are concerned with lies or maybe a better way to say it would be, half-truths, Frankie is perpetuating about a man she's dating. All of Frankie's other suitors were known to people, but this man, this mystery man, the only one to remain a mystery to this day, has never been decoded, one might say.

So, in the heat of all the passion, the fear, the ones with decent motive, this one man, this man of mystery remained unchecked and overlooked, forcing Frankie's spirit, for the past fifty years to attempt to connect through the Bible, the late-night visits to her home, the piggyback ride of Gregg's father and more.

John Peterson, whoever that is, killed Ms. Frances Bullock on July 26th, 1963." Tony triumphantly ended like a deep-south trial lawyer.

"And a pissed off lady," Dale mumbled like a child determined to get the last word in. Both men gently laughed at Dale's snappy insertion.

"We've got twenty seconds," Tony said like a game show host. "Gregg, we can't thank you enough for coming on tonight, and we can't wait to get to Franklin for some of your tours. To say it's been amazing would even be an understatement, and we will definitely be asking you back."

"Yeah," Dale hollered from somewhere behind. "We've got to get you back on to talk about Walpurgis Night and Banshees!"

"Thanks, guys. It's been great." Gregg finished and hung up the phone.

CHAPTER FORTY-TWO
A VERY SOUTHERN THING

I could never figure out why you chose that particular place to meet

From "Brownsville Girl" by Bob Dylan and Sam Shepard

SEPTEMBER 2, 2013 –MIDNIGHT

As Gregg ended his call with Little Rock, the stillness of his home was all but shocking, much the same feeling as trying to steady one's self after having disembarked from a roller coaster when the world is getting its act back together beneath your feet and fast.

His children were asleep. Pauletta, though he knew she always tried to trooper through for the gritty details, was also asleep on her favorite couch. She intentionally hadn't listened to the show, as it made her too nervous. She knew she'd hear about it the next day.

Gregg quietly walked through his home, ensuring his children were well. He smiled, as did Pauletta when he covered her bare shoulder with the blanket she'd wrapped herself in prior.

"How was it?" Pauletta asked without opening her eyes and without losing her smile.

"Great," Gregg replied. "I'll tell you all about it in the morning."

"Sounds good," She mumbled as she tugged at the blanket, this time pinning it beneath her chin. "I can't wait." She mumbled once more.

Far too awake with racing thoughts and feelings, Gregg didn't even consider sleep. Rather he walked over to the small eclectic bar his wife had recently purchased and placed in the corner of their living room. He poured himself a glass of Old Crow Bourbon Whiskey and smiled, his smile, the result of memorized comical insults cast out at his Whiskey's expense by friends.

No matter how he defended it. "It's one of Kentucky's oldest Bourbons!" He'd say. "President Andrew Jackson actually drank Crow's whiskey." Gregg would tell others. "President Harry S. Truman actually had his Oval Office Whiskey bar stocked with it, Old Granddad and Old Forrester." Nothing convinced the naysayers; however, Gregg was never one to care what others thought, so Old Crow it was.

Gregg stepped out onto his front porch. The cicadas and frogs were in full rumble on the outskirts of his dark yard and in the swampland below his driveway. The sliver of a moon, like an eye in finishing wink, made him think of her, Frances. *Was she happy she'd been talked about all night? Was she furious?* Gregg took a long swallow of Whiskey and walked from his front porch off into his yard; from there he strode down to the gravel road below. The lightning bugs were both bright and voluminous, flitting and flickering all around.

Gregg walked and drank, feeling the warm numbing sensation offered up by the Whiskey. One last mouthful by his mailbox finished up the Bourbon.

The euphonious frogs morphed with the cicadas as Gregg lifted his eyes to survey the night sky. The stars above and lightning bugs became a single tapestry of undulating, pulsing light. The flirting moon had slipped to sleep as Gregg opened up his mailbox and placed his empty glass inside. Maybe he'd remember to bring it in with him later. Maybe he wouldn't. It wouldn't matter either way.

"Who killed you, Frankie?" Gregg whispered to himself as he scuffed the heel of his boot into the loose gravel at the base of his mailbox post. And just like that, with the whispered question just having barely escaped his Whiskey-wet lips, a photomontage, frayed and ripped and burned, in stark black and white, then in Las Vegas Technicolor, and then back again and then upside down and then crooked and then slow, so very slow, was projected across the cognitive screen behind his eyes. Gregg saw....

Frankie as a teen plying bright red lipstick to her pursed young lips

Frankie on her wedding day throwing a bouquet of flowers Devil may care

Frankie clapping her hands at a birthday party amid Rose red balloons

Frankie playing peek a boo with a spit-bubble blowing baby

Then the images sped up, and the mental film in his mind took on sound, and new images joined the old. Gregg saw....

Frankie, clad in black, scaling the steps of a church for a funeral

Frankie holding her face in her hands as she wept

Frankie leaning her head back in laughter not born of comedy but of pain

Then, to the film, the killing came. Gregg saw....

The knife plunging Cobra-quick through the fabric of her dress and into her flesh

Then the images of her life both happy and sad took turns with the knife, and the mental film took on a life of its own when hundreds of clips and slivers of scenes and sounds filled the breaks and spaces between pictures, until the film was as

much a kaleidoscope as it was a movie, an explosion of au-
dio and visuals from the past. The soundtrack was the voices
from across the ages, voices of the dead, the living, songs, even
American Presidents. The movie rolled in Gregg's mind as the
night eclipsed him....

The knife raised and fell, raised and fell, raised and fell!
"I did something!"

*Frankie's tombstone without a date, then with a date, then
without a date again*
"Shazaam! Shazaam!"

*"Stop huffin' and puffin' like a damned old wolf! You hear me?
You hear me?"*

*Lipstick, clapping, church steps, wedding, crying, laughter, peek
a boo!*
"Slip the surly bonds of Earth to touch the face of God."
"Slip the surly bonds of Earth to touch the face of God."

"We've been playing a game, a game, a game, a game!"
The knife raised and fell, raised and fell, raised and fell!
"There go our two fearless leaders!"

"I mean she's been killed! I mean she's been killed!"
"Beware! Beware! Beware!"
"I did something!"

*"Crazy son of a bitch, damn high heels and all wrestled a big
black bear, a big black bear, a big black bear!"*
"Thrill Hill, Thrill Hill, Thrill Hill!"

"I know things!"

"It's witches night! Walpurgis."
Dogs are barking, barking, barking!

*Frankie's tombstone without a date, then with a date, then
without a date again*
"Green handed, Green handed, Green handed!"

*The rattle and roll of Pan Handle Pete clinked and clanked and
clinked and clanked.*
The knife raised and fell, raised and fell, raised and fell!

"Twenty-five lines in two days! Twenty-five lines in two days!"

Lipstick, clapping, church steps, wedding, crying, laughter, peek a boo!

"Naw, sir! Naw, sir! Naw, sir! Naw, sir!"

"Sleeps right up there with them corpses and caskets by God, by God, by God!"

The knife raised and fell, raised and fell, raised and fell!

Slick naked bodies in the golf course pool. Naked bodies in the golf course pool.

Dogs are barking, barking, barking, barking!

"I did something!"

"This must be yours, Mr. Clark."

"Slip the surly bonds of Earth to touch the face of God."

"Slip the surly bonds of Earth to touch the face of God."

"Go to Hell! Go to Hell! Go to Hell!"

"I know things!"

The knife raised and fell, raised and fell, raised and fell!

"Stop huffin' and puffin' like a damned old wolf. You hear me? You hear me?"

"3:16 in the window, 3:16 in the window!"

"It's witches night! Walpurgis!"

"Shazaam! Shazaam!"

"I mean she's been killed! I mean she's been killed!"

The knife raised and fell, raised and fell, raised and fell!

Frankie's tombstone without a date, then with a date, then without a date again

"She Wore Blue Velvet...!"

Lipstick, clapping church steps, wedding, crying laughter, peek a boo!

"Louie, Louie...!"

"Twenty-five lines in two days, Twenty-five lines in two days!"

"There go our two fearless leaders!"

"Beware! Beware! Beware!"

"Naw, sir! Naw, sir! Naw, sir! Naw, sir!"

CHAPTER FORTY-TWO

"Thrill Hill, Thrill Hill, Thrill Hill, Thrill Hill, Thrill Hill!"
"I did something!"

"I know things!"
The knife raised and fell, raised and fell, raised and fell!

Lipstick, clapping, church steps, wedding, crying, laughter, peek a boo!

Gregg blinked and the mad circus of words, pictures, and sounds was snuffed out like a candle. He inhaled deeply and looked toward his home.

"It's all I could possibly give you Frankie. It's the best I could do," Gregg mumbled as he walked slowly back toward his house.

One last time, Gregg turned around before going inside for the night. This time as he looked off toward the dancing lightning bugs and glittering stars, there was no roaring river of scenes and sounds playing out behind his eyes. This time it was just his father's face.

Again, as he'd done a million times before, Gregg envisioned his father standing at the Macon County Fairgrounds just before dawn as he'd done twenty years earlier after receiving the first solid tip in thirty years concerning the Frances Bullock cold case. Gregg imagined again the vein of life his father had stood beside, the headlights heading somewhere, a web of lives he'd never know anything of.

With his father's silhouette cast against the coming of dawn still the sole image in his mind, a sudden chill slithered across Gregg's shoulders, and something moved off in the woods to his right. A deer maybe, a possum, a skunk, Gregg silently assumed, but something in the air made him doubt his common sense assumptions, for Gregg felt eyes upon him. Something was watching him, of that he was certain.

Temporarily abandoning his path homeward, Gregg strode off into the darkness to where his yard met a field with thick forest beyond, to where the sound of movement had originated. At his yard's edge, in the bleak night, Gregg stopped and listened. Whatever had been there was gone, or at the least had grown still. Several moments passed, with the sound of Gregg's own breathing looped into and out of the song of a distant creek, the cicadas and the concert of frogs.

Given the relative stillness of the night and the late hour, Gregg finally turned and walked back toward home. From his front porch, with one hand firmly grasping his doorknob, Gregg looked back toward the yard's dark edge one final time. *Were they out there?* He wondered.

Gregg had read somewhere many years earlier that ghosts were like moths and stories told about them were like flames. Gregg often informed guests of his own tours that ghosts can be woken with a thought, that they lean it to listen to tales told of them—was he right? Were they indeed there, standing invisible in waist-high grass on the outskirts of his yard watching him?

Had they been pulled, one by one through the mists of time as he'd told their tales to a late-night summer Southland, all the ladies, and the lawmen, the town drunk, the suspects, the family, the friends, the killer, and Frances? Was Frances there as well?

Again a twig snapped in the darkness and Gregg smiled. He imagined them all bowing at the waist in graceful noiseless unison, a Southern Shakespearian cast of characters who'd played their parts with finesse and full steam, whose drama had closed with fifty years of rave reviews written on the pages of time itself.

Maybe not every mystery is destined to be solved. It may be sufficient that the story gets told, that the show goes on, that the curtain gets to fall proper with some cold tossed metaphorical roses and a hint of distant applause from the seemingly empty theatre that is life, Gregg thought to himself as he closed the door, shutting the night out behind him and leaving the ghosts in the darkness at the yard's edge and the Whiskey glass in the mailbox—a truly Southern thing.

APPENDIX

Christmas Recitation

He hadn't slept since Baton Rouge, and that was seven rides ago. Seemed it had snowed since Alabama, not a let-up, no noticeable ease, blinding in the night but awful pretty in the trees.

He'd heard seven snow stories, from blizzards to gales. One of his kind drivers told of snow on the ocean when he was back in the Navy manning the rails, and the snow stories brought on tales of Christmas, something he'd never really known. Seventy years out of seventy-seven he'd been all alone.

He knew every back road, every overpass, every alley and every trail, which boxcars you could sleep in, and he knew jailers in 212 jails.

He had nothing, but he had character. He wore a scarf and a long suit coat, both relics from a past, a past he never talked of, never hinted at, a past of which he never spoke.

He was like a ship with no sail, no direction, no beginning and no place to ever be, this American orphan in his ruined finery.

As the wind whipped the snow and headlights from oncoming cars weakened his tired old eyes, he listened about the star that arose and glowed and lit an old and distant sky.

Three drivers in a row from Montgomery to Rome talked of that ancient light that led a lost world home.

They talked of a baby, of a King and of a silent night, and three drivers in a row wiped their eyes as they described the sight of their own homes on Christmas mornings so many years before. They walked the stranger through towns and cities. They painted for him the shore, dirt roads and warm rooms and Christmas in all its glory. The old stranger, in his mind, like a phantom, walked through every story.

He smelled the roasting meats. He heard the popping of the fires. He felt the tender touch of babies, and he pushed aside the desire, and he quit his smile. He turned his head. Nothing brought more pain. His Christmas stories all involved missions, soup kitchens, snow, and freezing rain.

His present driver woke the drifter from his dreams of trains and wasted time, when he all but shouted, "Franklin's up ahead! This is the end of the line."

"But Georgia?" The drifter asked as the wipers beat the snow.

"You must have dozed old timer. We crossed into Carolina about twenty minutes ago."

As if he'd fallen into balmy water, swirling and whirling and wild, the ragged drifter's eyes went wide, and again he was a child, a child in his little mountain home hanging in smoke and hope and dreams. A thousand faces and places, as if on film, flickered across his mental screen.

"Franklin." He hadn't said its name out loud in over sixty years.

"What's that?" The driver asked, lightly cupping his ear.

"Oh, nothing," the old man remarked. The car slowed, then it stopped.

"This is where you disembark old friend. I'm hittin' back roads from here. They won't do you no good. There won't be no rides, and you might get lost in the woods. So Merry Christmas, and try to stay warm." The old drifter tipped his hat, and the car and driver rolled on.

The wayward relic blew warm air into his closed, clasped hands and buttoned his top coat button. He knew every step of this dance.

The old vagabond pulled his collar higher and tighter and lowered his eyes from the wind. He turned toward Franklin's snow-draped sign that wore the guise of a long waiting friend.

"Why should I go?" The old cold man queried himself in the night. "It's been so long. My people are all gone," but something pulled him inside. Something tugged and pushed him on. What it was he had no inkling, but he turned and walked with haste toward his boyhood home of Franklin.

The snow fell harder, and the wind blew wilder. A time or two he nearly fell, but in mere minutes, while lost in thought, he was climbing a steep town hill.

He recalled the looming statue, still dressed in Rebel garb, facing a long gone foe. To the North, it still stared hard, and in the shadows bending below, the streets were decked for Christmas, silver, red and green. Oh, how he had missed this.

Though his recollections were bright and warm were his dreams, the night was indifferent, and the wind began to scream.

Without a soul in sight to aid him, no charity in his needy hour, the wanderer curled up tight as could in the swallowing shadow of the town clock tower.

The time-worn old drifter was just slipping into slumber in the shadow of the tower on the dark side of the street when something shook him wide away, a strange rhythmic sound was emanating from up the street.

The half-frozen drifter, now wide awake and on both feet, stood in the darkest corner as the powder snow blew in sheets.

He'd heard the sound before, seemed a lifetime ago, and as recognition dawned, the wind died as did the blowing snow.

It was a horse he was hearing, and just coming into view, but what should have brought nostalgia made him tremble in his shoes, for the horse had a rider and not police as he'd assumed but a bearded clear-eyed soldier painted by a Christmas moon and not a soldier in green, no red white or blue but a wiry man in faded grey with spurs upon his boots, and there was something in his eyes, that he noticed didn't blink, a calm, like two cool pools of ink.

Was he a rein actor on such a cold late Christmas Eve? Just as the drifter raised his hand to the rider, he grew weak in the knees, for up strode another soldier, in saddle and with spurs, but this man wore a suit of blue. Was he seeing something rehearsed?

Was this some preparation for a Christmas scene to be played out later with laughter, cheers, and screams?

The soldier's horses, nose to nose, stopped silent in the street.

The old man held his breath, then amid the winter glow, both men dismounted, and he knew this was no show.

He heard the words Manassas spoke, Mary and Bull Run. Both men then led their horses as calmly as if through a pasture in the sun.

The old wanderer dared not move. He dared not take a breath, for he knew now in his heart both men had met their earthly deaths.

Both soldiers, once rivals, lay somewhere in the ground, but for reasons unbeknownst to him, they were walking through this town.

Just then another start, a man he hadn't seen, was setting up an easel. My God, was this a dream? He was a ragged man, not six feet from his side, securing a wide-high canvas as if to paint the night. By the weathered artist's side, on a bench, he carefully laid his paints, his brushes, edges and water and with no restraint, no gentle start, no taking of pains, with broad strokes he built the riders, the horses and their glistening reigns. Within seconds he was dotting stars that flickered and gleamed, but the painter didn't see him, at least that's how it seemed.

The drifter, then turned his gaze away from the midnight painter, for he heard more horses coming, more shouts and gentle banter.

One by one, others came upon the small town square laughing and swinging little ones into the cold night air.

The ragged aged drifter couldn't believe his ears at what followed. Voices from the street raised up in Christmas singing. The ground shook like it was hollow.

More soldiers came walking, some riding, some on canes. All a band of brothers, the denominator being pain. They all wore different uniforms from different centuries, these fighters of the Bloody Brother War, Vietnam and the War of

Independence.

Coming up the street, a fresh-faced lad in World War Two
fatigues laughed with a Civil War Major, no leg below his knee.

"What is this?" The old man whispered. Tears filled his eyes
as a dust snow whirled and his whole world changed there in
the night. He thought about running, screaming, leaving his
haunted home town, but just as he was turning, he heard a
whispering sound. A voice as soft as starlight, like lace upon
the wind, spoke from somewhere near him. "The show, it just
begins." The drifter spied a child standing in the powder-snow
that blew. Again he spoke, "And this show is just for you." The
little boy then ran across the street teeming with long-lost
souls, and just then bells begun ringing; from everywhere they
tolled. The bells they told a story too of a town lost in time,
and against his better judgment, the old drifter gave his old
home town his mind. And then, like the child before, a young
woman met his eyes and whispered, *"We all know that you
don't know us yet, but we beg you please don't leave. They've let
us know you need us, so we get one more Christmas Eve."*

Though the ghosts were strangers to the drifter spanning over
two hundred years, he found he was no more freezing, and his
eyes filled up with tears, tears at the passion and the laughter
and the smiles, tears as the bells tolled and echoed for miles,
tears as the soft snow fell and the bright silver moon shone,
tears for the way the children jumped and no one looked

alone, and though he'd left Franklin when he was just a boy, he felt faint recognition. He knew them, those who'd died before his birth, those born after he left. He knew them. He knew them! There's Dr. Angel and his wife. He knew no Dr. Angel. So long absent had he been, but he recognized their faces, all the women and all the men. He somehow knew their voices too, their stories and their ways, and one by one as they filled the night with life and Christmas praise, he watched them, and he listened, and all ages shared the gentle Christmas storm that whirled and swirled and tossed the hair of these long-forgotten forms.

There were Civil War soldiers, more than he could count of blue and dusty grey, World War One and World War Two, and he heard one mention D Day.

There were Korean War uniforms and Vietnam and Patriots with their hair still tied in bows with wives and children by their side all peppered with mountain snow.

Amid the soldiers, all clasping hands, grabbing shoulders and scuffing hair, stood their parents and grandparents so pleased to have them there. They never took their eyes from them, though the night was filled with friends and joys. They'd all waited for far too long to see their lost little boys.

Then, through all the festive gestures and the tear-filled eyes, someone shouted, "Peace to all," and their voices filled the night.

All eyes then turned down the street, and the chill air filled
with raves, for joining the pre-dawn miracle, came the ghosts
of all the slaves. They grabbed the hands of former masters,
each with Christmas written on their face, and all at once as if
on cue, they sang Amazing Grace.

Through the swirling, lifts and hugs strolled Dr. Samuel Harley
Lyle, the wind ripping apart the smoke that sailed from his
pipe in perfect doctor style. As if he'd heard a joke, he slapped
his leg and cried, when an old limping dog came running to
his side. The old dog had watched and waited, had jerked at
every white beard he sighted, and their eighty-year separation
melted as the Doc and Old Buck reunited.

Then an engine split the singing like sunlight through the rain,
as up the street came a motorcycle driven by Chief C.D. Baines
"Merry Christmas," He shouted, as he eased among the ghosts,
but he nor they seemed to notice the engine or the different
clothes.

The old chief parked his bike, and a Confederate boy leaned
near. They spoke as if their deaths had not been separated by
one hundred and thirty years.

Then other cars pulled up, from the fifties and forties and

Model Ts, and it didn't seem absurd that there were horses tied among the trees.

The ladies, all dressed to fit their age, winked slyly at their men. They giggled and shouted and danced and twirled unaffected by the wind.

They came from Cullasaja and Cartoogechaye, in sleek sixties Mustangs and wagons and on horse-drawn sleighs.

They came from Rose Creek and Burningtown Falls with snuff on their chins and in bib overalls.

They came from Nantahala, Oak Grove and Cowee with parasols and hats, the youngest no shoes and pants rolled up to the knee.

From Tellico and Hidgonville, Needmore and Elijay. North, South, East and West, they'd all come to play.

Some brought out guitars, fiddles and horns, mandolins and banjos, and into the air was born a new song out of old, from fingers aching to feel.

The archaic drifter knew their faces, and he somehow knew the names of the mountain musicians who'd never known fame, but there were others among them, faces he had seen. There among the local pickers who spun and sang and whirled was Roy Acuff, Grandpa Jones and a young dancing Minnie

Pearl.

Amid the voices, the singing, the music, and the engines
and all the love words were spoken, the drifter noticed no
sirens, no alarms, no man or beast was woken. The pre-dawn
Christmas party, both loud and filled with dances and toasts,
was only visible to him and of course the Christmas ghosts.

Up the street, on crooked canes, ambled all the witches, Vice
Borden, Anne Cameron, Granny Beck, and Aunt Mahalia,
skipping light like little girls, all donning bright regalia.

Amid the hustle and the bustle two old gunfighters strode,
eyes no more steely, but filled with charitable hunger. Both
men bent and scratched out an autograph for a boy, best
wishes they wrote, Franks James and Cole Younger.

On a fine black horse arrived Jesse Siler as if he'd entered
an arena. He was greeted by Julius, Mary, Alice, and little
Timoxena.

Major William Huffman Higdon and Lassie Kelly and
Governor James L. Robinson stepped into the street while
Sheriff Bryce Ingram, Ernie Caswell and Wayne Profit on
a park bench found a seat. From their seat, they talked of
heroes, of wars and of loves, and all of them were taken by the
brilliant stars above.

From Otto and Windy Gap, and from Buck Creek they arrived,
all long dead, but all so very much alive.

Old friends were brought together. The blue and the grey
blended. The men and women laughed until all were bent and
winded. The children chased each other black and white boy
and girl, as the moon hung high and the living slept. All was
right with the world.

Grover Cleveland and Walt Disney lit their pipes while telling
lies of lives and passersby to Tom Rickman in the night.

Mr. and Mrs. Bidwell rolled up in a fancy carriage. Mrs. Bidwell
was beaming due to the babe in arms she carried.

Old Mrs. Ada Munday came around the corner, and her old
heart began to wrench when young Mitchel Mozely took her
arm and led her gently to a bench.

The old drifter kept hearing a strange sound, a snapping, a
popping of sorts. He grinned when he looked up high and saw
the flag from Spanish Fort.

Silas McDowell was giving out apples, and Major Nathan
Rankin took three. He then gave them to the children working
hard at climbing up a tree.

From around the buildings where the dark began walked
shirtless men with rag-wrapped hands, street boxers from
days gone by. They were old and young black and white, and
they cheerfully joined the clatter of the night.

Old mailmen and firemen and businessmen and woman,
farmers and housewives dressed in silk, feed sacks, and denim,
sang and sank to their knees in laughter and praise, and the
drifter watching the whole scene in a daze wanted to join, for
his fear and trepidation had been replaced with desire and
need of reconciliation, but just as the ragged man set his mind
to step into the crowded happy street, his heart from inside
leaped, and he couldn't move his feet.

The children all stood still as well, and every conversation
paused when a primal chant came through the trees. The
drifter wondered at the cause. The ancient noise grew louder,
so real, so rich, so close. To join the pre-dawn party came all
the Cherokee ghosts.

The drifter, afraid, due to what seemed a fear-filled reaction,
thought about running, but to his great satisfaction, a mighty
cheer rose up that rocked the whole town square. Then there
were black men and woman Cherokee and children, all races
and faiths acting as kindling, igniting a fire, burning of one
accord, the slavers and enslaved calling out to the Lord. The

killers and killed, burned for their skin, arm in arm, walking closer than kin. The old Swami and his wife slow danced on the square as if no other person could see and watching their dance with a smile and a wink, was scientist George W. Meek.

They came from Iotla, Clark's Chappell and Holly Springs showing off lost teeth and shiny new wedding rings.

Up the street, on his old Palomino rode Nimrod Jarrett all smiles. He joined the old warriors who'd all won their wars single-handed and beat every trial.

Then, thinking nothing more could surprise him, the teary-eyed wanderer turned where light was arising. It came from behind the pines, and he jerked in fear as what sounded like cannons erupted too near. Then a roar in the distance made him shake like a baby, and a booming voice called out "Touchdown!" He was hearing Tom Raby!

The Panther Pit was wild with light and shouts and cheers. That's when the boys of fall appeared. Some were old. Some were young. All were wearing their numbers, no more in the shadows no more did they slumber.

Dink Love, dressed in Red and White, hugged all those football players, and the stranger, amid the laughter and prayers, watched the movie theatre bulbs, one-by-one spark, no more just a memory and no longer dark.

All the kids shouted and ran toward the glow, where Vernon
Stiles waited to tear their tickets for the show. Not only
children raced through the air. The Drymans ran too to see
Bogart, Heston, Ginger and Fred Astaire.

The old drifter was amazed, and he raised his eyes when
another screen in the distance lit up the sky. Cars from the
fifties with fins roared back to life when the dark Frog Town
Valley in a blink lit the night. The Drive-In was back, just like
a dream. Through the naked trees, the drifter could see Burt
Reynolds on the screen.

They came from Brush Creek and Skennah and Highlands
above, singing songs of forever of God and of love.

A little Cherokee girl running about, tripped and started to
cry, just as a kind-eyed doctor strolled casually by. He picked
her up and looked at her knee. He smiled like a diamond and
then set her free. He joked as he stood, sure rather that than
murder. Many voices called back: "Good job Dr. Berger!"

The town was alive with all the fair dead, ringing with singing.
The old drifter held his head. He felt he might faint. He had to
sit down, and he did, by a lovely girl in a long flowing gown.
She saw him not, just like all the others. It's then that he
recognized her as his very own mother. She'd died giving him
life, and she was buried so near. "My God," cried the Drifter.

"What have I found here?"

As the weathered drifter was wetting his lips to speak, his
attention was tugged upon by someone coming up the street,
a man in a dress, bad makeup, bad wig. Old farmers whistled
and catcalled as the man danced a jig. Then, pretending
to chase him with handcuffs and rope came Jimmy Clark
laughing. The man in drag spoke. "I'm with the band! I'm with
the band!! Jimmy don't get the jailor." A standing ovation rose
up for Guy Taylor!

All of a sudden the voices grew louder, the music faster, the
hugs more tight. It was anything but a silent night.

Though the party was raucous, the drifter noticed
transparency, a blurring as the morning neared, and one by
one the ghosts disappeared.

Next to go was the singing. Then all the music died. No horses
rode off. No cars sped away. It all just faded from sight.

The drifter stood, still in shadow, still watching, but all were
gone. Almost all were gone. He'd forgotten the ragged painter
who had been there all along.

The painter stepped back from his work to see how he'd
captured the mountain town, the colors, the snow, the faces,
the gestures, and the eyes, but amid the beauty, the old drifter
froze with surprise, for he too was in the picture. He too had

been painted within in the crowd. He'd been painted laughing and happy and shouting out loud.

"Who are you, and what is this painting?" The old drifter inquired.

"You can call me Rocky." The haggard artist replied, "and to understand the painting, you have to look deep inside."

The drifter stepped in close and timidly spoke. "I've never seen anything like it on a wall or in a store." The wild-eyed artist, through a wire-grey beard, spoke soft as moon dust:

"I call it The Door!"

The old vagabond, lost in the colors, the shading, and wild strokes, began again to hear the laughter, the singing and the jokes, the horses and ladies and legends so wild, and then, with the faith of a child, he closed his eyes, and he joined the merry scene. Everyone shouted out his name as if in a dream. They all knew his story, and he knew the songs, and with the last wisp of night, the old drifter was gone, lost in a masterpiece, trapped in a song.

Christmas morning dawned in the little mountain town, a town of many secrets, a town where spirits talk, a town where dreams come true, a town where shadows walk.

Gregg Clark is a native of the Southern Appalachian Mountains. An 8th grade History and English teacher in Franklin, North Carolina, Clark and his wife Pauletta, also a teacher, own and operate Where Shadows Walk, Historic Ghost Tours of Western North Carolina. Clark's deep and exhausting research, resulting in ghoulish tales, have been highlighted on the Travel Channel's Weird Travels and on various online radio broadcasts throughout the American South.

3 Days in 63 is Gregg's second novel following the great success of his debut novel, *Ghost Country*.

Sign up for his newsletter and visit whereshadowswalk.com

Please post a review on Amazon, Goodreads, and BookBub, to support this book and future works. Take a selfie with your book and post it on social media to spread the word.